LEE TOBIN McCLAIN

Low Country Christmas

HQN™

ISBN-13: 978-1-335-50502-6

Low Country Christmas

Recycling programs for this product may not exist in your area.

To my loyal readers...
Thank you for joining me in Safe Haven one more time.

Low
Country
Christmas

CHAPTER ONE

ON A MID-NOVEMBER EVENING, Cash O'Dwyer locked
the door of his luxury condo and trotted down the
steps, holding his phone to his ear to listen to the
third message from his CFO in Atlanta. "Urgent that
you return this—"

"Watch it!" The feminine voice was accompanied by a baby's cry.

Cash stopped with one foot halfway down to the
next step and squinted at the woman, who'd pressed
herself flat against the railing on the landing, baby
cradled protectively in her arms. He lifted a hand,
palm out. "Sorry, sorry, ma'am, wasn't watching
where I was going." He continued past them as he
listened to the rest of his message. And then, as he
processed what he'd seen, he clicked off his phone
and turned back, shifting his focus from Atlanta and
business deals to a very pretty young mother practically on his doorstep here in Safe Haven, South
Carolina.

The woman was still on the landing, gently joggling the baby, whose cries were already dying out.

"Can I help you?" As he spoke, he checked the

time on his phone. His brothers and their families would be waiting for him, the nieces and nephews getting more and more impatient, the wives ready to strangle him. His pockets full of candy and little toys wouldn't make up for a night of fussy kids. He'd *told* them to go ahead without him, that he'd meet them at the holiday tree-lighting ceremony in the park, but his sisters-in-law had insisted that they all have dessert together first, at the Southern Comfort Café.

His sisters-in-law were big on tradition, something he and his brothers were pretty severely lacking.

Three messages flashed onto his lock screen. His sales manager, his brother Liam and his brother Sean's wife, Anna.

Above him on the landing, the woman hadn't moved, hadn't spoken. The baby, who looked to be a girl and about a year old, settled against her shoulder with a gurgly sigh. "Can I help you?" he asked again. These stairs led to two condos, his own and that of an older businesswoman. "Are you looking for Hillary?"

"No." She stared into his eyes and hers were strangely familiar. "We're looking for you."

A spark of anxiety climbed up his spine. He didn't like it. "Is it an emergency? What's your connection to me?"

Her eyebrow lifted just enough that he realized

he sounded abrupt. Which was too bad, but that was how he was. Driven, impatient, materialistic. Not as bad as his father had been—at least Cash wasn't violent about it. But still. The old man must have known what he was doing, giving him the name Cash. It was why he didn't have a wife and kids, the way his brothers did.

"It's…a long story," she said. There was anxiety in her voice. "Is there somewhere we could talk?"

He glanced at his phone again, the time ticking away. "Not right now, no." He tried to keep the irritation out of his tone. There were a lot of people in the world, especially in the South, for whom time had a different meaning than it did for him. People who didn't mind having drop-in guests because their schedules were flexible or nonexistent.

Cash O'Dwyer wasn't one of those people.

"Does the name Tiffany Gibson ring a bell?"

"Tiffany…yeah." Involuntarily, he smiled. He'd shared a very lovely week with Tiffany, when she'd vacationed in a beach resort adjoining Safe Haven at the same time he'd been spending a rare week in his hometown. "I do remember Tiff," he said.

"She's my sister. I'm Holly Gibson." She was watching him steadily, like that was going to mean something to him.

But he and Tiffany hadn't spent their time together talking about their families. They hadn't talked much, period. He didn't think Tiffany had even mentioned she *had* a sister.

That must be why this woman's big grey eyes had looked so familiar. He didn't have time to piece together why Tiff's sister had shown up on his doorstep with a baby, but she probably had a sob story and needed money. That didn't even faze him anymore; as his bank account had expanded, so had the number of people who wanted to be his best friend. Couldn't blame 'em for trying.

But this one had a baby, which got to him. "Look," he said impulsively, starting down the stairs and gesturing for her to follow, "I'm late for this tree-lighting thing. It's a tradition, and there are kids involved, kids I can't disappoint. If you'd like to ride along, we can talk in the car. Or..." He frowned at the baby. "You can follow in your own car, if you'd be more comfortable."

"I came in an Uber," she said as she reached the bottom of the stairs, then half knelt and picked up a car seat she must've left there. "I can ride along with you."

She'd come in an *Uber*? That meant she didn't have a car. Definitely a sob story coming, but two more messages pinged onto his phone and he didn't have time to deal with it. He just took the car seat out of her hands, opened the rear door of his Tesla and slid it in. From his brothers, he'd actually learned how kids' car seats worked, so he attached the top tether strap to the anchor point, then stepped back to give her access.

"I'm impressed. Most guys can't do that." She bent over and carefully buckled in the baby.

Just as carefully, Cash tried to keep his eyes away from her sweet, shapely form. He focused on the sound of the waves lapping just beyond the parking lot, the sweet-smelling winter honeysuckle that climbed a lamppost, the stars emerging against the velvet-blue sky.

He loved it here, would have made it his permanent home if things were different. But he had never really fit in, and now that his two brothers were happily married and fathering families, he felt like even more of an outsider. He'd even gone into a funk about that back when Liam and Yasmin were getting together last year, had started to think about selling his business and finding something more meaningful to do with his life.

Fortunately, he'd come to his senses. He wasn't a family man and wasn't going to be. And despite his early midlife crisis, he wasn't the type to become a social worker or schoolteacher. Like his father before him, he was a player, money-oriented to the core. Accepting that, finally and for good, had helped get rid of the painful, gnawing jealousy he'd felt when he'd realized that both of his brothers were going to marry and find happiness in families of their own, and slowly pull away from the gang of three they'd always been.

Now, he was happy for them. He really was. Just as long as he didn't spend too much time in Safe Haven, milling around on the outskirts of their family lives.

The woman cleared her throat as she walked around the car to the passenger side. "You said you were in a hurry?"

"Right." He held her door for her, closed it once she was inside.

His brothers were going to think he was an idiot for bringing some stranger along to their family gathering. But he'd learned from experience that ignoring people who thought they had a claim on you could make for all kinds of harassment. And this one had shown up just when his family was demanding his immediate presence. So what choice did he have?

HOLLY SAT FORWARD in the front seat and turned to look at the baby, peaceful and sleepy. Love and worry squeezed her heart. This *had* to work.

But revealing her desperation would be a huge mistake. She sank back into the car's luxurious seats and studied the complicated-looking computer screen on the dashboard.

"Nice car," she said, and then felt stupid for the

understatement. The car accelerated like a silent spaceship.

"I like it." Cash smiled at her, as if he wasn't overly impressed with the car or with himself for owning it, which was nice. Also nice was the beautiful summer wool suit that fit his tall, muscular form perfectly.

So Cash O'Dwyer had a little class to go along with his wealth. But he'd acted like she and Penny were impediments in his journey to more important activities and people. That bothered her, especially given what she knew.

He'd lowered the windows partway, and the smell of the salty ocean blew into the car on a warm breeze. "You familiar with Safe Haven?" he asked. Again with the sexy baritone. The man had everything going for him.

But she *wasn't* attracted to him. Holly was known for keeping to herself, avoiding social connections, especially close ones with men. Too many bad relationships had caused her mother to neglect her and Tiff, and especially now that she had Penny, Holly was determined not to make the same mistakes.

"I'm not at all familiar with Safe Haven." She looked around at the tree-lined streets full of people strolling along, browsing the shop windows. It was well over fifty degrees—sweater weather to someone from the north, like her, but the people here wore leather or wool jackets, scarves and boots. "First time in the state, actually," she added.

Lots of small groups stood chatting. It looked like a friendly town, just as Tiff had described it. Kind of sweet that everything was already decorated for Christmas.

But could she live here? Make a life here?

She was opening her mouth to begin the difficult conversation they needed to have when Cash pulled into a diagonal parking space in front of an old-fashioned diner.

"Uncle Cash!" Two identical little girls, probably six or seven, ran toward the car. "We've been waiting forever!"

"Let me just check in with the family and then we'll talk," he said to Holly. "You need help with the baby?"

"I've got her," she said. It would give her another minute to experience this rich-guy car, the likes of which she'd probably never ride in again.

More importantly, it would give her a moment to figure out a little more about the man she was about to depend on.

As she pulled out the baby, trying not to wake her—thank heavens Penny was a good sleeper— more voices joined the two eager, childish ones around Cash. Propping Penny on her shoulder, Holly knelt to pick up the diaper bag and purse, taking her time so she could watch her target.

Two dark-haired men, one wearing a police uniform, the other in work clothes, were pounding him on the back. They were laughing, giving him a hard time about being late. A toddler lifted his hands, and Cash swung him up high, making him chortle, then he settled the child into the crook of his arm.

The twin girls were boldly sticking their hands into the pockets of his suit jacket.

"Hey, you little bandits," he said, laughing down at them. "Why would you even think I have candy for you?"

"Hope! Hayley!" A woman holding an infant just a bit bigger than Penny leaned down. "No begging!"

The biggest of the three brothers—for they were brothers, she could see now, all dark-haired and blue-eyed—knelt and talked quietly to the twins, and they nodded and stepped back from Cash, one of them with a lower lip pushed out.

"Aw, give 'em a break," Cash said. He reached into a pocket and pulled out two tiny gold boxes. He grinned winningly at the twins' mom. "Never too early to get them started on Godiva."

"Cash!" The woman laughed and shook her head.

"Don't worry," he said, "I brought you one, too." He fumbled in his other jacket pocket and handed her a slightly bigger box.

Standing there with a smile on his face, a toddler in his arms, giving extravagant gifts to people who obviously adored him, Cash O'Dwyer was so breathtaking that Holly swallowed and looked away.

"He's a good guy," said a female voice next to her shoulder.

Startled, Holly turned to see a curvy woman with multiple long braids. "That's…good," she said. She was hoping Cash was a good guy, because she needed him to step up.

"I'm Yasmin," the woman said. "Married to the cop." She nodded toward the brother in uniform. "Foster mom of the toddler he's holding, and for little Gino to let Cash pick him up is amazing. He was afraid of everything and everyone when he came to us." Without taking a breath, she added, "What's your connection to Cash?"

"I, oh, well, I…" What was she supposed to say, when she hadn't had the discussion she needed to have with him yet? "Friend of a friend," she said.

"And who's this little cutie?" Yasmin leaned in to study Penny.

The less information she shared, the better, at this point. "She's Penny, and she's one year old."

"Adorable."

A waitress came out of the diner—actually, it was the Southern Comfort Café according to the sign—and beckoned to Yasmin. "Can't hold the table much longer," she called across the crowd.

"Everybody inside," Yasmin yelled, and the whole gang started trooping into the café.

Holly bit her lip. This was a family gathering and she was completely out of place. And Cash was clearly at the center of the family, so he couldn't bail on them now.

She should have made arrangements for a business meeting with him, and she'd tried, but his secretary had set up a series of barriers that were almost impossible to breach, unless you disclosed your business.

Which Holly wasn't willing to do.

A hand touched her elbow, accompanied by the faintest whiff of spicy men's cologne, and Holly's stomach gave a little flip. Cash. She turned to him. "Hey," she said, keeping her voice cool and professional, "if we could just set up a meeting next week— tomorrow would be even better—I'll head out."

"In an Uber?" He frowned at her, one eyebrow quirked.

She nodded.

"No." He shook his head. "Come in and have some dessert. You haven't lived until you've tasted Abel's pies. And then things will settle down and we can go off in a corner and talk about whatever it is you came to talk about. And then I'll get you where you need to go."

"You don't have to do that."

He tilted his head to one side and met her eyes, smiling just enough to reveal a dimple. "What kind of gentleman would I be if I let a lady find her own way home?"

She sucked in a breath. The fact that Cash would bother to flirt with a woman holding a baby made him seem like an actual nice guy. No wonder Tiff had liked him.

Firmly, Holly pulled her mind away from the sad realities of her sister's short life. She tried for a different excuse to avoid the convivial group heading into the café. "It's a family gathering. I don't want to intrude."

"You won't be." He took the diaper bag from her and put a hand on the small of her back. "Look, they're already pulling up an extra chair and high chair. You'll hardly be noticed."

But Holly had seen the speculative way Yasmin looked at her. She had the feeling she *would* be noticed.

It was inevitable in a small town, which was why she wasn't very fond of them. But to fulfill her sister's wishes, she'd make the sacrifice and live here. Getting to know some people would be a good way to start. "If you're sure," she said.

His hand on her back increased its pressure, just a smidge, and heat suffused her chest. "I'm sure," he said in a husky voice.

You need him for cash, just like his name. Anything else will get you deep into trouble.

LATER THAT EVENING, Cash joined with his family talking and laughing as they waited for the giant, ancient oak tree to be lit, as it was every year in mid-

November. It was the town's traditional kickoff to the holiday season.

Holly seemed to be having an okay time, but they'd never gotten the chance to talk because his nieces and nephew wouldn't leave him alone. And he had to admit, he loved it. He'd shut down the whining of his CFO for the night. What good was owning the company if you couldn't take a night off to hand out candy to a bunch of kids you loved?

He knew he was too work-focused and impatient, could never be a good father, but he was determined to excel as an uncle. You didn't have to be the biological parent to help and influence a kid. He was living proof of that.

He glanced over at Holly now and noticed that she was shifting the baby to her other shoulder. He'd brought her here and he hated to see her looking so tired. Typical thoughtlessness on his part. "Let me hold her for a while," he said. "You've got to be worn out."

She tilted her head to one side and studied him as if evaluating his worth as a baby-holder. "Okay," she said, "if she'll let you. She's picky."

"As a lady should be." Gently, he lifted the baby out of Holly's arms.

The weight of the child settled something in him, felt good. Little Penny studied him with round blue eyes and then yawned, and when he patted her back, she leaned her head against his shoulder and sucked her hand.

Cash's heart expanded about three sizes.

Holly looked surprised. "She doesn't go to everyone."

He refocused on the here and now. "I'm a baby whisperer," he said casually, brushing off the often-paid compliment. "Listen, they'll light the tree any minute now. After that, we can have our talk and I'll take you back to your hotel. Where are you staying?"

She named a small inland town, not exactly known for tourism, and a motel he'd never heard of.

"How'd you land *there*?" Cash mostly met women who wanted luxury. Holly was different. Or maybe desperate.

"Cheaper," she said. "I don't know how long we'll need to stay."

Aha, desperate. But he didn't have time to think about it because the tree lit up in a blaze of white lights. Gasps and oohs and aahs went through the crowd, and then as more and more lights came on, kids started shouting.

"So pretty," Holly said, leaning closer. "Look, Penny—pretty!"

The baby stared and waved chubby arms. And for just a moment, he felt like he and this woman and this baby were a little family, doing a holiday tradition together, and his chest tightened with crazy longing. It must be the Christmas season that was making him soft and emotional.

He had to toughen up. The crowd was dispersing, all the little ones needing home and bed, and he handed the baby back to Holly and hugged everyone goodbye.

"Don't stay away so long next time," Yasmin, Liam's wife, said sternly.

Anna, Sean's wife, nodded. "The girls miss you when you're gone," she said.

They made it sound like he lived here, but he didn't. He lived in Atlanta. It was just that, with all the weddings and babies and family events in the past two years, he'd spent more and more time here.

Finally, he broke away and ushered Holly toward the car, hitching her diaper bag over his shoulder to lighten her burden a little. Funny how she'd seemed to become part of the group in just this one evening. He was a little reluctant to spoil the sweet, holiday family feeling with a conversation about whatever she wanted from him.

But that was ridiculous; best to get things out into the open right away. "So what did you want to talk to me about?" he asked. "Sorry it took so long, took up your evening."

"It's okay," she said as she shifted the baby from one arm to the other. "I'm glad to find out a little more about you and your family."

A strange uneasiness gripped him. "Why's that?" he asked.

She nodded down at Penny. "Because she's part of the family, too," she said. "She's your daughter."

CHAPTER TWO

HOLLY EXPECTED THAT her announcement would evoke surprise, even shock. What she didn't expect was laughter.

Cash actually did a full eye roll as he leaned back against his car and let out an unamused chuckle. "So I'm her father."

Affronted, Holly stepped back from the ridiculously expensive car and waited for his sarcastic smile to fade. Which it did, fairly quickly, when he saw she wasn't joining in.

"You're serious, aren't you?" He shook his head. "Holly, that's the oldest game in the book, and women have targeted me with it a number of times. Good try, though, and it's innovative to claim I fathered your baby when we never met before. Now, come on, let's get you back to your motel."

"She's Tiff's baby, not mine."

He tilted his head to one side as if he were thinking, then shook his head. "Nope. Not possible."

He was completely dismissing her. He was back to being that cold, heartless businessman he'd appeared to be when she'd first seen him at his fancy condo. All of a sudden, Holly felt exhausted. Her arms ached from holding the baby for what seemed like hours. She hadn't slept well last night, wondering whether the motel she'd chosen was safe, whether the bedbug epidemic she'd heard about on TV was real and, most of all, thinking about how to present the news about the baby to Cash.

As it turned out, that was the least of her worries, because he didn't believe her. Not even a little. And she didn't have the strength to muster up all the arguments tonight. "You know what," she said, "I'll just call another Uber. I assume you won't submit to a paternity test, so I'll start the court proceedings tomorrow." That would be the more expensive and time-consuming route, according to her online research, but it was worth it. Penny deserved to know her father, and she deserved a better life than Holly could provide on her own.

"You don't look so good." Cash seemed to ignore her words, but his face grew concerned as he studied her. "When was the last time you ate?"

She pressed a hand to her stomach. Now that she thought about it, she *was* hungry. "I ate two hours ago," she said. "Right here."

"You picked at a piece of pie. When before that?"

She thought back. "A granola bar this morning," she admitted.

"Come on." He gestured her toward the door of the café. "Half an hour isn't going to make a difference, time- and rest-wise, for you or the baby. Let's get you an actual meal."

She was too tired to argue and, anyway, her stomach growled at the notion of food. So she shrugged and followed him into the café, where they sat in a booth this time. Penny woke up and got social, so they put her in a high chair and Holly wiped the tray with a sanitary wipe and then dumped Cheerios onto the tray.

The same middle-aged waitress they'd had before came over and reached out to squeeze Cash's shoulder. That made him uncomfortable, even Holly could see it. Weird.

"Umm… Rita," Cash said awkwardly. "Did you meet Holly before? Anyway, she needs something quick and nutritious."

"We've got plenty of choices, though we're only open another forty-five minutes." Rita smiled at her. "What do you like, hon? Bean soup? Eggs and grits?"

Holly was grateful not to have to look at a menu. "Eggs sound good," she said. "Scrambled. Thanks." As Rita walked away, she turned to Cash. "I'd like to go freshen up, wash my hands."

"Do it," Cash said. "I'll take care of Penny here. We're bonding. Since we're, you know, father and daughter."

She didn't bother to get mad; she just looked at him and shook her head. Clearly this was a joke to

Cash, and if she had the energy she'd strangle him, but she didn't.

She went into the bathroom, washed her face and considered applying some makeup, but decided against it. Who was she trying to impress?

She studied her pale, drawn face in the mirror. Her life had changed insanely in the past month, and the changes hadn't stopped coming. A part of her longed for the carefree days in Manhattan as a mobile dog sitter, living out of a small suitcase in the finest of apartments, spending her days with the canines who were so much more understanding than people. She'd had the ideal life for someone who wanted zero attachments.

Attachments—the wrong ones—had caused her mother to neglect her children and ruin her own health. Holly had no interest in repeating her mother's mistakes.

Tiff had laughed at her independent lifestyle, told her she was avoiding reality. But Tiff hadn't been any better; in fact, she'd been much, much worse. Zero attachments was better than destructive ones.

And yes, she was exhausted, but as she left the restroom and caught sight of her niece giggling up at Cash, Holly straightened her back and put a smile on her face. She had the privilege and responsibility of raising her niece, and it gave her life a purpose she'd never had before.

By the time Holly got back to the table, Rita had

gone to the pass-through window and back and was bringing a plate of hot food that smelled amazing. "Thank you," Holly said, and dug in. She only looked up after she'd eaten half the plateful, at which point she realized that Cash and Rita were watching her with...what? Amazement? Amusement?

Heat climbed into her face. "Sorry. I didn't realize how long it had been since I'd eaten, and this is fantastic food. I haven't had grits in ages."

"Let me know if you need anything else, and meanwhile, you listen to what he has to suggest," the waitress said, and went back to wait on others.

"Look," Cash said, "Rita gets off in a few minutes, and she said you can stay with her."

"What?" Holly stared at him. "You got her involved?"

He nodded. "Sorry," he said, "but Safe Haven is sort of an involved community. And...well, she's my mother."

That was strange. "I thought I heard you call her 'Rita.'" *And a waitress mom doesn't exactly match a son with a Tesla.*

Cash's face reddened. "It's complicated," he said. "But the point is, she's sympathetic when she sees a mother and child in need. Let's just say she's been a woman in a tough spot herself."

"Okay, that explains her, sort of." She studied him narrowly. "But what about you? If you don't believe me about the paternity stuff, why are you still being nice?"

He shrugged. "You're in a spot," he said. "Look, the baby isn't mine, but maybe Tiff told you she was and sent you here to meet me. That's not your fault. I'm impressed you're helping out with your sister's child."

Holly blew out a breath, wondering whether to believe him. Either way, she and Penny needed nourishment, so she hunkered down and finished her meal, putting bits of toast and egg on Penny's tray and helping the baby guide the food to her mouth.

Cash was going on about how Rita's place was right down the street and how she had a guest room and loved kids. Then Rita came back and urged her to accept the help, that she could sort out everything tomorrow. "Doesn't a real bed sound nice?" she asked. "I even called my neighbor and asked her to put her Pack 'n' Play outside my door, so the baby will have a crib."

This had the feeling of being inevitable, and she could see in Cash's face that he felt virtuous for helping the poor stranger. And she didn't feel too bad about it, because Penny was related to both of them.

Unlike him, she knew it and was certain of it. Tiff had left a letter with her will that spelled it out and urged Holly to go to Cash for help. She wouldn't have lied. Not about something as important as a child.

THE NEXT MORNING, Rita O'Dwyer poured coffee for Holly, who'd been her reluctant overnight guest, and her best friend, Norma, who'd stopped over to visit. She liked living by herself, but it had been fun to get up this morning, fix breakfast and listen to the cooing of a baby.

Plus, Norma had brought fresh cinnamon rolls, which made any day feel like a celebration.

Holly sat at the kitchen table spooning banana pieces into baby Penny's mouth. She wore Rita's old shorts and T-shirt and looked a little more rested than she'd seemed last night. She still wasn't exactly forthcoming about what her story was, but it wasn't any of Rita's business.

There was a knock at the door, and Rita jumped up to get it. Cash. "Come on in," she said, absurdly happy. He was her son, and even though she didn't remember raising him, she felt a mother's love in her heart. "Try a cinnamon roll," she suggested.

"Jean Carol's?" he asked automatically. Jean Carol's cinnamon rolls were legendary in this town.

"Of course! Norma brought them."

"They're heavenly," Holly added, taking a bite and closing her eyes.

"Thanks, Norma," Cash said, but he didn't look at Rita's friend. Instead, he watched Holly lick a crumb off her lip, a hungry expression on his face.

He's got it bad, Norma mouthed to Rita.

Rita studied her son through narrowed eyes.

What was the connection between Cash and this pretty young stranger?

"You about ready to go?" Cash asked Holly. They were going to go pick up Holly's belongings at the motel where she'd been staying, because Cash, in his typical business-executive way, had talked the management of Rita's apartment complex into renting an empty apartment to Holly short-term.

"Not quite. I'm sorry," she said. "I didn't realize you'd be quite so punctual."

"Let me hold the baby while you wash up and get your things together," Rita said. She loved babies, probably because she knew she'd had her own, but she didn't remember any of it.

"I'll be quick. I just have a few things to pack up and we'll be ready. Out of your hair," she added to Rita.

"No rush," Rita said. "You're a welcome guest."

Holly looked confused, as if she'd never heard those words before. Poor kid.

Once she was gone, and the sound of water running indicated she was out of earshot, Rita turned to Cash. "What's the story with Holly and baby Penny?"

Cash helped himself to another cinnamon roll. "She's just another pretty girl looking for a handout."

"Harsh," Norma said, and Rita flinched inside. Was Cash really as cold as he acted sometimes?

Cash shrugged. "I know her kind and I know how to deal with her."

"She doesn't seem to have a lot of experience with babies," Rita volunteered. "Says this is her sister's, and that she's only been taking care of her for about a month."

"A month?" Cash lifted an eyebrow. "I knew Tiff was a free spirit, but I didn't think she'd dump her kid on her sister for that long."

"What's *your* connection with all of them?" Norma asked. "Is there a paternity suit coming your way?"

"Norma!" Rita exclaimed.

But Cash just shrugged. "Wouldn't be the first time. I know better than to make a baby. I'm always careful. But Tiff knew I had money. I guess she didn't have the guts to come to me herself, so she sent her sister." He watched Penny gum the pieces of banana Rita was handing her. "Is that okay for her?"

"Of course," Rita said. "Banana is one of the first things babies can eat."

"How do you know?"

Rita looked at him. "What?"

"Sorry. What I mean is, how do you remember what babies should eat? From—from us?"

Regret clutched at her. "No, Cash, I'm sorry. I know it from being around other women's babies and helping with them."

"I figured." He looked away.

Of all her three sons, he was the one who was taking longest to come around. Sean, her oldest, had been thrilled to learn she was his mother and had connected with her right away. Liam, her youngest, had been outright angry and resentful about the fact that she'd abandoned them in Safe Haven as young teenagers, however unintentionally. That open anger had been easier to deal with because it had forced them to talk things out, explain their sides of the argument, apologize and cry and hug.

Cash was another kind of person. He'd been polite to her from the beginning. Polite and distant. Which kind of seemed to be his modus operandi, and she worried about her middle son. When would he find love and happiness if he kept to himself, kept his distance from everyone?

"I sure do wish I remembered what you boys were like as kids," she said.

"No big deal." He shrugged like it didn't matter and scooted his chair forward. "Can I hold her?"

"Sure. Let me wipe her off." Rita rinsed a cloth and cleaned the baby's banana-goo-covered face and hands, and then Cash swung her up into his arms.

"You look good with a baby," Rita said, leaning back against the kitchen counter and smiling at him. "Like a natural. Ever think about settling down and becoming a dad, like your brothers?"

"Nope," he said, catching Penny's hand to keep her from pulling at the chain he wore around his neck.

"Why not?"

"I'm my father's son, but I don't want to make his mistakes."

Rita couldn't help shuddering. Cash's father had beaten her nearly to death, giving her the brain injury that had caused her amnesia. But for Cash to think he'd possibly do the same...no. "Cash, you can't let yourself be tied to the past like that. You're nothing like him."

He lifted an eyebrow and held her gaze.

"You want to know how I know, since I don't remember Orin. It's because of what you and your brothers have told me. And because you're a good man."

He blew out a breath and handed her the baby, who was starting to fuss a little. "Not a family man, never gonna be," he said, grinning easily. "Too busy doing deals. Besides, somebody's got to work late while all the other guys are at their kids' soccer games."

Despite his lighthearted expression and words, he seemed sad, and Rita didn't like it. She changed the subject. "What about you, Norma?"

"What *about* me?"

"We've delved into Cash's personal life. When are you gonna get one?"

"At my age, really?"

"It happened to me." Rita felt compelled to play matchmaker because she'd found a wonderful man herself: her boss at the diner, Jimmy Cooper. Not like they were planning a walk down the aisle or anything, but they'd been having a blast together. Rita wanted her best friend to be as happy as she was.

"We should get together with Jimmy and that neighbor of yours," she said. "The good-looking, cranky one?"

"No."

Rita didn't push it, not now, because she understood Norma's reason for keeping herself closed off from men. But that didn't mean she wouldn't keep encouraging her.

Holly came out and lifted Penny, who was still fussy, into the sling she wore across her chest. "This always calms her down. She likes being close."

"Is your little one content to ride with you in that thing?" Norma asked. She was obviously trying to shift the focus off herself, but Rita hoped she'd planted a seed.

"She seems to love the sling." Holly ran a hand over the baby's fine hair, smiling down at her. "Pretty soon, though, I'll have to invest in a backpack. She's getting heavy."

"You might not need one," Rita said. "She'll be walking soon."

"I don't think so," Holly said. "She hasn't even started crawling yet, not really."

Uh-oh. Rita sucked in a breath and looked at Norma.

Norma frowned and opened her mouth to say something, but shut it again.

"What?" Holly asked. "Why are you guys looking at me like that?"

"It's just unusual," Norma said, "for a baby of that age not to crawl." She hesitated, then added, "If you'd ever want to have her tested, we could set something up through the women's center."

"Tested for *what*?" Holly's voice rose to a squeak.

"Just see if the fact that she's a little behind on crawling is cause for concern. See if she has other delays." Norma's voice was reassuring, but Holly didn't look reassured.

"I didn't know the center did that kind of testing," Rita said.

"Yep. A lot of our clients have faced abuse, and sometimes their kids haven't had the support they need for normal development."

"That wasn't Tiff's situation, I don't think." Holly frowned, deep lines forming between her eyebrows. "But she *did* neglect Penny early on, I'm sorry to say. Could a baby have delays from that?"

"She could. But it's almost never irreparable. Early-intervention services are free, and they can help a lot."

"Ready to go?" Cash stood abruptly. He always

made himself scarce when the women's center was mentioned. Just another part of him avoiding the past.

"Um, sure." Holly shrugged at Rita and Norma, and the two of them left.

"She's got a lot on her plate," Norma said as soon as the door closed behind her. "Wonder if Cash will take it upon himself to give her some help."

Rita lifted her hands, palms up. "Your guess is as good as mine. I don't even pretend to understand Cash, even though he's my son."

HOLLY WASN'T GOING to worry about what Rita and Norma had said, not today, anyway. They were kind, but how could they know anything about Penny just from the fact that she wasn't very mobile?

No, Holly was just going to enjoy the ride inland to pick up her stuff. Today, Cash had brought his SUV. The better, he said, to haul her things.

How many cars did the guy have?

He'd agreed to the paternity test, even offered to pay for a faster analysis from a private lab. Which he'd obviously done because he thought the result would get him off the hook. So he had a surprise coming in a few days, and undoubtedly, he'd be angry at her for bringing it to his attention.

Although, maybe not. He seemed to really like Penny, and children in general. Maybe he'd be happy.

Maybe he'd want custody.

The thought chilled her. She hadn't even considered it before. What if he wanted to take the baby to Atlanta and put her in the charge of nannies, send her to private school and have her raised by one of the girlfriends he doubtless collected by the dozen?

She reached back and rubbed Penny's leg. They'd known each other only a month, but already, Holly couldn't imagine parting from her. Penny was all she had left of her beautiful, troubled sister, but it was more than that. Penny was a happy, expressive baby, and Holly already loved her desperately, wanted the best for her, couldn't wait to help her grow up right. She wouldn't let Cash take her away.

"So… Thinking about if you're Penny's father," she said, trying to feel him out on the topic, "your life isn't really set up for a baby, right?"

"Absolutely not." He glanced over at her. "I don't think anybody's really ready for a baby, me in particular."

Now was the time to show that she was, in fact, prepared to raise Penny. "I'm ready," she said, then quipped, "I have a grand plan."

"Grand plan, huh?" A smile quirked up the corners of his mouth, and there was that dimple again. It gave him a boyishness that loosened up the look of his expensive, preppy clothes.

Her mouth went dry. She nodded, cleared her throat. "As soon as I'm settled in, I'll start step two."

"Wait, you're really moving here? For good?"

She nodded. "Yes. That apartment that's available

in Rita's complex looks perfect, so I called the manager and negotiated a longer lease, six months. It's the right size, comfortable and it's walking distance to town. I won't need to rush into buying a car."

"You didn't choose Safe Haven because of me, did you? Because I'd hate to see you pin your hopes on a paternity suit that's not likely to go your way."

"No," she said, ignoring his negativity. "It's not all about you, though you're a part of it. It's because I know it's what Tiff wanted. She thought this town looked like a great place to raise a child. She'd even considered moving back here herself, once she got clean." Her throat went tight on the last word, so that she had to choke it out.

"Wait, where's Tiff now? She shouldn't use you as childcare for much longer, right?"

She felt her eyes go wide as she stared at him. *He doesn't know.*

CHAPTER THREE

HOLLY LOOKED AROUND at the thick vegetation speeding by, gathered herself and drew in a breath. "I just assumed you realized," she said.

"Realized what?" Cash accelerated, passed another car.

There was no easy way to say it. "Tiff's dead."

His head snapped to face her momentarily. "What?" The word cracked out like a gunshot as he turned his attention back to the road.

She swallowed, cleared her throat. "She OD'd three months ago. Penny went into the system for a little while until they could find me and I could get custody."

Cash signaled, then pulled onto the berm of the highway, the SUV cruising smoothly to a stop. He shook his head back and forth slowly. "Tiff's dead? You're sure?"

"Of course I'm sure!" Then she took a deep calming breath. Cash wasn't implying she was stupid or joking; he was just shocked and wanting to deny it.

She recognized the feeling. She hadn't believed it herself, at first.

Soon enough, her grief had morphed into a heaviness that weighed down her shoulders, a quivering, aching sadness that hovered between her stomach and her heart.

"I don't know what to say. I'm shocked." Cash stared off into the distance, where trees lined the highway. His eyes looked shiny.

"I guess I didn't realize you were that attached to her," she said.

He shook his head and drew in a huge breath. "I wasn't, not exactly. It's just that…she was so full of life, you know?"

"I know." She bit her lip, her stomach churning. "I try not to think about it too much. Can't," she added, "because of Penny. I have to take care of her."

"Penny." He turned around and held out a finger for Penny to grasp, almost like he needed the comfort of human touch. "Do you think she knows what she lost?"

"She does know," Holly said. "I talked to a social worker about it. No matter how young they are, babies who are attached to their caregivers experience grief."

Cash still stared off into the distance, not talking.

And for once, Holly let herself think about her sister. They hadn't been close as adults—their lifestyles had been so different—but they'd loved each other. The utter finality of the thought that she'd never see Tiff again pressed down on her like a stone.

After a few minutes Cash started the SUV again, and they drove the rest of the way to her motel. He didn't speak as he turned into the parking lot, as she directed him to a parking space in front of her room. He cut off the engine and got out of the car.

She and Cash made quick work of bringing her humble belongings out to the SUV. Cash arranged everything neatly, and there was still plenty of space for more. "A function of living in a bunch of different places," she explained, feeling apologetic about how little she owned, but also wanting to bring their conversation back to everyday stuff, to show Cash he didn't need to keep talking to her about Tiff. What else was there to say, really? "It didn't make sense to accumulate a lot of possessions."

"I've got way too many possessions," he said. "I like my toys."

Penny woke up then, fussy from being in the car too long. "Put down a blanket and let her crawl around a little," Cash suggested, waving an arm toward the grassy side lawn of the little motel.

"You don't mind? I figured you'd have somewhere to be."

"Kids come first," he said without an ounce of resentment in his tone, and her heart warmed toward him, just a little.

He even spread the blanket for her, pulled a couple of toys out of the diaper bag and proceeded to make Penny laugh while Holly got out some baby food. She sat cross-legged and fed Penny, changed her diaper. Even then, Cash didn't seem in a hurry to leave. "How are you going to manage here?" he asked. "I mean, for a job and childcare and the like."

"I have a few plans," she said, not sure if she wanted to go into it, if he wanted to hear it.

He was quiet a minute. Then he tilted his head, studying her. "I heard you telling Rita you lived in New York. What did you do back there? Where'd you live? I'm pretty familiar with the city."

This was always hard to explain. "I didn't have a home address," she said.

He glanced over at her. "I can't believe you were homeless."

"Oh, I lived in the finest of places," she said.

"Explain."

"I was a pet sitter for the rich and famous. I went from ritzy apartment to ritzy apartment, taking care of people's dogs."

Most people were shocked by that, by the unsettled nature of it, but Cash actually looked impressed. "So you didn't have to pay rent."

"Right. Which, as you probably know, is exorbitant in the city."

"Very clever," he said. "What would you do if you didn't have a client?"

"That was rare," she said. "But I'd either book a hotel for a few nights or stay with a friend."

"Boyfriend?" he asked.

She didn't answer. That was a way too personal question.

He seemed to realize it. "Sorry," he said. "Not my business. I can actually identify with a lifestyle like that. I haven't wanted to put down a lot of roots, either."

"There's something to be said for freedom."

"There's something great about freedom, yes," he said, "but there's also something to be said for having a place to call home."

"I wouldn't know." She remembered when she and Tiff had laughed about small towns and made fun of the whole apple-pie-and-family-down-the-street business; as kids, they'd eaten pizza on holidays and they certainly hadn't put up Christmas decorations very often.

Maybe, though, they'd laughed out of defense? Because they'd never had the opportunity for the traditional things, not with their mom and her string of boyfriends.

Time to change the subject. "I'm hoping to start a dog-walking business here. I have great recommendations, and I can bring Penny along in a carrier while I get on my feet financially."

"Sounds a little rough," he said.

She shrugged. "I think it'll be fun. I want to do it. I want to spend as much time with her as possible."

He nodded, then entertained Penny by hiding a toy from her and then showing it. "Speaking of that," he said, his voice hesitant, "what do you think about what Norma said? Do you think she might have some delays?"

Holly's heart lurched. "I didn't until this morning."

He shrugged. "It's not like I know much about babies," he said. "But Anna's son, that's my nephew, the one I was holding last night—he's crawling and standing up. Doesn't seem like Penny is doing a whole lot of that."

She certainly wasn't, but Holly hadn't been around enough babies to know what was normal.

"Did Tiff...? Did she use drugs while she was pregnant?" His voice sounded tight, controlled. Like he was trying not to express the condemnation he felt.

Defensiveness for her sister flared up. "She worked so hard to stay clean while she was pregnant," Holly said. "She said in the letter she left for me that she'd managed it, and I believe her. When I got custody of Penny, I also got her hospital records, and I saw her Apgar score. She was perfect."

"But..." Cash prompted.

Holly sighed. "But Tiff had to have a C-section, and afterward, they gave her opioids for pain. They didn't have the sense to check into her history, and she didn't have the strength to turn them down."

Cash blew out a breath. "That stinks. Do you think it's why Penny is...behind the curve? Because of neglect?"

Cash was voicing questions she didn't want to deal with.

Had Tiff's neglect, due to her addiction, set back Penny that much? If so, how could Holly forgive herself for not stepping in?

Guilt, her perennial companion, wrestled her down. When Tiff had started abusing drugs, Holly had tried to get her into rehab time after time, but Tiff had always refused to go. She'd taken up with bad characters and stolen from Holly over and over, and finally, they'd had a terrible fight and stopped speaking.

Holly hadn't known how bad her sister's addictions had gotten. Hadn't known she'd even gotten pregnant, let alone that she'd had the baby, gotten addicted again and neglected her. She'd just lived her carefree, New York life.

Was Penny paying for it now?

Two EVENINGS LATER, Cash climbed the steps to Holly's new second-floor apartment.

He couldn't stay away. This would all be over soon; the DNA test results would prove to Holly that he had no connection to the baby. She'd get on with building a life here, and he'd head back to Atlanta, and that would be that.

Precisely for that reason, he felt okay about indulging himself in his odd attraction to Holly, just for tonight. He shifted the pizza and the six-pack of cola to his other hand and rang the bell.

When she opened the door, her eyes widened. "Cash! Wow, did you...? Wow. I was going to call you, ask you to come over tomorrow."

He got a little jolt from that: Did she like him, that she wanted him to come over? "I saw you walking two dogs today, carrying the baby," he said. "It looked tiring. Thought you might welcome not having to cook dinner." He held up the pizza.

"Oh, you didn't have to..." She broke off and inhaled, her eyebrows lifting. "That smells amazing."

"Bert and Bimbo's best," he said. "And I brought up the cola. But there's wine in my car." Which he hadn't planned to offer, but all of a sudden, he had a get-lucky feeling. Maybe she'd be open to getting closer.

You're not doing that anymore.

He ignored his conscience. Yeah, drive-by relationships had started to seem empty, especially since his brothers had gotten married to women they were crazy about. But one more time wouldn't hurt. Holly Gibson was a very pretty lady.

"Oh, soda's fine. I'm not much of a drinker. Come on in," she added, holding open the door.

He walked into the furnished apartment, strewn with toys. There was a half-eaten banana on the table and newspapers scattered across the couch.

"Let me clear a space for you," she said, and collected the newspapers into a stack so he could sit down.

He liked that she didn't apologize for the state of her apartment. "I'm sorry to drop in on you," he said. "I should have called first."

"I don't mind," she said, "as long as whoever drops in realizes he has to take it as he finds it."

Penny chose that moment to blow a raspberry, and the sound made her laugh with delight and do it again.

"Yes," Holly said, all animation, kneeling beside the Pack 'n' Play. "You're so funny!" She handed Penny a baby cup. "Juice," she said, and Penny seized it and drank.

"I've been thinking more about what Norma and Rita said, and I'm worried about her," Holly explained. "I'm trying to talk to her a lot and get her to move around, and I have an appointment with this developmental pediatrician next week."

She seemed upset about it, and understandably so. Cash even felt a little guilty. No, he hadn't been truly close to Tiff, but he should have followed up, remained a friend. Seemed like she'd needed one. "Can I hold the baby?" he asked.

"Sure. She seems to like you. Well, of course she

does. She should." Holly sounded flustered as she handed him the baby, but then, caring for a kid all day was tough.

Penny was a cute little peanut, dressed in a soft pink one-piece outfit and smelling like baby powder. She fit right into his arms. They ended up on the couch together, all three of them, Holly and Cash taking turns holding Penny and scarfing down a slice of pizza each. He talked nonsense to Penny, laughed at her when she grabbed for his slice, and when her face screwed up like she was going to cry again, he distracted her with a rattle Holly handed him. Slowly, they got her calmed down.

It was dangerously close to the domestic fantasy Cash had in his weakest moments. The times when he blatantly envied his brothers, when he longed for what he'd never have.

"I'm going to put her to bed," Holly said finally. She looked up at him, her face close, uncertain. "Do you… Would you like to come?"

"Sure, why not?"

After they'd put Penny into the Pack 'n' Play, which Holly had moved into her bedroom—she planned to give Penny the other small bedroom, she said, but not just yet—they walked out of the room together. When Holly looked up at him, her flushed cheeks and smile had turned her face from pretty to beautiful. He couldn't resist moving closer.

The way her pupils dilated and her breath caught

was very subtle, but Cash knew how to read women. She was interested in him, at least a little. Good, because he was interested in her.

"You're doing a great job with Penny," he said, leaning one hand against the wall, looking down at her.

She started to smile, and then something crossed her face, some concern. She stepped out and away from him and searched his eyes. "I don't... Look, we should talk."

"Talking's overrated." He smiled at her. He didn't necessarily like the part of himself that said that, not anymore. But it had always been effective.

The next step she took away from him was bigger, more decisive, and she held up a hand. "Whoa. I'm sorry if I gave you the wrong idea. That's not what this is about."

"Is it my fault you're irresistible?" She was, but what a line! He could do better.

"Come out to the living room," she said, and strode out there. "Have a seat." She gestured to a chair. Not, he noted, to the couch.

Too bad.

"Look," she said, "I was hoping you'd find out the same way I did, by mail, but I'm just going to tell you."

"Tell me what?" He was still thinking about seduction possibilities. He should definitely take her out before making a move. Maybe to one of the expensive restaurants that overlooked the ocean. She seemed far from affluent and would probably appreciate a good dinner.

She swallowed, and her hands tightened on the edge of the couch. "The DNA test results are back," she said.

"That was fast. What did you find out?" She looked upset, and that was understandable; she'd probably hoped he could help her as the baby's father. But maybe he'd be able to help her a little bit, just because. He could certainly afford it.

"The baby's yours."

"I can maybe… Whoa. What did you say?"

She repeated it. *The baby's yours.*

"That's got to be wrong," he said while a great, swirling noise rose up inside his head. *The baby's yours.*

She was saying something about how the results should come to him, too, would be waiting in his mailbox, but he couldn't follow the details.

The baby's yours.

Total disaster. It just couldn't be, because he was the last person who should be parenting a child.

She walked over to the kitchen counter and picked up a special-delivery envelope. "It's all right here," she said, opening the envelope in what seemed like slow motion.

He couldn't move.

"Don't you want to see?" she asked, beckoning him over.

He forced his legs to walk to the kitchen area, forced his eyes to skim the chart, the "alleged father" column, something about alleles and double Xs and Ys.

She leaned over and tapped the bottom of the page. "Paternity practically proven," it said.

Practically proven. He seized on that. "What's that supposed to mean?"

"It's a greater than 99.9 percent chance," she said, holding up another page, dense with writing. "It's all explained here." She pointed him to sections here and paragraphs there, talking him through it.

Cash looked at her. Looked back toward the bedroom where Penny was sleeping.

He felt like something was constricting his throat, like he couldn't breathe.

"I want to keep this copy," she said, "but like I mentioned, you should have the exact same report in your mailbox when you get home. Do you—do you want to talk about it?"

Talk? He could barely breathe. "No," he said. "No. I need to think." Stiff as a robot, he walked over and picked up his jacket.

"But we didn't finish the pizza." She nodded toward the forgotten box. "And we do need to talk. As soon as possible." She straightened her back and faced him.

"Not now," he said.

"Look," she said, "I'm not asking you to have custody of Penny, or even take care of her. I just need you to step up to the plate with child support. So can we meet tomorrow?"

Dimly, beneath the shock, he felt a twinge because, of course, she only wanted his money.

That was usually the case with women, but this time, apparently, the child was actually his.

He had a child. "Sure. Tomorrow." He turned and practically ran out of the apartment.

He *couldn't* be a father. He'd always known that. He wasn't suited.

What was he supposed to do?

CHAPTER FOUR

THE NEXT MORNING, Holly decided she needed to do something concrete to enrich Penny's life, stimulate her, work on any delays she might have. Taking her to the baby lap-sit at the library seemed like a good—and fortunately, free—way to do it.

She needed to get Cash's stricken expression out of her mind and stop worrying about what he'd do with the knowledge that he was Penny's father. He was supposed to get in touch with her today and talk things through; if he didn't, she'd figure out her next step. No point in sitting inside her apartment worrying.

When she walked into the Safe Haven Public Library, she inhaled the old-book smell and listened to the quiet voices, and felt her tight shoulders relax. She'd always loved libraries; they'd been refuges when she was a kid. This one was particularly homey, with lots of polished old wood and comfortably shabby carpets and furniture.

She followed the "Baby Lap-Sit" signs upstairs and soon was sitting in a circle with about ten other parents and babies.

Holly felt nervous, like the new kid at school; all the others seemed to know each other. But unlike when she'd been in school, several of these women were friendly. A couple of them made eye contact with her and smiled, and the mom next to her looked at Penny. "Why, aren't you the cutest little thing!" she said in a singsong voice, making Penny laugh.

Three women stood off to one side, talking intently about something that made them smirk and snicker as they held their babies loosely on their hips. One, a little girl, struggled to get down, but her mother just pulled a big bag of marshmallows out of her purse and started popping them in the baby's mouth.

The white-haired, rosy-faced woman who was leading the group introduced herself as Miss Martha. "We'll go around the circle," she said. "Everyone introduce yourselves and your babies. Tell us the age of your kids. You don't have to reveal your own age," she joked, and the moms laughed.

As the mothers introduced themselves and their babies, it became obvious that Penny was one of the older babies in the group, even though Holly was probably one of the youngest moms, or rather, mother figures. She didn't clarify that she wasn't Penny's mother; that wasn't a concern of any of theirs.

One of the few babies that looked bigger and older than Holly—a toddler, really—was lying beside his mother, thumping his clunky shoes on the floor over and over, only pausing to give his mother the occasional hard kick.

"Oh, Jason, don't," his mother said, but didn't do anything else to stop the child.

The marshmallow mom nudged one of her friends, whose lip curled. Jason's mother seemed to notice, because her mouth turned down and her shoulders slumped.

The marshmallow-eating baby broke free from her mother's arms and grabbed Jason's truck, causing a small tussle.

"Come on, Tyla, you have a toy to play with." The mom dug into her bag and produced a rubber doll.

Tyla took the doll, glanced at it and then hurled it at Jason. Fortunately, her aim wasn't good enough to hit her target.

"Well, okay, let's get started!" Miss Martha said. "This playtime is about you connecting with your baby. Eye contact, smiles, giggles—all of it is crucial to your child's socialization."

"Some kids could use a little help," Jason's mom muttered.

Miss Martha had them all sit with babies in their laps, facing outward, then showed them a simple finger-play game. As Holly manipulated Penny's tiny hands, Penny looked back over her shoulder and gave Holly a wide-eyed smile.

Love for her niece exploded in her chest, and

tears pushed at the backs of her eyes. She kissed the top of Penny's head and made a silent promise: *I'll do everything I can to help you catch up and grow up right*.

"Patty-cake next," Miss Martha singsonged. Clearly, she was determined to keep them busy so the babies—and mothers—stayed focused instead of turning on each other.

All the moms obediently encouraged their children to clap their hands, which the babies did with varying degrees of success.

All except Penny, who didn't seem to have a clue about clapping, even after Holly showed her how. She had to hold Penny's hands in her own and move them in a patty-cake motion throughout the whole rhyme.

Covertly, she looked around to see if anyone else's baby was struggling. Nope, just Penny.

As Holly wiggled her fingers in front of Penny for a counting game, she was painfully aware of how little she knew about how to raise a baby.

She'd tried to read and research and watch videos when she could, but since she'd brought Penny home she'd been so busy, what with closing down her dog-walking business in New York and moving to Safe Haven, that she really hadn't had a lot of time for a conscious plan of how to do a good job as Penny's new mom; it had mostly been catch-as-catch-can.

Now, she felt inadequate, especially compared to the

other parents, who seemed so comfortable and knowl-
edgeable with their babies. One of the kids actually
threw up, which would have made Holly panic. But her
mother just held her over a blanket until she'd finished,
rolled up the blanket and stuffed it into her diaper bag,
then swiped a tissue over the child's mouth.

Again, the snotty moms sneered. But Holly was
just impressed with the throw-up mother's aplomb.

She tried to soak in everything the leader said
about child development. She'd get a library card
and check out some of the books the leader was
holding up, and would try to play these types of
games with Penny every day.

After the official baby lap-sit ended, the leader
encouraged them to stay a little longer and let the
babies play together while the parents got to know
each other. Holly sat Penny beside a colorful bolster
and watched her as she took in her surroundings,
feeling shy around the other mothers.

Penny got herself onto her hands and knees and
scooted backward, but unlike the other babies,
she didn't pull up. Even babies who were younger
seemed able to do more, much more. As she watched
Penny's awkward semi-crawl, Holly's heart twisted
in her chest.

It was becoming more and more apparent that
Tiff hadn't taken good care of Penny. And now,
Holly was continuing that tradition. She'd started
to realize that Norma and Rita had been right—

Penny had delays. But now she saw, with a sinking feeling, just how far behind Penny was.

Miss Martha was making her way around the room, chatting with people, and she soon approached Holly and Penny. "We're glad you joined us this week. Can I answer any questions for you?"

"She's so far behind," Holly blurted out. "She can't really even crawl yet, and I don't think she's ever done anything like this—" she waved a hand to indicate the busy circle of mothers and babies "—in her whole life."

"You don't *think* so?" Miss Martha cocked her head to one side. "Are you a new foster or adoptive parent?"

"I'm her aunt, but I'm raising her now. Since last month, and I feel like I don't know anything."

"You'll figure it out," Miss Martha said reassuringly. "She's adorable. I might be able to point you to a specialist or play therapist, if you'd like to hurry her along."

"Yes, that would be great." Holly scribbled down the names the woman gave her with a sinking heart. How was she going to pay for a special therapist when her savings were depleting so rapidly?

Penny's father, that was how. She had to get in touch, motivate him to help his child.

She shot a text to Cash and then took a couple of videos of Penny sitting and watching the other babies. No one seemed to mind; in fact, a lot of the other moms were taking pictures.

As soon as Cash texted back that he was on his way, she collected Penny's things, hoisted the baby into her arms and hurried down the stairs.

Minutes later, Cash joined her in the little outside sitting area. "You said you needed to talk to me."

"I want you to see something." Unceremoniously, she plunked Penny into his arms and held her phone so he could see.

"So she's playing with the other babies and... Oh. She's not."

"Right. She's just watching them, even though they're all younger than she is. Sometimes she crawls, but just barely. She's really behind, Cash." Her voice caught a little as she said it.

He settled Penny closer to his chest and brushed a kiss on top of her head, and worry lines appeared on his forehead. Holly could smell his cologne—expensive—and feel the heat from his body so close to hers.

One of the snotty moms walked across the courtyard and did a double take when she saw Cash. "Well, hey, Cash," she said, smiling. "You have a new little friend, do you?"

"Yeah," he said without elaborating on the relationship. "You've met Holly, right?"

"We just had a fun time together," the mom said, sparing a quick smile for Holly.

"And this is…Tyla, right?" He reached out and tickled her baby's chin, making her giggle. "When did Tyla start to crawl?"

"Oh, gosh, she was scooting around at six months, but a real crawl? Just a few weeks ago. At nine months."

"Smarty," he said, tickling the baby again.

He was so much better with babies than Holly was. So much better with people.

And he was charming to everyone, obviously, so when he treated Holly nicely, she couldn't take it personally.

After Tyla and her mother left, Cash turned back to Holly. "We have some work to do," he said.

"Remember, you don't have to be involved," she said quickly. "I just need money to get help for her."

The friendly light went out of his eyes and his lips flattened. He looked from her to Penny. "Of course. I'll do some research and draw up a child-support plan." He stood, handed the baby back to Holly and left.

She sensed she'd offended him again and she felt bad about that. It was clear that Penny would benefit from his involvement. But Cash was too dangerous. Dangerous because he could take Penny from her. And dangerous because he was a little too attractive for a woman like her to handle.

AFTER LEAVING HOLLY and Penny, Cash headed for the center of town. Ever since Holly's bombshell revelation last night, he'd known he needed to see his brothers, immediately.

And since there was no other way to do it, he'd agreed to join them for the worst holiday duty around: managing their kids in the long line of families that snaked through Safe Haven's downtown park, waiting to see Santa. Their wives had dumped them off here at the park and escaped to shop and have a late lunch.

He'd agreed to help his brothers, but he hoped he'd find a chance to talk to them about the crazy results of the paternity test and the implications, which he was still trying to process. Even if the kids kept them too busy for a heart-to-heart, he craved a sense of normalcy and the support he got nowhere else but with his brothers.

They were the only people who understood him. Who'd understand why it was such a disaster for him to learn he was a father.

The smell of kettle corn and hot chocolate filled the air, and Christmas carols played over loudspeakers. Cash had to admire the business model of the early Santa visit: a captive audience, foods that played up everyone's sense of tradition, hungry, cranky kids and parents who were feeling indulgent. Or maybe just desperate.

He spotted his brothers about halfway back in the line and headed over. No surprise, they barely had energy to say hello to him. Liam was busy with his foster son, Gino; the toddler had never visited Santa before and was scared at the prospect. Probably uncomfortable with the crowd and the noise, too. Sean was joggling his baby, Hosea, affectionately known as HoHo.

"Uncle Cash!" Sean's twins, Hope and Hayley, rushed over to hug him, and it lifted his spirits even though he'd forgotten to stop to buy them anything. He had been so frazzled that he hadn't stocked up the way he usually did.

What kind of father would he be when he couldn't even remember the basic gifts required by his nieces?

"If you could just…keep them entertained." Sean sounded harassed. "I've got to go change HoHo's diaper."

HoHo laughed and waved his arms, and Sean held him out at arm's length, his nose wrinkling. "Be still, buddy! I forgot to bring a spare outfit."

Cash had to chuckle. Sean did great as a dad. It was fun to see his brother totally embracing the role. "I've got the girls," Cash promised.

Gino looked up at Cash fearfully and then buried his face in Liam's leg.

"Hey, little buddy, you remember me," Cash said. "We hung out just the other night." But Gino kept his face hidden.

"He's going through a fear stage, according to the social worker," Liam said quietly. "Not really a surprise with all he's been through. He'll get used to you again soon."

"I'll be here when he does." Cash knelt in front of the twins, more certain of his welcome. "Hey, ladies. Are you excited about seeing Santa? What are you going to ask him for?"

Hope and Hayley looked at each other, and then Hope beckoned him closer. "He's not the real Santa," she said with a worried frown on her face, patting his shoulder as if the news would be crushing to him.

"Is that right?" Cash actually wasn't sure where the girls stood in relation to Santa. Did they still believe in him? They were seven, so they probably did, but kids were pretty sophisticated these days. No telling what they had heard.

Fortunately, a vendor walked by just then, carrying a rack of old-fashioned toys—ball and cups, wooden dolls that danced when you squeezed the base they stood on, brightly painted cars and trucks. Cash waved the man over. "Pick out what you want, girls," he said, and when Hope couldn't decide, he bought her both toys she liked, and then bought a second one for Hayley, to be fair. He picked out a colorful dog pull toy for Gino, too.

Liam rolled his eyes as he helped Gino figure out how to pull the toy. "Good thing you're just the rich uncle. You'd go broke if you had kids of your own."

Cash felt a chill skitter up his spine.

Cash waved down another vendor and bought giant candy canes for the twins just as Sean came back with the always-cheerful HoHo. Around them, the noise of families rose, joyous and fussy in turn. Someone jostled Hope, who was the sensitive twin, so Cash positioned himself between her and the rest of the crowd, moving her more tightly into the family circle.

Sean lifted an eyebrow at the candy and toys. "You don't have to do that, you know," he said to Cash. "They'll love you even if you don't spend a fortune on them."

"I like buying them stuff," Cash said, defending himself.

"Yeah, but when it's junk food like that, it's me and Anna who have to pay the price."

"Sorry." Again, worry flashed through him. "It's not like I know anything about kids."

Sean and Liam looked at each other and frowned. "Chill, bro, I didn't mean that," Sean said.

"Cash!" A pretty woman—what was her name, Chelsea something-or-other?—came up with her little girl, just the twins' size.

"Hope! Hayley!" The little girl rushed to stand in front of the twins, smiling hugely. "We're going to the playground. Want to come?"

"Can we, Daddy?" Identical pairs of puppy-dog eyes looked up at Sean. "We don't want to miss Santa," Hope said.

"We won't," Hayley assured her twin. "Will we, Daddy?"

For some reason, hearing the twins call Sean "Daddy" choked up Cash. The twins' biological father had been a scumbag and was serving a long prison sentence. They'd accepted Sean as a father and he loved them dearly, as dearly as he loved HoHo, his own son with Anna.

Now, he knelt to discuss manners with them and Chelsea stepped closer to Cash. "How *are* you? I haven't seen you in, like, forever!"

"Doing fine, thanks. You're looking good." He'd dated Chelsea a couple of times but they hadn't really clicked. "You sure you don't mind taking my nieces over to the playground?"

"Glad to," Chelsea said with a winning smile. "You could come along."

"I, um, have to talk to my brothers about something."

"Sure," she said easily. "I'll bring 'em back when you get close to the front of the line. Maybe we could get some dinner later."

"Can't, not tonight," Cash said.

The twins stuffed their new toys and candy into Sean's arms. Chelsea shrugged and waved and headed over to the swings and slides, the three little girls orbiting her.

"Whoa, you're losing your touch, brother." Liam was kneeling beside Gino, who was varooming the dog toy as if it was a car. "Chelsea turns a lot of heads over at the Palmetto Pig. Can't believe you let an invite like that go."

"Other stuff on my mind," Cash said.

"So you really do want to talk to us?" Sean put HoHo into his stroller and handed him a blue vinyl duck, which he proceeded to stuff into his mouth.

Liam looked up, then touched Gino's chin. "You can play, but stay right here by my legs, understand?"

The toddler nodded solemnly, then squatted beside the wooden dog Cash had bought him.

Liam stood. "So what's up?"

"A lot," Cash said, looking from him to Sean. His heart rate jumped a little. "You know Holly, that woman I brought to the tree lighting?"

"Pretty," Sean said, and Liam nodded.

"You remember her baby?"

"Sure," Sean said. "About HoHo's size."

Cash nodded, swallowed. Looked around to see if anyone was listening in, but the crowd was noisy, as everyone focused on their own family groups. "She's, um. She's mine."

Sean caught on first. "Your *baby*? Did you and Holly—?"

"No, no," Cash interrupted, waving a hand. "Her sister. Tiff. It's her baby. Holly's raising Penny because Tiff…" To his complete embarrassment, his throat tightened to where he couldn't get out the rest of the words.

His brothers waited, watching him.

"Tiff died," he choked out finally, and then knelt and tickled HoHo's chin while he pulled himself together.

He had no idea what his reaction was all about. He wasn't usually emotional. It was like he'd caught some kind of pregnancy and childbirth hormones from being around Penny.

"Sorry, man," Liam said, his voice gruff. "When were you seeing her? Was she from Atlanta?"

Sean extended a hand and pulled Cash to his feet. "Why didn't you tell us you were serious about someone?"

"I *wasn't*." He drew in a breath, calmer now. "It was casual. We spent a week together when she was here on vacation and I happened to be home." He shook his head. "I never planned to have a baby. Thought it was all taken care of, you know?"

"You sure Holly's not scamming you?"

He nodded. "Paternity test."

"Wow."

They were all quiet for a few minutes. Then the line moved forward, and Gino clung to Liam's leg. "Don't wanna see Santa."

Liam scooped him up, along with the wooden dog. "You don't have to, buddy. You can just watch."

"Yeah, Santa already came to this crowd." Sean

eyed Cash as he shifted the armful of new toys the twins had left in his care.

Pretty soon they reached the front of the line. The twins rushed back, worried they'd miss their chance, and everyone focused on the Santa visit. HoHo sat cheerfully on the exhausted-looking Santa's lap, and Gino crept close enough that a photo could be snapped, even though he refused to interact. The twins each had a turn reciting a list of their wants.

"So what are you going to do?" Sean asked him as the twins posed.

Cash shrugged. "Pay child support. See if there's any other way I can help a little." Ironic that he, who was always doing his best to avoid people trying to get their hands on his money, was willing to help out with Penny.

But this was different. Penny was his child, according to the DNA results. That made it right for him to provide for her.

"Throw money at it and that's all?" Sean frowned.

Cash lifted his hands, palms up. "What else can I do? I've had a million relationships, all bad." And he didn't want to say it out loud, but he knew the truth: he was like his father. Looked just like him, according to Sean, who remembered their father the best. More than that, he shared a lot of his father's inner qualities, like loving money and always trying to find a way to make more of it. He remembered following their father around, even when his brothers and mother avoided him, listening to the way he talked to people, always making some kind of a deal.

Cash had been his father's favorite, and he'd admired him. Which said a lot about who Cash was, considering what type of person their father had turned out to be.

In high school, even though Cash's foster parents gave him plenty of material things, making money had been like a drug. He'd started a business helping people program their remote controls or video players and made a ton; he'd become president of the business club, organized fund-raisers that had financed every member's trip to the state capital, and made the business club the cool place, gotten lots of cute girls to join. His brothers had just rolled their eyes at him. "Just like Dad," they'd said, and, "You're Dad's son."

He walked away from Sean toward the twins and Santa, who were talking with a picture-taking elf.

The Santa cleared his throat. "I remember you, young man," he said, pointing a bony finger, which was at odds with his probably fake plump belly. "You created quite a disruption at the party for foster kids, oh, about twenty years ago."

Cash remembered all too well, and stared at the not-so-jovial man in the red suit. "You were there?"

Santa nodded and then gestured for Hope and Hayley to smile for the camera.

From behind him, Liam snickered. "I remember, too. You were the worst of all of us."

"Still am," Cash said, turning away in time to catch Sean's frown.

They collected all the kids and their things and headed toward the spot they'd planned to meet the wives, a gazebo at the center of the park. "This is serious stuff," Sean remarked as the twins coaxed Gino to run ahead with them. "You've got to figure out if Holly is even fit to parent that child. If she's not…you need to take over."

"Me?" Cash stared at Sean. "I can't take care of a baby."

"If it's the right thing to do, you can." Sean was implacable in his big-brother mode. "You've got to figure out a way to get to know her, get some perspective." He looked at Cash, then at Liam, and a smile started to cross his face. "And I know just how and where you can do it."

Liam nodded slowly. "Out at Ma Dixie's. Bring them both to the crab crack after Thanksgiving. Holly and the baby."

Cash frowned. "That's a lot to spring on her. She's not from around here. And she's kind of quiet."

"But seems like she's settling in," Liam said. "What better way for her to get to know the area?"

What could it hurt? It certainly wouldn't make things any *worse*. "I'll think about it." And maybe he'd take her to meet Ma and Pudge first, one-on-

one. Seeing her and Penny in that environment would definitely give him more information.

He'd figured to limit his involvement to money, both because that was what Holly wanted and because he wasn't good at deep relationships.

But Sean was right; he had a responsibility to make sure his own child was being raised right.

"My little brother, a daddy." Sean pounded Cash's shoulder, none too gently. "That's almost sweet."

Except it wasn't. Not at all. His brothers hadn't freaked about him having a baby, but when they gave it more thought, they'd realize just how ridiculous it was.

Maybe Ma and her longtime boyfriend, Pudge LeFrost, would have some ideas for how to handle the situation. Because Cash was fresh out of them, himself.

THE NEXT DAY, Holly trudged back to the apartment complex with Penny whimpering in her carrier. Penny, who suddenly seemed to weigh four hundred pounds. Walking two mastiffs while carrying a baby on her chest had been no joke. Especially when they'd been preceded by an excitable beagle and a pair of fussy, feisty Maltese mixes.

At least she wouldn't need to join a gym.

Even though it was only midafternoon, her dog-walking duties were over for the day. Most working people wanted a lunchtime walk for their dogs, and she didn't yet have any clients with afternoon or evening jobs. She tried to shove aside the tight feeling in her chest, but it wouldn't stay away. It was going to be a lot harder to make a living when she could only walk dogs, not stay over to care for them while their owners were away. That had been the main moneymaker for her in the past, with a few dog walks in the middle of the day adding extra income.

Now, with a baby to care for, the dog-walking was the main event. And people in a small Southern town wouldn't pay the same high rates she'd gotten so easily in New York. Yeah, the cost of living was lower, but she still wasn't convinced her budget would balance.

"Hey, Holly!" Norma's voice drew her to the pool enclosure, where multicolored Christmas lights already glowed on this overcast afternoon. Rita and Norma sat at one of the tables by the pool, both bundled up in thick coats. When Holly saw Norma put out a cigarette, she understood why the ladies were sitting outside even though it was chilly.

Rita stood and came over to the gate. She reached out a hand and cupped Penny's head. "How's the little sweetie?"

"That's going to kill you, walking dogs with a baby strapped to you," Norma added as she propped up her feet.

"Anytime I'm not working, I'm happy to watch her," Rita said. "After all, I'm her grandma."

Holly's jaw dropped. "You know?"

Rita nodded. "Cash told me today."

Holly studied her to see whether that revelation had upset her, but she was all smiles. "I love being a grandma," she said. "It's a real thrill to have another little one to love."

"Hand her over, and you go take a nap," Norma suggested. "You look beat."

A part of Holly would've liked nothing better. But she was responsible for Penny. She and no one else, and you couldn't count on other people—they let you down or wanted something in return. "That's a nice offer," she said, "but I'm fine." She turned and headed toward the steps up to her apartment, trying to inject some energy into her walk so the ladies would believe her.

Before she got halfway up the steps, the sound of loud music assailed her. Penny started to cry.

Hmm, maybe she should have thought twice before taking the apartment here. It had been so quiet in the last few days, but this music was seriously loud. Not only that, but she also knew the song and cringed, waiting for the obscenity in the chorus.

It didn't come. Someone was at least playing a family-friendly version.

When she reached the top of the stairs and looked down the walkway, she was stunned to see Cash gesturing and pointing as a couple of men carried boxes into the apartment next door. A speaker, small but obviously powerful, seemed to be the source of the music.

"What are you doing here?" she yelled over it.

He strode toward her, frowned, then called back over his shoulder, "Turn it down, guys." He took the key from her, opened her apartment door and held out his hands for the baby.

She hesitated, then lifted Penny out of her carrier so Cash could take her. After all, he was her father, and although she wasn't looking for him to be involved, she couldn't deny him the right to see his child.

Besides, Holly was really, really tired.

Cash seemed to see that. He followed her inside and pulled out one of the kitchen chairs for her. Then he tapped at his cell phone and spoke rapidly into it in a language that sounded Asian, the tones rising and falling.

"Hope you like Chinese food," he said. "It'll be here in thirty minutes." He opened her refrigerator, found a pitcher of tea and poured her a glass.

"Make yourself at home, why don't you," she said, but without heat. It was kind of nice to have someone taking care of her.

"I *am* making myself at home. I'm moving in next door."

"What?" Her heart lifted dangerously at his words.

"I'm your new neighbor," he said. "Don't look so shocked. I'm subletting until Christmas."

"But why? You have another place just a few miles away."

"Converting that into an office, a temporary one," he said. "Look, I know you said you don't need for me to be involved, but I figure I should at least help out while you get settled."

Whoa. Holly's stomach knotted, and sweat broke out on her forehead and neck despite the cool day. Cash, here? Right next door? Staking a claim and invading her privacy?

Despite her tension, she was surprised to feel her shoulders relax a little. It would be nice to have some help from Penny's father, just for a bit. And she was reluctantly impressed that he seemed to want to be close to Penny, even if it meant setting up housekeeping in a place decorated with inflatable Swimming Santas.

After she'd gulped down some tea and Cash had gotten Penny to stop crying, Holly warmed up a bottle and fed her. Cash went back next door to give more instructions to the guys who were moving him in.

She couldn't believe that, within thirty-six hours, he had accepted his paternity and moved his residence to take responsibility for it. On the one hand, she knew it was a good thing. She needed Cash to step up to the plate and it looked like he was going to do that.

The only problem was, what she actually wanted from him wasn't hands-on parenting, but money to help support Penny. She would have to figure out a way to talk to him about it.

The food came, and Cash waved aside her offer to pay. He pulled out a big wad of bills—it figured that was how would pay for things, flashy as he was—and again, spoke to the delivery guy in that tonal language. As he opened cartons at her small kitchen table, she asked him about it. "When did you learn to speak Mandarin?"

"Cantonese," he corrected. "I do a lot of business in southern China."

"What other languages do you speak?" She was kind of joking.

He waved a hand in a dismissive gesture. "Oh, Spanish and a few other Asian languages, but I'm not very good at them."

She lifted an eyebrow. "Are you good at Cantonese? Because that man seemed to understand you pretty well."

"I get by. So what do you like? I ordered some Szechuan, because I like spicy, but there's pork-fried rice if you'd rather have something more plain. And this is a tofu eggplant dish, in case you don't eat meat."

"Don't you think of everything." She smiled up at him. "It all looks fantastic. Thank you."

After they'd eaten their fill, Cash held Penny while Holly put away the rest of the food. By the time she had wiped down the table, Penny was dozing off. "Since she didn't have much of a nap today, I'm going to put her to bed now," she said. Then she added, "Unless you want to do it." Such a strange feeling, having Cash here for Penny's bedtime again.

She should worry about it, and no doubt she would. But having him here, having another adult she could talk to and share her concerns with, made muscles loosen that she hadn't known were tight.

He smiled with what looked like gratitude. "Thanks for the offer. I'd better watch what you do one more time."

"Sure. I guess it's something you'll need to learn, since you're her father."

He drew in a deep breath. "I'm still trying to get used to that word."

"Seems like you're doing a pretty good job, considering that you moved in next door." She shot a glare over her shoulder. "And told your mom."

"Did that bother you?"

She shook her head. "I was just surprised."

"What can I say, I'm a man of action. Lead on."

That made her nervous.

She took Penny into the bedroom and stopped, surprised. "There's a rocking chair here."

Cash held up his hands, palms out. "Wasn't me. The ladies in the rental office found one to bring in for you. Apparently it circulates through the furnished apartments, depending on who has a baby that needs rocking."

"That's nice." It was. And it also made her nervous. How could she keep a safe distance from people who were acting so helpful and kind?

She put Penny on the floor to change her diaper, but Cash waved her away. "This, I actually know how to do," he said.

"You do?" Even men who loved their role as uncle rarely got this down and dirty about it.

"My brother Sean insisted. Said it was something every man needed to know. I think he was really just making sure I'd be available to babysit when he wanted to take his wife out." While he spoke, he deftly did the cleaning, wiping and diapering. He swung up Penny, but when she started to chortle, he tucked her quickly against his chest. "Sorry. I know it's wrong to get her excited right before bedtime."

"I think you know more about babies than I do." She held out her arms for Penny and cuddled her close, sniffing her sweaty, baby-shampoo-scented head. Then she sat down in the rocking chair. "She'll love being rocked to sleep. You can stay if you want."

"Should I be quiet?"

"You can talk a little, but not loud." Holly rocked

gently, the weight of the baby in her lap and arms anchoring her. She loved these quiet moments with Penny. She was almost sorry that the baby was so tired she started to drift off immediately.

Cash leaned against the doorjamb and watched, and only when Penny had sighed and nestled closer to Holly, indicating that she was asleep, did he speak. "I drew up a child-support plan, with the help of my lawyer." He named a monthly figure that was three times as high as what she'd expected him to offer.

"It's too much!" she blurted out, and then clamped her mouth shut. That much money made her uneasy even though she'd come here wanting financial help from Cash, and she needed to think about why.

"Huh." Cash let out a short laugh. "Never heard a woman say that before."

She stared at him. "How many times have women asked you for child support?"

"More than you might think." He shoved his hands into his pockets. "But they weren't my kids. Penny is, and I've been thinking about it. Penny's more my responsibility than yours. I'm the one who had a relationship with Tiff that ended up making a baby. You had nothing to do with that, and you're taking care of her out of the kindness of your heart."

"She's my family, too!" Holly didn't like the turn this conversation had taken. Cash had so many advantages over her—money and connections. And now he'd realized he had a closer biological relationship with Penny as well.

"You shouldn't suffer for something I did," he went on. "She's my daughter. So I want to pay whatever is needed for her to have a good life."

Holly's grip tightened on the baby. She wasn't comfortable with Cash focusing on how much more Penny belonged to him than to her. It sounded... possessive. "I want to pay and contribute. She's my niece. She's my responsibility, too."

He waved a hand at the room. "I want her to have more than this."

"Excuse me?" Holly stood up too fast and Penny twisted in her arms, her face crinkling like she was about to cry.

The thoughtless judgment in Cash's gesture, in the way he looked around the humble bedroom, made her want to smack him, a totally uncharacteristic feeling for her, and certainly not a way for a caregiver to act.

She drew in a calming breath, biting off the angry words she wanted to say. Carefully, she placed Penny in the Pack 'n' Play, put her favorite snuggly toy in her arms and patted her back until she settled again.

It gave her time to think. "Look, Cash, if you feel like that's the right amount of child support to pay, I'm not going to argue with you. I'll just put what we don't need in a savings account, for college. But I'm not going to quit working or move into some fancy place just so you feel more at home. This apartment is perfectly fine for a baby, and seeing me work is good for her."

He studied her, frowning. "You're your own person, aren't you?"

"Of course," she said, and led the way back out to the living room. She hoped he would leave now. She needed time to process everything that had happened today.

No such luck. "I want to talk to you about something I'm going to do on the advice of Rita and my brothers," he said.

"Oh, what's that?" She didn't sit down, didn't offer him a seat or a drink. *Go home*, she tried to say without words.

"There's a parenting class at the women's center." He pulled out his phone and scrolled while Holly's mind reeled. A parenting class? What was he implying?

"Here it is," he said. He showed her an informational page. "Rita told me about it. It's for parents of infants and babies, or people who are fostering or have a court-related order. Emphasis on special needs." He glanced toward the bedroom and then back at Holly. "I'd like to take Penny and do these classes," he said.

The tightness in her chest got worse. "Are you trying to take her from me?"

"No!" He stared at her. "I'm just trying to learn and figure this out, so I can see her and know her. Take care of her without completely screwing up."

But Holly was suspicious. All she'd heard was "take Penny."

She started toward the door, hoping he'd follow, then stopped halfway to look at the picture of Tiff she'd hung on the wall.

I know you wanted me to bring her here and get Cash's help, but how well did you know him, really?

But Tiff wasn't here now, couldn't answer, couldn't help Holly make decisions about her baby. She turned abruptly, causing Cash to stop. "You can do the parenting class," she said, "and you can take Penny. But only if I can do it with you."

CHAPTER FIVE

RITA KNOCKED ON the door of Norma's high-end condo, then turned and leaned over the railing to see the ocean just beyond. She loved the sight and sound of pounding waves.

For a moment, she let herself envy her friend. An insurance settlement from a company Norma had worked for long ago meant that Norma had all the money she needed. She could afford to live in a luxury, oceanfront condo, the same complex where Cash lived, and yeah, the place was nice.

But, she reminded herself, Norma's life was far from perfect; the envy went both ways. Rita had it good. She lived in a small rental, yes, but she had friends and a good man to keep her company. Money couldn't buy that.

Norma's front door had a painted sign as a Christmas decoration: Be Naughty. Save Santa the Trip. Knowing Norma, it was in defiance of everyone else's classy Christmas wreaths. Her friend loved a lot of things about this condominium complex, but she railed against the slightly snobbish attitude held by some of the residents.

Like her neighbor, affectionately known to the two of them as the Silver Fox.

Norma opened the door and, even though Rita hadn't called in advance, gave her a big smile and opened her arms for a hug.

It was wonderful to have a close, drop-in-anytime type of friend nearby.

"I'm so glad you moved to Safe Haven," Rita said as they walked inside, where the smell of something baking pervaded the air. "Muffins? Coffee cake? It smells fabulous."

"Blueberry muffins." Norma opened her built-in, stainless-steel oven and pulled out a tin of golden brown muffins, their rounded tops rising high. She opened a canister of sugar, the fancy crystalized kind, and sprinkled some on top. "You want one?"

Rita's mouth watered, but she patted her belly regretfully. "I'd better not. At least, not unless we take a walk first to preburn the calories."

"Can't," Norma said. "I promised Cash that I'd wait for his wireless guy. He's supposed to come sometime this morning."

Rita's heart gave a painful twist. Why would Cash ask Norma for help when Rita was his own mother and perfectly willing? Was it an on-purpose slap in the face, or just a general lack of trust?

She was too embarrassed by her son's coldness toward her to say anything about it. "Is he having problems with his wireless?"

"He's setting up an office here," Norma explained. "Got an okay from the condo association and everything."

Oh. Rita swallowed. Something else she hadn't known about.

Norma paused in the midst of turning the muffins out onto a plate. "What's wrong?"

"Nothing!" Rita made a show of studying Norma's salt and pepper shakers, then gave up and met her friend's eyes. "It's that obvious?"

"Yep. You don't exactly have a poker face."

Rita sighed. No keeping anything from her therapist/friend. "Cash runs hot and cold on me. Mostly cold. Hurts that he'd ask for your help, but not mine."

"Well," Norma said, leaning back against the counter, "to be fair, I live in this complex and you don't. Maybe he didn't want you to have to drive over here and wait. Maybe he was just being thoughtful."

"He wasn't being thoughtful. He won't ask me for help moving into his new place, either, even though I'm just two doors down." She pulled out a kitchen chair and sat, looking out the sliding glass doors at the tossing waves. "Let's face it, I was a bad mother. The other two have let me off the hook about that, but Cash won't. He's the tough one."

Without asking, Norma brought a mug of black coffee over to Rita, and another one for herself. She sank into the chair across from Rita. "Did you have a choice?"

"How would I know?" Rita bit her lip when she heard the bitterness in her own voice.

"You know what happened to you," Norma said, her voice patient, "because your boys and other people told you what happened. The boys' father abducted you and beat you nearly to death. When you came to, you didn't remember anything. Right?"

"Right," Rita said. Put so baldly, it sounded horrible. She would have felt great sympathy for such a thing happening to someone else. But the fact that she had no memory of the events somehow rendered them hard to believe.

"So," Norma continued, "how could you know that you even *had* kids, let alone neglected them?"

They'd been through all this before. Rita had gotten to know Norma because Norma had been her counselor at the Maine clinic where she'd ended up after being rescued by T-Bone, the man who'd become her husband, and was now deceased. Norma had to be kind and understanding about issues like this, because she was a trained counselor.

Cash wasn't. He wasn't letting her off the hook. Which Rita totally understood. Although Cash acted easygoing, he was anything but. Not only that, but from what she'd been able to glean from her other sons, Cash's foster parents, with whom he'd landed after the Orin disaster, had also been cold. Wealthy, but cold.

She still couldn't believe she'd let it happen. What

kind of a person had she been, anyway, that she'd hooked up with a man so evil, then stayed with him to have not one, but three children? Had she been stupid or just passive? Why hadn't she sought the resources of a shelter or domestic-abuse hotline sooner, in order to save her boys, if not herself?

She had the feeling that, if her current self met her earlier self, she wouldn't have liked her. Because what kind of mother let things get that bad for her children?

The whole thing swirled painfully in her mind. She shook her head a little bit, sipped coffee and met Norma's eyes. "I'm not here to talk about me and my problems. I wanted to ask a favor of you. Actually, I have a proposition for you."

"Don't get a whole lot of those anymore," Norma joked. "What's up?"

"This request actually comes from Yasmin over at the women's center," Rita said, "and you've heard it before—they need help. They have a parenting class starting up soon, and their normal instructor got a new job and can't do it. Could you step in?"

Before Rita finished speaking, Norma was shaking her head. "I don't really want to work," she said. "I know I told Yasmin I'd consider it when she asked a while back, but I'm not really up for it."

"Hear me out," Rita said. "It's a class for parents who need help with their special-needs children, or their kids are having discipline problems, or they've been somehow neglected because of whatever it was that brought them to the women's center. Right up your alley. The kind of stuff that you worked on for your whole career, so when Yasmin told me they needed an instructor for that particular course, I thought of you right away."

"Yeah, but standing up in front of a bunch of people and talking? I hate that kind of thing. I do better one-on-one."

"But you turned down that volunteer job of offering counseling to kids in trouble," Rita reminded her.

"Didn't suit my schedule," Norma said, her tone offhanded.

Rita didn't get it. "Are you going to just sit here and rot? You're too young to retire."

Norma glared. "I'm not rotting, I'm baking muffins and helping out your son."

Ouch. "Don't rub it in. I would love to be the one helping him, but he doesn't want anything to do with me, I already told you that."

"Are you sure you're not being oversensitive? Taking offense where there's none meant?"

"I thought a therapist was supposed to let you be oversensitive." Rita wasn't really mad, that was the kind of relationship she and Norma had, but she wasn't going to let herself get sidetracked. "Just like a therapist is supposed to want to help people. As in, teach that class."

"I told you, I'm off duty. I don't want to work anymore, and that goes for acting sympathetic when someone just might need a kick in the pants!"

"*I* need a kick in the pants? Why did I even come over here?" Rita took one of the muffins and broke a piece off it.

Norma slapped her hand and went to the sink to wash the mixing bowl and muffin tin.

Rita turned away. Outside the windows, the November sun was finally high enough to heat up the day. There was no noise outside, though, not like at Rita's apartment complex. This place was dead. She was glad she didn't live here. Especially since living here would mean living closer to her impossible best friend.

"What are you doing for Thanksgiving?" Norma asked, her voice gruff. "If you're alone, you can come with me to the meal the civic association is putting on." She gestured at the muffins. "That's what these are for. We're serving breakfast while the main meal's being prepared. Could always use another helping hand."

It was Norma's way of apologizing for her sharp words, and it also made Rita feel guilty. As the person who'd been in town longer, she should have thought to make sure Norma had something to do for the holiday. "Jimmy and I are going to Sean's place," she said. "And I'm one hundred percent sure there's plenty of food and space for another person, if you'd like to stop by after you help with the civic group's meal."

"Thanks, maybe I will." Norma reached out and gave Rita a half hug. "You know I love you, kiddo, right? If I mess with you, it's for your own good."

"Yeah, because you know it all." But she hugged Norma back.

The tap-tap-tap at the door broke into their love-fest. Norma went to the door, and Rita couldn't re-sist looking over her shoulder to see who was there. Maybe it was Cash.

But instead, it was the Silver Fox, whose name was actually Stephen. Norma spoke with him at the entrance. When the exchange got longer, Rita cleared her throat, and Norma looked back at her. "Invite the man in!" she said in a stage whisper.

"That would be…much appreciated," Stephen said.

"Fine, come in." Norma held open the door and beckoned him toward the kitchen. "I suppose you want a blueberry muffin, too."

Rita stared at her friend. Norma was a tough cookie who didn't put up with nonsense, but she wasn't usually this ungracious.

She soon understood the reason, at least the su-perficial one: this was a conversation about Christ-mas decorations, and the rules that governed them, in this complex. "I'd be happy to cover the cost," he said. "I just thought it would look better if we coordinated my outdoor display with yours, since we're next-door neighbors."

Norma cackled. "You just don't want me to do something tacky," she said.

Color suffused Stephen's face. Looking at him, Rita wasn't sure whether he had really not wanted Norma to decorate, or whether he was looking for an excuse to come by. She couldn't get over the notion that he was drawn to Norma, although two more different people could hardly be imagined.

She also thought that Norma's testy attitude might have everything to do with her own feeling of attraction for Stephen. She was so insistent that she didn't want to get involved with a man again, but Rita knew for sure that was mostly fear talking—fear of what a man would think of her mastectomy scars.

"If you're too busy, I can do the decorating," he said, sounding uncomfortable. "I didn't think you worked."

Norma looked at him with head tilted to one side, frowning. Then she looked at Rita. "When does the gig at the women's center start?"

Score one for me and the Silver Fox, Rita thought. "I think it starts the last week of November. Are you in?"

"I'm in."

But as she let herself out, leaving Norma and Stephen to their bickering, she had to wonder. Norma was growing, albeit against her will. But what about

Rita? Was she growing, or stagnating? Maybe she was the one who was rotting.

Her ringing phone offered relief from her thoughts. She pulled out her phone, but the caller was unknown.

She clicked on the call, and to her surprise, it was Holly. "Hey, you know how you offered to help out?" she asked. In the background was a baby crying and a dog barking.

"Whatever you need," Rita said promptly. "Where are you?"

"I'm taking home the worst-behaved dog in the history of dogs," Holly said. "And I'm afraid his owner's going to put him out on the street. Any interest in adopting him?"

A dog. She hadn't thought about a pet, not lately, but she was surprisingly intrigued. "Doubtful, but I'm willing to meet him," she said, and immediately, inexplicably, felt a whole lot better.

HOLLY LOOKED AROUND at the low-hanging Spanish moss and overarching oak trees that made the road they were traveling seem more like a dark tunnel, the sunny day more like twilight. "I'm not sure this is a good idea," she said.

Cash looked over at her from the driver's seat. They were in the SUV again, due, Cash had said, to the rutted road that led to Ma Dixie's place.

Ma Dixie. Even the name sounded completely

obscure to Holly, like a character in a TV show about the South.

"It won't be bad. It's not her big Friday-night supper. It's just…" He trailed off, looking embarrassed or maybe shy.

That roused her curiosity. "It's just what?"

"I want Ma to meet Penny and vice versa."

Holly tilted her head to one side, studying him. "Was she your foster mom?" She hadn't gotten that impression.

"Not exactly, but kind of." He navigated around an especially big dip in the dirt road. "She was Sean's foster mom, but she made me and Liam feel welcome. When we were kids, and after we'd grown up, too."

She nodded, looking out at the deep shadows of the bayou. "Screws you up, doesn't it? Not having a regular mom."

He looked at her sharply. "You and Tiff?"

"We had a mom, just not… Not someone who wanted to be a mom."

"Ouch." He looked thoughtful. "Rita, she wanted to be our mom, I guess. She just couldn't. The right was taken away from her."

"You don't hold that against her, do you?"

"I shouldn't. I try not to."

Sudden anxiety squeezed her stomach. "Do you think Penny will blame Tiff, when she grows up? That she wasn't here?"

"Let alone blame me for all the mistakes I'm

likely to make." Cash heaved a sigh as they turned down an even narrower road. There, in a clearing, was a rustic-looking cabin on stilts. A porch wrapped around it, and a green lawn sloped down to a narrow, muddy river.

Cash was lifting Penny out of the car before Holly could grab her purse and climb down from the passenger side. He shouldered the diaper bag and waved off her offer to carry it. "This way," he said, then went up the porch steps and pounded on the door. "Ma! Pudge! You've got company!"

After a few seconds with no answer, he pounded again, then led the way around the house to the back door. But there was no response there, either.

"Did you call?" she asked.

He shook his head. "No. They're always here." His voice sounded bleak, and she caught a fleeting glimpse of the lonely, forsaken teen he must have been at one time. But he shook it off almost instantly. "Let's hang out on the porch for a few, at least. Get Penny used to the marsh air."

They sat on an old-fashioned glider, shoulder-to-shoulder, knee-to-knee. Cash held Penny, who looked at everything, wide-eyed, and let out a shriek of excitement when a blue jay landed on the porch railing and cawed at them.

Holly drew in deep breaths and tried to focus on the scent of the flowers growing around the porch rather than on the warmth of Cash's leg beside hers.

She couldn't help the way her breathing quick-ened, though, and when their fingers brushed as he passed her a packet of crackers to open for Penny, she sucked in a breath. She'd never been one to get all keyed up about a man. She'd always shrugged it off when a girlfriend talked about how hot and sexy a particular guy was.

Now, all of a sudden, she got it.

The overly loud sound of a car with muffler prob-lems broke the mood. *Good.*

A big old sedan pulled up directly in front of the house. An enormous man opened the passenger door and started out, then looked back at a sharply spo-ken word from the driver. A moment later, a woman who must be Ma Dixie bustled around the car and braced herself.

"Okay, on three," she said.

"Wait, Ma!" Cash thrust Penny into Holly's arms and hurried down the porch steps. He spoke to the woman and then stepped in front of her to help the man hoist himself out of the car. Cash walked slowly to the porch, the man clinging to his arm, breathing hard. The steps, only four of them, were a challenge, but with Cash's help the man made it up, and they both disappeared into the house.

When Holly realized that Ma Dixie was collect-ing bags from the back seat, she shifted Penny to one hip and went down to the car. "I'm Cash's friend, Holly," she said. "Let me help you with that."

"Thank you, honey. I'm Ma, but I expect you know that. And the big one's my man, Pudge." She waved a hand toward the house.

Between the two of them, they got several bags of what smelled like barbeque into the house. In the kitchen, Ma directed her to put the bags on the counter and then gestured toward the table. "Have a seat. Would you like some sweet tea?"

"Yes, thank you." Holly wanted to offer to get them drinks herself, because the other woman looked tired. But Holly was the guest and she didn't know if Ma would welcome the assistance or be offended by the offer.

Ma brought ice-filled glasses and a pitcher to the table. "If you could pour, I'd surely appreciate it," she said, holding out her arms for Penny. "And who's this little lady?"

"Her name's Penny," Holly said as she poured tea. She didn't know how much Cash had told Ma. "She's a year old."

"Such a pretty little peanut," she said. "Yours?"

Holly opened her mouth and then closed it again. *Was* Penny hers? Yes, in every way that mattered, she decided, and nodded her head.

She was pretty sure Ma had caught the hesitation, but she didn't push it. "I'm right glad the two of you showed up today," she said. "I told Pudge we'd better get enough barbeque to feed a few more mouths than just ours."

Cash came in, followed by Pudge, and they poured more tea and settled down around the table. "First he's eaten all day," Ma Dixie said, nodding at Pudge.

"Why's that?" Cash asked.

Ma and Pudge exchanged glances. "Some medical tests. Nothing to worry about."

"What kind of tests?" Cash crossed his forearms on the table and looked from Ma to Pudge.

"Like she said, nothing to worry about." Pudge smiled at Penny, his broad face creasing. "What's more interesting is this little lady." He looked at Cash. "Anything you want to tell us?"

"Pudge, mind your manners. He'll tell us in his own good time."

"That she's his?"

Ma slapped his hand. "Just for that, I'm serving you last," she said and then stood to dish up barbequed ribs onto four plates. "Cash, if you could dip out the potato salad and string beans, I'd be obliged."

Cash did as instructed, a sheepish look on his face. Once they'd prayed over the food and started to dig in—and man, was it good—Cash put down his fork and looked from Pudge to Ma and back again. "It's true. She's my child. I only just learned about her myself. Now the question is, how did *you* find out?"

"Your doings are news in this town." Ma smiled

at Cash, then at Holly. "We're glad to welcome you and Penny to the family."

Holly's chest tugged with a mixture of longing and apprehension. She didn't belong to any family, not really. Didn't know how to be in a family.

"Holly's raising Penny, but her sister, Tiff, is the one who…was Penny's biological mother." Cash looked a little embarrassed, but determined, as if he wanted to set the record straight.

Was that to save Holly's reputation, or because he didn't want to be associated with her romantically?

"So I heard," Pudge said, smiling at Holly. "Good for you, taking in your sister's child. You'll fit right in here in Safe Haven."

"You know," Ma said, "I could take care of this little one. Babysit, I mean."

The offer startled Holly so much that she didn't know what to say. What kind of place *was* Safe Haven, that a stranger would offer to take care of your kid?

Cash wiped his mouth and looked at Holly. "She did it for Anna, when she moved to town with her twins and needed day care for them. In fact," he added, turning to Ma, "I'm surprised you don't have any foster kids here now."

"Oh, well, we will again soon. I hope." She glanced at Pudge. "Which is why it's the perfect time for me to take care of little Penny, here. I miss having a little one around."

Near panic rose in Holly. She didn't even know this woman; she wasn't about to become obligated to her, or to trust her with precious Penny. "It's a lovely offer," she said, "but I've got it covered for now."

Cash frowned. "You're carrying Penny around while you walk dogs. It's got to be exhausting to you and her both."

"Cash was telling me about your business," Pudge said. "Good idea, that. Around here, at least out in the country, people have tended to leave their dogs tied up outside while they're at work. Or else they're cooped up in the house all day."

Holly's shoulders relaxed. "That's what I like about my job," she said. "It's a chance to spring the pups out of jail and give them some attention and fun and exercise."

"I could connect you with some of my clients," Pudge said. "And I hope you're walking Liam's dog, Rio. He's full of beans."

"Yes, Rio was one of my first clients." Cash's doing, she suspected. Holly smiled to think of the big Lab-rottweiler mix. "And he *is* a handful, but he's a great dog. I'm glad I can help Liam and Yasmin out. They're pretty busy, it seems."

"Still," Ma said, "it must be tough to walk dogs with a baby strapped on."

"You should really think about Ma's offer," Cash said.

Holly's ease with the group around the table dissolved, and she pushed away her plate. "We're fine," she said, only keeping her voice level with effort.

Just because she was receiving child support from Cash, did she have to dive into his family as if she'd known them all her life?

She glanced at the wall clock and wondered how long until they could leave this overly friendly, threatening place.

CHAPTER SIX

SATURDAY AFTERNOON, Cash pulled away from the pediatric developmentalist's office with Penny in her car seat in back and Holly white-faced beside him. He felt like going back to his luxury condo, blasting his state-of-the-art flat-screen TV with some mindless sports show and downing a six-pack.

But he was a father now. And even though his impulses showed what he was made of, he was trying to be better than that.

They cruised along the highway at a fair clip. Holly didn't seem inclined to talk, and Penny was sucking on a bottle; she'd actually napped during their long wait at the doctor's office.

It gave Cash the chance to think about what the doctor had said. Cash had known Penny most likely had some developmental delays, but he'd figured a few therapy sessions would take care of it.

It looked like things might be a little more serious.

What got to him was that the doctor had spoken to him and Holly as if they were Penny's mother and father, as if they both had equal responsibility for

Penny's care. Technically, that was true. In fact, just looking at the facts of the case, Cash should have more responsibility, because Holly was only Penny's aunt, while Cash was her father.

Sean's words came back to haunt him: *You've got to figure out if Holly is even fit to parent that child. If she's not...you need to take over.*

Everyone seemed to think Cash should jump in and take charge of Penny's care, but they didn't know what he knew: that deep inside, he was the one who was unfit.

Still, he knew what Sean meant. If Holly wasn't doing right by Penny, then Cash had to figure out another plan. He'd had that in mind when he'd latched onto the idea of Ma Dixie helping out with Penny, but Holly had shot that down.

It gave Cash a worried feeling. Holly was great in a lot of ways, but she didn't seem aware of the concept that it takes a village. She wanted to do everything on her own, but particularly since Penny had special needs, that just wasn't going to work.

He came out of his thoughts enough to realize that they were close to the Sea Pine Cottages, managed and lived in by Sean and his family. "Mind if we stop and see my brother for a few?" he asked.

Holly looked over at him with a wide-eyed, deer-in-the-headlights expression.

"Not for long," he said. "But it's right on the way, and the doctor said the more stimulation—"

"It's fine, we can stop there," she interrupted. She didn't give an audible sigh, but she definitely implied it.

He opened his mouth to needle her about her attitude and then closed it. Just didn't have the heart.

Penny had delays that could be serious, and needed further evaluation. They already knew that she was underweight with a small head circumference. Physical signs of the neglect she'd experienced on Tiff's watch, and Cash wanted to shake the woman. To shake Holly, too, because she'd let it happen.

But when it came down to it, *he'd* let it happen by not following up with Tiff, checking in, making sure.

And inadequate as his efforts were bound to be, he had to do his best to make up for it. Stimulation, affection, talking. Doing things together with Holly so that Penny could get to know them both, feel secure in them being her family, which would help a lot with the grief she was experiencing.

He turned into the Sea Pine Cottages and Holly *did* let out a sigh.

"What's wrong?" he asked, although he knew.

"Nothing. Well, it's just that…you have a lot of family."

"You're about the only person in the universe who'd say that. For a long time, it was just me and my two brothers."

"Being on your own isn't so bad." She sounded defensive. "Families can cause a lot of grief."

"Is family so awful to you?"

"That's not what I meant," she snapped. "Why would you say that?"

"Because of how you acted back at Ma's the other night. Refusing to even consider her offer of baby-sitting."

A wail, thin and reedy, rose from the back seat and quickly gathered steam.

"Sorry." Cash blew out a sigh of his own as he pulled into the sandy driveway in front of his brother's amped-up beach cottage. "I've upset her now." *Bad father, bad father.*

"She just isn't used to people arguing," Holly said. She got out of the car and beat him to the back seat, pulling Penny out and cuddling her close, burying her face in the baby's neck.

He was trying to watch her parenting, like Sean said, to see if she was doing an okay job, but it was hard to maintain that detachment. Because clearly, she loved the child. So much. And this whole neglect nightmare was hitting her at least as hard as it was hitting Cash. He put an arm lightly around her shoulders and gave her an awkward pat.

He, who was so comfortable making a move on a woman, found it much harder to give the simple human comfort that would make her feel better.

She looked up at him with a shaky smile, but she couldn't conceal the worry behind it.

"Come on," he said. "You don't know Sean and Anna well yet, but they're great. They'll make you feel at home."

"Do they know we're coming?"

"No," he said, "but we're family. We don't have to call first."

"Right," she said faintly.

Cash looked around the Sea Pine Cottages. The rustic little resort had been on its last legs when Sean had undertaken the remodeling and renovation of it. Now, it was thriving, with a mix of young families and vacationers and, from what he'd heard, an eccentric artist well-known for her seascapes.

They mounted the stairs and knocked. Hayley, the bolder of Anna's twins, answered the door, with Hope peeping behind her.

"Baby Penny!" Hayley cried. "Mom, Uncle Cash and baby Penny and that lady are here!"

Anna came out, wiping her hands on a dishcloth, wearing an apron. "That lady has a name," she said. "She's Ms. Gibson. Hi, Holly, Cash. Come on in. We're just messing around, making lasagna and cookies. Lazy day. Good to see you."

Holly smiled down at Hayley. "You can call me Miss Holly if you like," she said.

Cash walked in and right away, he saw the huge Christmas tree that dominated the big family room, smelled the piney scent of it. Christmas music was playing softly, and HoHo was dressed in a green-and-white-striped one-piece outfit that made him look like a chubby elf. "Christmas comes early at your house, huh?"

"We love it," Anna said. "We had a lot of years when we could barely celebrate, so we go a little overboard now that we can."

Sean was on the floor, propped on one elbow, with boxes and instruction sheets in front of him. He beckoned to Cash. "Get in here and help me figure out how to put together this train set," he said. "Hope and I have been working for an hour, but it's slow going."

"Mom and I are almost done with the gingerbread men," Hayley said. "Maybe baby Penny and—and Miss Holly can help us decorate them."

Cash looked over at Holly to see how she was reacting. "Sound okay to you?" he asked.

But she didn't answer. She was staring up at the Christmas tree, as wide-eyed as a kid herself.

He nudged her. "Pretty, huh?"

She nodded. "It's beautiful. You have a beautiful home," she added to Anna. "Penny and I would love to help you decorate cookies. Or at least watch and give advice." She looked seriously down at Hayley. "She's a little young to help, but it's good for her to see the colors and hear you all talking."

"Oh, if it's talking you want, Hayley's your girl,"

Anna said, rubbing Hayley's shoulders absentmind-edly. And then she and Hayley and Holly and Penny disappeared into the kitchen.

"Daddy?" Hope shifted from foot to foot while Cash marveled, once again, at how quickly Sean had become the twins' daddy. "Would it be okay if I went in the kitchen with the girls? I can stay here if you need me to."

Sean knelt down and put his arm around Hope. "Tell you what, I'll see if your uncle Cash can help me. You go in the kitchen, and if I need you I'll call you to come back." He winked up at Cash. "Hope's a real good helper."

"I'm sure she is." And they both watched the little girl run off into the kitchen.

"You'll be there one day," Sean said as he gestured for Cash to get down on the floor with him. "They grow up real fast. Before you know it, Penny'll be walking and talking and going to school."

"I hope." He settled down, pushing a truck around for HoHo's entertainment while Sean studied the diagram for the train set. "We're just coming from the pediatrician."

Sean's eyes flicked up to Cash's. "Anything wrong?"

"A lot," Cash said. "None of it irreparable, but she's got delays we're going to need to work pretty hard on."

"Tough news." Sean fumbled for a screwdriver

and started putting together the complex elevated track. "But you should know, more than anybody, that history isn't destiny. There was a time when all three of us were considered most unlikely to succeed."

"Yeah, only Miss Vi wouldn't let it happen." Cash smiled at the memory of the librarian who'd taken an interest in all three of them, sat them down to read the classics, scolded them for any grade below a B and generally bullied them into achieving the most they could. "In fact, Holly's already taking Penny to baby lap-sit at the library."

"That's good. The folks at the center could help, too."

"We're signed up for a class there. Rita told us about it."

Sean leveled a glare at him. "You mean *Mom* told you about it?" Of all the brothers, Sean was the one who'd embraced Rita most completely as their mother. He'd spent the most time with her and talked to her about the past, trying to help her remember it.

"Yeah. Mom."

"You know who else would be good? Ma Dixie and Pudge," Sean said. "For when you and Holly are working. They're so great with kids, including kids who struggle."

That brought up Cash's other worry, and he told Sean about how Ma and Pudge hadn't been home when they'd visited, how Pudge had a doctor's appointment and Ma hadn't cooked.

"They're not young, I guess." Sean frowned. "I'll talk to them." As their actual foster son, Sean had more of an in to finding out what was going on with Ma and Pudge.

"And, anyway," Cash added, "Holly doesn't want them watching Penny."

"She doesn't? Why not?"

He shrugged. "Guess she just got uncomfortable or something. Says she doesn't like to impose on them."

Sean grunted and got more involved with his construction project while Cash played with HoHo. Then the girls came out into the room with a plate of heavily frosted and decorated gingerbread cookies that smelled fantastic. Cash ate four of them. Holly seemed fully initiated into the twins' club, and they were telling her everything they were planning for Christmas.

"See," Hayley said, "this is the ornament we picked out this year. We did it last year, too, and we're gonna do the same thing every year."

"Because it's a tradition," Hope said seriously. "A *family* tradition."

Cash's throat tightened. These girls had had precious little in the way of family tradition, but obviously Anna and Sean were making up for that now.

Maybe he and Holly could do the same for Penny.

Except he wasn't like Sean—good-natured and methodical and handy around the house. He was loud and impatient, just like his father had been.

He should try, though. He took a sparkly ornament from the tree and dangled it in front of Penny. "See, pretty," he said, imitating the way Holly had started narrating all kinds of life events to her.

"No!"

"Cash!"

"She can't have a glass ornament!"

Sean's, Holly's and Anna's voices all converged to remind Cash that he knew nothing about parenting and wasn't good at it. Sheepishly, he handed the fragile bauble to Hope to hang safely out of reach.

After Sean and Anna had talked them into staying for lasagna, and they'd eaten, and the twins were yawning, and HoHo had fallen asleep, Penny—who'd gotten a second wind just when the other kids were going down—started making her way toward the tree with her funny, awkward crawl.

Cash watched her as the others talked. This time, he knew to make sure she didn't grab an ornament.

She got to an ottoman that impeded her path toward the tree and her little face started to screw up, and Cash braced himself for a big fuss. He was just starting to stand up to get her when she gripped the edge of the ottoman and pulled herself to her feet. She swayed there, staring at the tree in what looked like an awestruck way.

Not wanting to take his eyes off her, Cash reached out a hand to Holly, found her arm and nodded toward the baby.

Holly gasped. "She pulled herself up."

Cash nodded, and then he did look at Holly, and the joy on her face matched the joy in his heart.

In all the world, they were the only two people who knew just how monumental that move was.

Sean and Anna had gone over to a card table set up in the corner of the room, where they had an ongoing battle about who'd finish the jigsaw puzzle first.

The twins were focused on the Christmas movie playing quietly on the old television, sleepy-eyed.

Cash slid over and put an arm around Holly, and they stood and watched Penny—their daughter—as she swayed, staring at the tree.

A few seconds later, of course, she sat down hard. But Cash had seen a moment of hope.

If she was pulling up, she'd soon learn to walk. And that was the first of many important steps.

She was going to improve, to catch up. And no matter how inadequate, he was going to help her.

THE NEXT DAY, Rita practically dragged Norma out to take a walk. "It'll help you quit smoking better than anything else—getting exercise," she said.

"I know, I know." Norma patted the pocket of her jacket as if for reassurance, and Rita rolled her eyes. Ninety-nine chances out of a hundred, she had a pack of cigarettes in there.

"You're going to have to chuck those away sometime."

"You ain't the boss of me," Norma said with a stuck-out tongue and wrinkled-nose sneer that was classic middle grade.

"Besides," Rita continued, ignoring the expression, "I need support. Holly wants me to meet this rascal of a dog on neutral ground, and you have to help me resist adopting him."

"That I can do. I'm not the sucker that you are."

They walked at a brisk pace—not as brisk as Rita wanted, but probably a little brisker than Norma did—and were soon at the designated meeting spot in the town park. Holly was already there, sitting on a bench. But instead of having one dog with her, she had two.

As Rita and Norma approached, the two dogs left their sniffing and ball-chasing to jump at them, barking hysterically. One was big, what looked like a poorly groomed standard poodle; the other was a fluffy yellow terrier mix with soulful brown eyes that immediately tugged at Rita's heart. She knelt to pet it, looking up at Holly. "Don't get any ideas," she said. "I'm not certain about taking even one dog, and I'm definitely not taking two."

Holly grinned. "I'm not asking you to. But there

are two of you, so…" She looked expectantly at Norma.

"No way. Me and dogs don't get along," Norma said.

"But you haven't met Snowball," Holly coaxed. "Come on, Snowball, show Norma what a great dog you are. Sit."

Promptly, the white poodle sat.

The little yellow dog ran and yapped and tangled its leash with the other dog's.

"Rita, could you…?" Holly held out the leash to her.

Rita couldn't keep her eyes off the little dog. She knelt down to touch its soft fur as it leaped at her, joyous at the attention. "Aren't you a cutie, though?" Instinctively, she cradled the dog against her chest and held it, loose but restrained.

"Snowball, catch!" Holly threw a treat into the air, and Snowball snapped it out of the air with her big jaws.

Holly stood and held out her arm. "Paws up," she ordered, and Snowball stood, front paws on Holly's arm.

"Well, isn't that something," Norma said, reluctant appreciation in her voice.

"So," Holly said, "the owner of these two took them on because his parents had to move into assisted living and couldn't bring their pets. But he works long hours and doesn't have time for them.

He's got plenty of toys and crates and dog food that he'll give you along with the dogs."

The yellow dog had settled against Rita's stomach as she sat cross-legged on the ground, a warm, welcome weight. "I wish I could take them. This one especially. But my apartment complex only allows small dogs. I checked last night. And you wouldn't want to separate them."

"Well, that's just it," Holly said. "They're not a bonded pair. Apparently the couple that went into assisted living didn't get along, so the husband took Snowball and trained her and the wife took Taffy and spoiled her. They had separate bedrooms and separate TV areas and so the two dogs know each other, but they don't especially like each other."

"So I could just take Taffy?" Rita's heart tugged for the little girl. With some training, she'd be a terrific dog. Well, maybe a lot of training, she reflected ruefully as the dog started chewing on the edge of Holly's shoe.

"Yes," Holly said, beaming as she tugged her foot out of the dog's mouth, "and I thought maybe Norma would like Snowball."

"Why?" Norma squawked. "I told you, I don't like dogs."

"Poodles aren't the same as other dogs," Holly said. "Look how smart she is, and how calm. She's six years old, and if she were groomed nicely, she'd be beautiful, almost a show dog."

"I don't think my condo allows pets." Norma scratched Snowball's head and the poodle leaned against her, panting up at her, tongue out.

"Call and check," Holly suggested. "It would be so perfect if you'd each take one. Then they could see each other sometimes, but they wouldn't have to live together and drive each other crazy."

Rita laughed. "Sort of like you and me, lady," she said to Norma. "I love you, but I can't imagine living with you."

"Call now," Holly urged. "I'm seriously afraid he's going to take them to the pound."

"The condo office isn't even open."

"Call Stephen," Rita suggested. "Isn't he on the board of the condos and everything? He seems like he'd know all the rules."

"No, I'm not calling him."

"Then I will." Rita scrolled through her contacts.

"Give me his number." Norma whipped out her phone as Rita sent her the contact. "And I'm *not* saying I'll take her. I'm just saying I'll consider it."

Stephen didn't answer, so she left a message. Rita committed to take the smaller dog, Taffy, after she'd had a couple of days to arrange things. Holly promised to continue walking them for as long as needed, gratis.

"No, that isn't necessary. I walk a lot, but when I work a long shift I'll call you. And I'll pay you, and no arguments."

"If there's any problem," Holly said, "I'm sure there are trainers around. In fact, the owner kept planning to take them to a trainer, but when he found out he'd have to actually work with them instead of dropping them off, he didn't want to."

Rita snapped a few photos of Taffy, joyous about getting her for no particular reason. It was good to be single and have enough money to do something spontaneous. And she'd instantly fallen in love with the butterscotch-colored pup.

After Holly headed off to take the dogs home, Rita and Norma spent the rest of the walk arguing amiably about them. Rita was definitely planning to adopt Taffy, and Norma was definitely *not* planning to adopt Snowball. "She's a beautiful dog, or she could be," Norma said. "But I want my freedom. I don't want to be getting up in the middle of the night for bathroom runs."

"She's six. She isn't going to need to go out in the middle of the night. T-Bone and I, we always had an older Lab or mix, and none of them gave us much trouble." She flashed a smile at her friend. "Just a whole lot of love."

"Love, I could use," Norma admitted.

"A dog's going to be less demanding than a man," Rita teased her.

"Less judgmental, too. They don't care what you look like."

"That's for sure." Rita put an arm around her

friend. "If they *did* care you'd get high grades, my friend. You're a beautiful woman."

Norma snorted but didn't answer.

Norma needed something to give her confidence and cheer her up, Rita reflected. And Snowball might just be the ticket. She probably shouldn't press Norma on it; she was old enough to make her own decisions. Plus, she had a lot more education than Rita had.

But there was more than one kind of smarts. Norma didn't always know what was good for her. Insight about other people was one thing; insight about yourself was something else.

They stopped at the diner so Rita could pick up her paycheck, and wouldn't you know it, there was Cash at the counter. Rita walked over and said hello, feeling awkward for all that he was her son.

His coffee cup was empty. Good. Something she could do for him. "Want me to get you a refill?" she asked, reaching for it.

"No, it's okay. Brenda will do it." He smiled at her, a brief, impersonal smile.

Rita pulled back her hand and tried not to feel hurt. It wasn't easy. Cash was never rude to her, but he definitely kept his guard up.

Norma patted Rita's shoulder. She understood.

Man, Rita wished she could remember the past. Especially with Cash—she felt like knowing what he'd been like as a kid would unlock the key to his cryptic personality.

It helped that when her boss and now boyfriend, Jimmy Cooper, saw her, his handsome face lit up and he came over and put an arm around her. "There's my favorite employee-slash-girlfriend," he said, smiling as he looked from her to Norma, nodding at Cash. "What's up with you two? You out walking?"

"That, and making foolish decisions," Norma said. "You ought to hear what your girlfriend-slash-employee is thinking about doing."

Thinking about Taffy made all Rita's complicated emotions fall away. "You've got to see this dog I'm gonna get," she said, pulling up the photos she'd snapped on her phone. "She's absolutely adorable. She's going to be a handful, but I think I can help her calm down. I just really connected with her."

"You're getting a dog?" Jimmy sounded surprised.

"Yeah, I think so." She looked at him. His smile had vanished, replaced by a tight little frown she'd never seen before. "What's wrong? Don't you like them?" When she thought about it, Jimmy had never paid much attention to Rio, Liam's dog.

He shrugged. "I'm not a fan." Then he got very busy wiping the counter and busing a table, things that as the manager, he didn't need to do, especially when a couple of his employees were standing around idle.

She slid down a couple of stools and tugged at his sleeve. "Hey, what's wrong?"

He tilted his head to one side and looked at her. "Did you ever think that I might want to have some say in whether you got a dog?"

She looked at him blankly. "No. Honestly, I didn't."

"Really?" He scrubbed at a nonexistent spot on the counter.

"Really. Why would you have a say in whether I get a pet? It's not like we live together."

"No, but we might someday, right?" He leaned back against the counter then, not looking at her. "Rita, a dog's going to live ten or more years. It's going to be a big part of your life, take a lot of your attention. I'd rather you'd consulted me before you made a commitment."

"I… Really, Jimmy? You're jealous of me giving attention to a *dog*?"

"That's not what I meant and you know it. Just think about how you'd feel if I, oh, decided to move to a different town or take up a time-consuming hobby. It would affect you, right? So I should talk to you about it before I decided."

She drew in a breath and let it out in a sigh. "I guess I see what you mean. But, Jimmy, I just feel so drawn to this dog, so excited about it. Do you really want to kill that in me?"

His forehead wrinkled as he looked down at her.

"We're not going to solve this right now, and I have work to do." He turned and headed back into the kitchen.

Norma and Cash had been talking desultorily and probably eavesdropping, she guessed from the expressions on their faces as she slid back down to them. "That didn't go too well," she said glumly.

"Sorry, kiddo," Norma said, patting her shoulder. "For the record, he *doesn't* have a say and you *don't* have to consult him. Not until he puts a ring on your finger or signs a lease with you."

"Yeah. But I don't necessarily want to have this little sweetie be a constant source of friction between us." She bit her lip as she stared down at the photo of the little dog.

"Let me see," Cash said. He seemed to be attempting to reach out to her, and even with her concern about Jimmy, she appreciated it. She held out the phone to him so he could see the picture.

He took it, studied it, then raised his eyes to meet hers. "You know why you like it, right?"

"What do you mean?"

"You don't know, do you?" he said, looking from her to the dog's photo and back again. "Wow."

"What is it?"

"This dog looks almost exactly like the dog we had—the dog we left behind when we came to Safe Haven."

Rita stared at the dog's picture as her heart started a deep, steady pounding.

"I've got to go. See you ladies." Cash put a twenty—way too much for his meal plus tip—on the counter and walked out.

"Do you remember anything about the dog?" Norma asked after they'd watched Cash get into his fancy car and zoom away.

Slowly, she shook her head. "No, I don't," she said. "But I want to find out about it. And I definitely want to get this new dog. I *need* to get it. No matter what Jimmy says."

CHAPTER SEVEN

HOLLY TOOK ONE look at the adults in the parenting class, talking and laughing as if they'd known each other all their lives—which they probably had—and felt a strong urge to turn around and leave. She didn't do well with groups like this, full of people who'd always belonged.

It was Wednesday, four days after their warm and lovely Saturday afternoon with Cash's brother's family. There, she'd felt welcome from the start.

In fact, having Cash at her side at the pediatric developmentalist had been an incredible comfort. She knew she couldn't handle Penny's special needs alone.

So the fact that he'd texted her the last couple of mornings to check on Penny, and had stopped by last night to see if they needed anything... Well, she'd welcomed it. He was the only one who cared about Penny's minuscule changes and adorable antics as much as she did.

It turned out she *didn't* want Cash just for his money; she wanted his co-parenting, too. Needed it.

A disconcerting thought.

Being here at the parenting class was disconcerting in a different way. It took her back.

That sound of talking, laughing voices, growing quieter as she, the new kid, walked in, was familiar from her eight school changes during her growing-up years. Mostly, that uncomfortable new-kid feeling passed when you were an adult; you met people one-on-one. But this parenting class was school. Back to school, again.

Cash shifted Penny to his other arm—he always insisted on carrying her, so Holly just carried the diaper bag—and looked over at Holly. "Are you ready?"

Their eyes met and held. "I'm not sure," she admitted.

"Should we turn around and run away?" He quirked a smile at her, and those clear blue eyes seemed to read her reluctance and understand it. The spark that passed between them lifted her spirits. She wasn't going to do anything about it, but she had to admit that walking into a gathering with a hot guy like Cash was...comforting.

"We'd better not run away," she said. "We have to be grown-ups."

"Really?" He gave her a mock sulky look and she laughed.

They edged quietly through the door of the big, shabby multipurpose room at the women's center, housed inside a church and filled with that dusty old-church smell. There were about fifteen adults here, mostly couples, most holding babies of a year or younger, although there was also a toddler with Down syndrome who looked to be two or three.

They stowed their things on a table heaped with coats, purses and diaper bags. "Come on," Cash said, and urged her toward the little crowd with a hand on her elbow.

He was instantly noticed.

"Cash!"

"Hey, O'Dwyer!"

"Long time no see!"

It rapidly became clear that Cash was a minor celebrity in this area. People looked at Holly and Penny with open curiosity.

Why hadn't she thought of the fact that he'd have to explain Penny to all his friends? Given that, she was pretty impressed that he'd suggested doing parenting class. He wasn't ashamed of Penny, wasn't trying to hide her existence.

"Okay, everyone, let's get started." Norma, Rita's friend, stood at the front of the room wearing a colorful caftan-style shirt and jeans tucked into high boots. She looked cool and stylish.

In fact, most of the women looked stylish, when Holly stopped to notice. And here she was, dressed in her standard black T-shirt and jeans. She hadn't thought of dressing up for a parenting class—hadn't had time.

Oh, well. It wasn't like she was expecting to fit in here or anything.

As soon as she had the thought, she scolded herself. This wasn't about her—it was about Penny and helping her build a life here.

"Seems like a lot of you know each other," Norma said, "but I'm at a disadvantage since I moved here not that long ago. So if you don't mind, I'd like everyone to introduce yourselves. And your kids, too."

That was nice. Holly tried hard to remember everyone's name, laughed when the little girl with Down syndrome corrected her mother, insisting that she was "four *half*." When it was Holly's turn she floundered a little, wondering what to say about Penny and Cash. She settled for explaining that she'd recently moved here and that she was Penny's aunt and guardian.

She wondered what Cash would say, but just as he opened his mouth to speak, Liam and Yasmin came rushing in, Liam holding the toddler they were fostering, Gino. "Sorry to be late," Yasmin said to the group at large. "We had issues."

It was a nice distraction from people's speculative looks at her and Cash. Liam and Yasmin felt like friends, especially when they came immediately over to the empty chairs next to Holly. Gino was crying, loudly, so it took a few minutes before he quieted down and class could get going again.

But then Norma came right back to it. "Cash, we didn't get to hear from you," she said.

"I'm this little sweetheart's papa," he said easily. "I don't have custody, but I'm going to do my best to help. I have a lot to learn."

And with that, Holly could see, he charmed all the women in the audience.

Once the introductions were over, Norma talked a little about what they'd be doing in the class. Today was a short lecture about the various developmental delays and ways to stimulate babies and children who'd gotten off to a rough start. "It's not possible to do it alone," she emphasized. "Our kids need socialization, seeing other families, new experiences and opportunities to interact. And we, as parents and caregivers, need support, too, and I hope this class will be a place where we can give that to each other. So to finish up…" She paused and looked around. "I need to do a drumroll here. We have a whole tray of Jean Carol's cinnamon rolls, and we're going to have a social hour. Try to get the names and contact information for at least two other families to set up playdates or get-togethers with."

The group broke up and people moved toward the cinnamon rolls as if drawn by a magnet, and Holly turned to Yasmin. "Is it cheating to have one of my playdates with you?" she asked.

"Nope. That would be lovely." Yasmin looked around, clearly checking to make sure that Gino was okay in Liam's arms, and then turned back to Holly. "It's a lot, coming into a small Southern town from outside, huh?"

"Yeah. It is." But Holly forced herself to get up and mingle with a few of the other parents. Most were kind and welcoming. And curious. "Why'd you move to Safe Haven?" one woman asked. "Why not to Atlanta, where Cash normally lives?"

She overcame her usual sense of privacy and explained that it had been a desire of Tiff's. The comment served as a reminder, though, that Cash didn't normally live here and that his stay in Safe Haven was temporary. He had a business empire to manage.

"Don't you have people back in New York?" someone else asked.

"Not really," she admitted, and the pity on the other woman's face hurt.

Another couple came over and introduced themselves, then politely inquired about Holly's work as a dog walker. "If you're running a small business here in town, you should think about joining the SHSBA."

"She doesn't know what that is, hon," the wife said, rolling her eyes but with a smile on her face. "It's the Safe Haven Small Business Association, and Ronald is obsessed with it. We run a fruit stand out on the edge of town and we're trying to build it up into a little store."

"That's nice," Holly said.

"We share ideas and work together," Ronald explained. "It's tough to go it alone."

No, mister, alone is the only safe way to go. "I appreciate the offer," she said, "but I'm pretty busy right now."

"We meet for breakfast every two weeks. Not that time-consuming."

"Thanks. We'll see."

"Ronald," the wife said, "she doesn't want to join. Let it go." Her eyes on Holly had gone cool.

Cash seemed to detect that she needed help. He came over and put a light arm around her, basically protecting her from the others. Where his arm touched her neck and shoulders, a tingling sensation danced. It made Holly really, really happy and really, really nervous.

She was having the strangest feeling that she wanted the little artificial family she'd formed with Cash for tonight to become real, a permanent thing. Which couldn't happen. For one, Cash wasn't sticking around Safe Haven. Also, he was an important businessman with women chasing him wherever he went in the world. Experienced, sophisticated women. Not practically penniless dog walkers who forgot to wear makeup and jewelry.

Letting herself have these soft feelings for him put her at risk of being just like her mother. Getting involved in impossible relationships, falling hard, neglecting her duties as a parent.

Holly couldn't take the risk of getting closer to Cash. And she didn't need to have them thought of as a couple among the small-town gossips, not when it was never going to be that way for them.

She shrugged out from under his arm and frowned at him. "Do you mind?"

Hurt flashed across his face so quickly she wasn't sure she'd really seen it. "Sorry."

The small-business couple had seen the interaction. Of course, they didn't look askance at Cash; they looked askance at her.

She blew out a sigh. This was so complicated. She didn't care for herself if she was liked or ostracized in Safe Haven—at least, she didn't care much—but for Penny's sake, she didn't want to be that weird mom. She knew from experience what it was like to be from the oddball family in town.

Figuring out how to walk the right line between encouraging Cash to be an involved father and discouraging herself from falling for him wouldn't be easy.

THE DAY AFTER the parenting class, Cash walked into the car dealership to get his SUV inspected. It was something he usually had his assistant do, or had when he'd been in Atlanta. But he had time now, and it felt important to do it right away when a child's safety was riding on it.

In the waiting room, the TV blared a morning

talk show, and the grease smell from the service department contrasted with the new vinyl smell from the showroom. Ads for tires and stain-prevention treatments for upholstery decorated the walls. Out on the sales floor, balloons and Christmas decorations drew the eye to the new cars, and Cash was tempted to take a look, but he resisted. Giving in to that temptation was the reason he owned three vehicles.

Without the distraction of car-shopping, though, he was left with his thoughts about Holly. She'd pushed him away pretty decisively at the parenting class, and it was clear that she could settle into the community and take care of the baby herself.

All she needed was his money. All she *wanted* was his money, a common refrain in his life.

Trying to shake off his depressing thoughts, he poured himself a cup of bad coffee and picked up a Motor Trend magazine. Then he heard a familiar voice talking to the cashier. A minute later, Pudge LeFrost came in and settled heavily onto the waiting-room couch.

They greeted each other, two customers who couldn't be more different. Cash was getting his late-model expensive SUV inspected, and Pudge was trying to keep his ancient pickup running. Cash was dressed casually, for him, but his sweater was cashmere and his shoes Italian leather. Pudge wore overalls and work boots.

Despite their differences, there were few men Cash liked and respected more than Pudge.

"Any more doctor visits?" he asked, because Pudge didn't look so good. Maybe it was just the fluorescent lights; he usually saw Pudge outside, training dogs or playing his ukulele or fishing.

"Nothing to speak of." Pudge waved a meaty hand. "How *you* doing? How's fatherhood treating you?"

Cash shrugged. "Okay for a guy who doesn't have a clue what he's doing."

Pudge didn't try to protest; he knew all about Cash's background, his lack of a role model. He just nodded, and they sat for a few, listening to the talk show and the Christmas music playing over the speakers. Absently, Cash watched the salesmen schmoozing, showing off cars to the few customers there on a weekday morning.

"You looking for joint custody of that baby?" Pudge asked finally.

Cash shook his head, because he wasn't. Not unless Holly proved to be an unfit mother, which seemed less and less likely to him. "I'm gonna see if I can get once-a-month visitation, as soon as we're past this initial phase. Probably after Christmas."

"Once a month isn't much for a baby," Pudge said mildly. "They grow fast, change fast."

"Might be best for her." Cash shrugged. Penny didn't need him, not really.

Pudge frowned and picked at a spot of dirt on his overalls. "Just don't live in a way that gives you regrets."

There was something about how he said it. "Voice of experience?"

Pudge rubbed at his chest and stared unseeingly into the car showroom. "Ever wonder why Ma and I didn't get married?"

They all had; he'd discussed it a time or two with Liam and Sean. "We figured it's your preference not to, is all."

"Nope. I'd marry her in a minute." Pudge shook his head back and forth, letting a sigh out through pursed lips. "Problem is, I'm already married."

"What?" Cash stared at the older man. He'd seen a lot, knew that fidelity in marriage wasn't everyone's approach, but he'd never have pegged Pudge for a cheater.

"I know what you're thinking." Pudge sighed. "My wife wants nothing to do with me, hasn't for years. I let her dictate that, and the result is I have no relationship with my kids, either."

"You have children?" Cash stared. He'd spent a lot of time at Pudge and Ma's place, a lot of holidays, a lot of long, after-dinner conversations that bounced from topic to topic. But this was the first he'd heard of Pudge having kids.

Pudge nodded. "But I didn't visit, didn't get involved. Paid my child support, yeah, but that's it.

Not that I didn't want to—I missed them like crazy, especially right after I moved out—but their mom wouldn't let me see them, and I didn't fight it like I should've."

"Wow." That just went to show you that you shouldn't assume people had simple lives. "Are you able to keep up with them? Do any of them live nearby?"

Pudge shook his head. "They're busy with their own lives. I figure the least I can do is stay married so if something happens to me, they'll get the death benefits from my pension. My wife doesn't want anything to do with me, but she doesn't mind taking my money."

Didn't that sound familiar. And Cash understood Pudge's thinking but wasn't sure he agreed. It just didn't seem fair to Ma. He opened his mouth to say something to that effect, but Pudge beat him to it.

"Ma's the kind of woman who understands complex situations. And for whatever reason, she loves me." He shook his head, looked down at his enormous body, then back at Cash. "I wish I could do better by her. Wish I'd done better by my kids."

"That's rough." Cash didn't know what else to say.

"Yes, it is, so don't you make the same mistake." Now Pudge was looking at him hard. "I'm telling you, whatever pride or doubts you have, it's not worth living with the fact that you've done the wrong thing."

Cash's mind was being blown, right here in the Chevy dealership. He didn't know anyone who was a better man than Pudge. Yet the man had made mistakes, big ones that obviously weighed heavy on him.

"I know your own father had faults far worse than mine," Pudge said. "Regardless, you don't have to carry on what your father did. You're your own man."

"I wish," Cash said. "Whatever I do, I have Orin O'Dwyer's blood in me."

"Pudge LeFrost?" the woman at the counter called.

"That's me. Guess they got the old truck running again." Pudge started to heave himself up off the couch.

Cash stood and held out a hand to help him pull himself upright, then turned and walked beside him to the counter.

Pudge slapped Cash on the back. "You think about what I said."

"I will." And he would. Pudge had made a good point. Life flew by fast and so did a baby's early years, and he didn't want to live with regrets about how he'd handled fatherhood.

But with the taint of Orin's blood, it might be better just to keep his distance.

He walked over to the service bays and watched a couple of guys working under the hood of an old Chevy, pulling out an air compressor, tinkering with it. Moments later, it was fixed and fitted back in.

If only Cash himself could be repaired like a car or a truck.

CHAPTER EIGHT

OKAY, HOLLY THOUGHT as she sat at Ma Dixie's kitchen table dangling a toy in front of Penny to cover her discomfort. Point taken. Cash was mad at her for rejecting him at the parenting class. But he'd brought her out to Ma Dixie's and abandoned her in the midst of a family gathering, or at least the preparations for one, and she really, really didn't appreciate it.

It was the Saturday after Thanksgiving, a holiday that she and Penny had spent alone despite several invitations to join others for dinner—most insistently Cash's brothers and their wives, who'd gathered at Sean's place.

She hadn't wanted to impose. Hadn't wanted to see Cash.

But she had to admit, it had been a really lonely day. Every TV show and commercial, the family groups gathering at the homes around the apartment complex—all of it had made her feel her isolation keenly.

She'd thought she wanted to be alone, thought that was safer, and it was, but it hadn't been much fun. Even Penny had seemed to look at her with reproachful eyes, as if to say "*this* is what you have to offer for the holidays?"

Her refusal to join the family, her keeping Penny to herself on the holiday, must have further alienated Cash and the rest of his family, too, even though most of them were still acting perfectly nice.

You did it to yourself. It's your own fault.

The internal reminder annoyed her as she fiddled with Penny's shoes, watching Cash's sisters-in-law shred carrots and cabbage for coleslaw. She didn't belong here, didn't *want* to belong, didn't trust this overfriendly family.

Anna, Sean's wife, looked at the old-fashioned clock on the wall. "We'd better head out if we want to see the guys crabbing," she said.

"Right." Yasmin hurriedly washed her hands at the white porcelain sink. "Come on, Holly, this is a sight you've got to see."

Holly weighed the merits of going along with staying here. "I... Sure, okay. Just let me grab my diaper bag."

"Oh, leave the baby with Ma and Pudge. They'll bring the kids out later."

"That's what we're doing," Anna added. "Believe me, I can use a break from the girls and HoHo."

Holly wavered, but in the end, it was she who was responsible for Penny, and she didn't want to start down the road of letting that responsibility slide.

She didn't want to be like Tiff, or their mother. "No, I couldn't."

Both women looked at her blankly. "It's fine. It's Ma," Yasmin said.

"What's Ma?" The older woman bustled into the kitchen.

Anna smiled at her. "It's you who's willing to watch our kids while we run out ahead of everyone and see the guys."

"Oh, my, yes. Pudge and I will bring them out in the van in a bit. Rita and Norma, probably a few other folks, will be here any minute, too. They'll give us a hand if we need it."

"Go ahead, Holly, hand her over to the expert," Anna said. "Grab some freedom while you can get it. Believe me, I know it's hard for a single mom to come by."

Holly stood, frozen against the wall, clutching Penny. She couldn't leave her precious baby in the hands of these strangers. Strangers who considered themselves family, maybe, but not a one of them, Rita excepted, was related to Penny by blood.

Yasmin stepped in front of her, frowning, hands on hips. "You're hurting her feelings," she said quietly.

Anna patted Holly's arm. "She's a certified foster parent. She's not going to hurt your child!"

Yasmin glared at her. Ma held out her arms.

This was the price of taking Cash's generous

child-support payments: she had to become a part of his family and his community. She definitely wasn't comfortable with that, which was why she continued to work her dog-walking business and live frugally.

But Penny needed a family and a community and the things Cash's money could buy. So Holly was going to have to sacrifice some of her independence for Penny's sake.

"I... Okay." She handed Penny to Ma. "She's about ready for a nap, so she might be fussy."

"Fussy babies are my specialty, honey. You go have fun."

"I have a bottle for her in the diaper bag." Holly hurried over to the coatrack, grabbed the diaper bag and thrust it into Ma's hands. "Let me write down my phone number in case there's any problem." She grabbed a pen and Post-it note from the kitchen counter and scribbled down her number.

"Got it. We're going to have fun, aren't we, Penny?" Ma smiled down at the baby, her eyes crinkling.

"Thank you." She turned, and then turned back and put a hand on Ma's arm. "I mean that. Thank you. You're very kind." Then she followed the other two women out the door, stopping on the other side of the screen to give one backward glance.

Penny was smiling up at Ma, beating her arms. She was fine. The separation anxiety was entirely Holly's problem. And it seemed to have ticked off Cash's sisters-in-law, who rode along in silence.

They traveled only a few miles down the road, then pulled off into a parking area along a large body of water.

As Anna parked, Holly cleared her throat. "Look, I'm sorry to be so tense. It's just that I didn't grow up having a whole lot of people to trust."

Yasmin glanced back at her. "I hear you, but Ma has done an incredible amount for our men. We're pretty protective of her."

"And Holly's protective of her child," Anna said. "It's natural. I was the same way when I got to Safe Haven. Lighten up, Yas."

When they climbed out of the car, a salty ocean breeze was blowing in, and the marsh grasses shone red and gold. In a circle of stones, a fire burned, a giant pot of water boiling over it.

And there, on the edge of the inlet, were the three O'Dwyer men. Liam and Sean held what looked like fishing lines, while Cash was farther out on the edge, peering down into the water. As she watched, he jerked a line and started hauling something out of the bay. A wire trap, sporting three large crabs. Even from here, she could see their claws opening and closing.

"All right!" Yasmin said. "Blue crabs. I can almost taste them." She took a step toward the men.

Anna put a hand on her arm, holding her back. "Let's just admire the view for a few minutes."

Yasmin smiled. "It's a fine view, for sure." Something in her voice made it clear that she wasn't talking about the blue sky or sparkling water. No, she was talking about the laughing, muscular men. Two of them—Sean and Cash—emptied the trap's snappish contents into what looked like an old laundry basket. Liam tugged at a line that held another crab at the end of it.

Holly forgot, for a moment, that Penny was in the care of someone she barely knew and that Cash was mad at her. She just enjoyed the sound of deep laughter, the sight of the three men who looked so much alike punching and joking with each other in that strange way men had of showing love. Enjoyed it so much that she lifted her phone and snapped a couple of pictures.

"I think it was hanging out by the water that healed them, way back when," Anna said.

"They needed healing?" Holly asked.

Both women looked at her as if she was stupid. "Yeah, they needed healing."

"They had things pretty rough," Anna explained quietly. "When they came to Safe Haven, their mom was abducted by their dad and they were left in foster care. I'm sure you heard that, but what you might not know is that they had bad reputations and got in a lot of trouble. They've worked hard to pull themselves up."

"I actually didn't know," Holly said, staring at the three men before her with new eyes.

"The whole town kind of rallied around them," Yasmin said. "My dad helped Liam get a college scholarship, but that's just one example."

"Sean's made peace with his past," Anna said. "I think Liam has, too, wouldn't you say, Yasmin?"

"Mostly yes." She frowned. "Cash, now…"

"Cash hasn't," Anna said flatly.

Guilt ate at Holly. She'd been judging Cash for his materialism, when he'd actually had a poorer and more difficult childhood than she had herself. Her mother had been preoccupied and sometimes neglectful, but at least she'd been around.

Cash wasn't just a rich man Tiff had taken advantage of. He was a survivor with scars.

They walked closer to the men, enough to hear their banter.

"Who'd have thought the O'Dwyer boys would be crabbing legally," Liam said as he measured the crab he'd just pulled in.

"Who'd have ever thought they'd amount to anything," Sean said. "And now, look, we've got a genuine millionaire right here." He pounded Cash hard on the back.

"Jealous?" Cash taunted.

"Yeah, well, get to work, millionaire," Liam said. "Your fire's about to go out."

Cash turned to poke at the fire, topped by a huge pot of steaming water, and that was when he spotted her. There was a light in his eyes for just a moment, but they quickly clouded.

Holly's heart ached for him. She'd treated him badly, pushing him away for no apparent reason. Underneath all his confidence was a troubled mind.

While the other two women joined the men, talking and laughing, Holly sat on a rock and just watched.

An old, rusty van and a newer pickup pulled into the parking lot. Kids poured out of the van, and there was Penny, perfectly safe and content in Ma Dixie's arms.

A couple of men she didn't recognize pulled planks and sawhorses out of the pickup under Pudge's direction and put them together to make a long plank table, which they covered with newspapers. Rita, Norma and another woman did an informal assembly line, passing dish after dish to set along the table.

Holly took Penny from Ma's arms, thanking her. "Was she good?"

"A little angel." Ma frowned. "Not where she should be, though. You're having her tested?"

"We are."

"Good. She's going to be just fine, but she's behind by a few months with gross motor skills."

So it was obvious, at least to an experienced foster parent, Holly thought as she tied a sun hat on Penny and smeared sunscreen over her arms and legs.

The crabs were tossed into the pot of water boiling over the fire.

She felt awkward sitting down beside Cash at the long table, but she didn't feel comfortable sitting by anyone else, and after all, he was Penny's father.

And then her excuse for sitting with him was taken away, because Anna spread a blanket beside the table and scooped Penny up to sit with HoHo and Rocky, a teenage boy who, along with his mother, was visiting from out of state and who apparently loved babies.

"And I don't like seafood," he said, "so I'll just give 'em baby food or whatever you want."

"They say you can feed them shellfish at a year old," Anna added, "but I'm a little nervous. I'm going to wait a few more months. I brought leftover chicken, way more than HoHo can eat."

"I have a whole box of crackers," Holly said, and dug them out for the babies to share. Apparently, in this family, you just passed babies from person to person. It did require trust, but it also gave mothers a considerable amount of freedom.

She stretched in the warm breeze and inhaled the

smell of fresh-baked rolls someone was unwrapping. She could get used to this.

Soon the crabs were done boiling—they were bright orange-red now—and were laid out in heaps on the newspaper. Holly looked at them blankly.

"Don't know how to eat 'em? Here, I'll show you." Cash put a crab in front of her. "First, you break off the legs. Throw those away, but keep the claws." He showed her how to use scissors, a knife and her fingers to extract the meat. "You're going to get messy," he said, and then turned to the twins, who sat across from them. "Hang on, let me do the knife part and then you can dig in."

The twins acted as comfortable ripping apart the crabs as if they'd been born on the water. Holly, though, cringed a little at the messy-looking innards.

"Here, get rid of those, those are the lungs. There, now. There's the good meat." He indicated a section of the crab, and when she just stared at it, he pulled it out for her. "Open wide," he said.

Her cheeks heated.

"She's not a baby, Uncle Cash!" Hayley said. "Still," she added to Holly, "you should eat it. It's really good."

So Holly opened her mouth, and Cash popped in the piece of crab. When she tasted it, her eyes widened.

He grinned. "See? We wouldn't steer you wrong."

Was it her imagination that his eyes lingered on her lips?

Probably so, because he quickly turned away and occupied himself with helping the twins extract more of the delicious meat from the claws.

When they'd all eaten their fill, Rita and Norma walked up and down the table with bowls of lemon water and stacks of soft washrags. Holly wiped her hands and mouth.

Then she reached over and squeezed Cash's hand. "Thank you," she said. "I've been sort of awkward with your family, and I'm sorry. I'll try to do better."

He studied her, his gaze level. "I can't figure you out," he said. "You sure do run hot and cold. What's with the mixed messages?"

She bit her lip and shook her head, pretending simple shyness, because what could she say when she didn't understand her own feelings?

THE NEXT THURSDAY MORNING, Holly shoved her hair off her sweating forehead and unlocked the door of her client Mitch Mitchell's town house. From inside, she heard the hysterical barking and jumping of his shih tzu, Daisy.

She had another dog with her, something Mitch didn't like. He wanted Daisy to get her full attention on walks, but it wasn't possible today.

She tied the Lab mix to the front-porch railing, went inside and shrugged her child carrier off her back. Its design, comfortable and breathable on a rigid frame with a sort of kickstand, was priceless on occasions like this. She set the carrier on the floor, made sure Penny was well-supported and steady and then knelt to properly greet Daisy. The little dog was sweet and impeccably groomed, but hyperactive.

"Come on, Daisy, let's get your harness on." She held up the pink contraption, enticing the pup with a contraband dog treat. She was running behind schedule. Penny had been out of sorts this morning, had spit up and struggled against getting dressed, and all of it had taken longer than it should.

After Daisy and Gus the Lab mix, two more dogs were eagerly waiting for their lunchtime walks. She stretched her back. It was noon and she felt like she'd put in a full day already.

A traitorous thought penetrated: if only she'd taken up Rita on her offer to babysit. Today would have been much easier if she wasn't worrying about Penny, constantly stopping to check on her or readjust the straps of the new backpack carrier—an expensive purchase, but necessary if she was going to make this dog-walking-while-mothering gig work.

She just had to get more organized, that was all. She could do this. The blessing was that business was booming as more and more people heard about her and her services.

Abandoning the effort to get Daisy's harness on for the moment, she looked out onto the porch.

Gus, bless his patient heart, had lain down and was snoozing.

Next, she kissed Penny's forehead. Was it a little warmer than usual? She thought so, but wasn't good at judging such things and she hadn't brought a thermometer.

The baby's temperature had been normal this morning, though. No doubt she was just a little hot from the excitement.

She turned back to Daisy again, and by a mixture of pleading and scolding and luring with treats, finally got the ridiculous ruffled harness on the dog. As she fastened it, she caught a whiff of the dog and frowned. Did Mitch Mitchell actually put perfume on poor Daisy?

They headed out the door, Holly feeling a little guilty. Gus's owner wouldn't mind her doubling up on his walk, but Mitch was another story.

Holly had weighed her options and decided it was more important to get Daisy out on time, or close to it. Besides, Daisy might benefit from a few lessons in doggie decorum from big, gentle Gus.

As they walked toward Safe Haven's downtown, Holly's spirits lifted. A few people greeted them, both passersby and folks in their yards. She hadn't realized how many people she'd meet working as a dog walker in a small Southern town. Half the community seemed to know who she was, and most called out friendly greetings.

Initially, she'd wanted to keep to herself and be anonymous. But she was finding the friendliness appealing, was starting to learn a few people's names just from the daily encounters while she was out walking.

Downtown, lampposts sparkled with tinsel-covered decorations, and most of the storefronts had Christmas displays or lights. A cinnamon smell emanated from Jean Carol's bakery; if Holly hadn't been in such a hurry, she might have stopped in to grab a roll, since she'd had to skip breakfast. She'd already learned that Jean Carol, like most of the shopkeepers here, was dog-friendly.

Cars passed at a leisurely pace, and a mother with a baby and a toddler smiled and said hello. Belatedly, Holly recognized her from last week's parenting class and returned the greeting.

Usually, she worked on teaching Daisy to heel during walks. Today, she decided to let her do as she pleased. Mitch had been advised by a trainer—for some reason, Holly thought it was Pudge LeFrost—that the dog needed more exercise. That was the only reason he'd gotten a dog walker, and he was a fairly reluctant customer. Hopefully, with Daisy getting more of her energy out during the day, she'd behave better when Mitch came home from work and he'd start to see and believe in the benefits.

As her day settled down into its regular routine, with Penny and the dogs all content, Holly's thoughts returned to the place she'd been trying to distract them from: Cash.

He'd definitely cooled toward her since she'd rebuffed him at the one parenting class. Which was what she'd wanted, right? But at the crab boil, she'd wished they could be closer. And every morning her phone didn't flash his number, every evening he didn't knock on her door as he walked past it to his apartment, regret nudged at her heart.

Cash was incredibly handsome and had real charisma, an aura of success. Of course, all of that attracted her; she was human, hardwired to be drawn to a good provider, the alpha of the tribe.

But it was more than that. He cared about his brothers and was a great uncle to their kids. He gave back to the community of Safe Haven; she'd heard Yasmin talking to him about what they were doing with his big donation to the women's center, had seen him sneak a hundred-dollar bill into the church collection plate.

He wasn't exactly outspoken about his emotions, but he had a slew of them. She'd seen the struggle in his face when he'd talked about Rita, and had watched him kiss Penny's head, then close his eyes and pull her close.

She reached Mitchell's Men's Shop, glanced in and waved, knowing that Mitch enjoyed catching a glimpse of Daisy during his busy days. Gus seized the opportunity to mark the fire hydrant in front of the store.

The store's door opened. "What on *earth*?" Mitch came out, consternation written all over his face. He knelt down and Daisy rushed to him and jumped into his arms, yapping.

"Hi, Mitch." Even though she suspected he was angry that there was another dog on Daisy's walk, Holly figured that ignorance might be the best defense. "Is something wrong?"

"It certainly is." He glared up at her as he stood, Daisy in his arms. "Look how traumatized she is."

Daisy was alternating between licking Mitch's face and struggling to get down, her face relaxed, tongue out. "I—I don't think she's upset," Holly said.

"Not only are you late, but you're walking my Daisy with that—that *beast*."

Holly glanced down at Gus, who'd flopped onto the sidewalk and twisted himself into a pretzel to lick his own hindquarters. "Gus and Daisy are getting along great. Sometimes it can be good for a dog to interact with other dogs, and Gus is supergentle."

"Daisy is very sensitive," Mitch said severely. "Aren't you, sweetheart?" He turned her over to cradle her like a baby while she struggled to escape.

"I'm sorry," Holly said. "I was running a little late and I'm trying to get back on schedule." She resisted the urge to look at her watch.

Mitch flipped Daisy back over to right side up and looked sternly at Holly. "I'm reconsidering hiring you as a dog walker," he said.

She actually wouldn't mind losing Mitch as a client, though she felt bad for Daisy, so full of pent-up energy. "Of course, that's your decision," she said. "It's kind of like a babysitter. There has to be a good fit. Maybe I'm not the right person."

Mitch looked annoyed, probably because she hadn't begged him to keep her on. "I'll be telling other people in town that I've been dissatisfied with your work," he said.

Holly's heart sank. "Do you want me to at least take Daisy home?"

"I'm debating that," he said, setting Daisy down and examining her carefully, as if she might have sustained injuries during the treacherous walk from his house to his shop, a distance of a few blocks at most.

She cleared her throat. Time to cut her losses. "I need to get moving," she said. "I'm running a little late." In the backpack, Penny shifted restlessly.

"Whose fault is that?" he asked. "I should have known not to hire a woman with a child."

A thin, white-haired African American woman who'd been standing behind Mitch, looking in the shop window and poking at her oversize cell phone, spun, strode over and faced the man, hands on hips. "Did I really just hear you say that, Mitch Mitchell?"

Mitch seemed to shrink, just a little, and recognition welled up in Holly. This must be the famous matriarch of the town library, Miss Vi.

"I'll have you know," the woman continued, "that someone raised you and took you places and put bread on your table. We're all indebted to our mothers, and we should support the young mothers among us." She turned to Holly. "I'm known as Miss Vi around town. And you are…Holly Gibson, is that right?"

Holly nodded and held out her hand to shake the other woman's thin, calloused one—she was rendered a little speechless by Miss Vi's energy. Penny wiggled hard in the backpack, and Holly patted her leg, hoping to calm her.

"I just don't see," Mitch said, his voice petulant, "why those of us without children are always expected to make accommodations for people who have them. I open my shop on time whether or not Daisy is causing me trouble."

"It's not comparable," Miss Vi said briskly. "You can put a dog in a crate and shut the door. Last I heard, that was frowned on with a child."

Holly pressed her lips together to keep from laughing. Or crying. She wasn't sure which.

Penny didn't have any such restraint; she started to cry. Loudly. Right in Holly's ear.

As Mitch and Miss Vi went on arguing, Holly drew in a deep breath, willing herself to relax. Both

Miss Vi and Mitch were dressed and groomed beautifully, while she was wearing jeans and a hoodie. There'd been no time for makeup this morning; she'd barely managed to run a comb through her hair.

Though she appreciated Miss Vi's backing, she felt at a disadvantage, like a poor relation.

A silent flash of silver arrived at the curb. Cash in his Tesla.

Could this day get any worse?

He climbed out and strode to the three of them, earning excited barks from Daisy and a low woof of greeting from Gus. He reached up and pulled Penny out of Holly's backpack in one smooth swoop. "What's the problem here?"

Relief from the weight of the baby vied with embarrassment about her unkempt state. "I don't need rescuing," Holly said, even though it wasn't true.

TEN MINUTES LATER, after figuring out what was going on and helping Holly and Miss Vi calm Mitch down—to the point where he'd agreed Holly could at least take Daisy home—Cash turned to Holly. She looked exhausted, and there were shadows under Penny's eyes as well. He had to do something about that.

"Go home and take Penny," he said. "I'll be there soon. We need to talk."

Holly visibly straightened her shoulders. "I can't.

I have to take these dogs home, and then I have two more clients."

"Not for long," Mitch quipped over his shoulder as he walked into the shop.

Holly flinched.

Cash's eyes narrowed as a caveman protective impulse washed over him. "Wait here," he ordered her, giving a meaningful glance to Miss Vi. She'd gotten herself involved by sending Cash a text, telling him Holly and Penny needed him. Now, he was sure she wouldn't mind staying to help set things right.

She gave a little nod, reading his unspoken request. She'd stay with Holly and Penny until Cash came back out.

He followed Mitch into his shop. "Not that anyone will listen if you do a smear campaign on Holly," he said, "but just don't."

"I'm only going to share my experience," the other man said. "There's no law against that."

"You and I both know," Cash said, "that there are a lot of different ways to share experiences. Don't trash Holly's name or you'll have me to contend with."

Mitch's eyebrow flicked up, and the faintest trace of a sneer crossed his face. Cash took a step closer. He wasn't the biggest of the O'Dwyer brothers—that honor fell to Sean—but he had a few pounds of muscle on Mitch. More than that, he had a background of street fighting that Mitch, one of Safe Haven's privileged sons, couldn't touch.

Still, he was beyond his street-fighting days. He had other tools at his disposal now. "I buy clothes from you because I believe in supporting local businesses," he said. "Those I believe in, with owners and business philosophies I respect."

"Are you threatening me?"

"I'm only going to share my experience," he said, quoting Mitch. "Good or bad. Think about that." He turned on his heel, giving the man the opportunity to stay out of a fight he couldn't win, and walked outside to find Miss Vi standing alone.

"I couldn't keep your friend here," she said, her voice apologetic. "If you head down there—" she gestured toward a side street "—you might catch her."

"Thanks. And thanks for the text." He patted Miss Vi's arm, and would have hugged her, except he still held her in the fear and awe she'd commanded in all the O'Dwyer boys when they'd landed in town as teenagers.

"In Safe Haven, we take care of our own," she said.

"Some didn't get the memo." He nodded toward Mitch's shop.

"That man." She pursed her lips. "You go after her. I'll do some damage control around town, see if I can counteract any smear campaign Mitch starts up."

Cash grinned as he turned away. Mitch didn't stand a chance.

Taking long strides, he soon caught up with Holly, Penny and the two dogs. "Let me take Penny," he said.

"No, it's… Well, okay. Sure." She turned, and he lifted the backpack off her shoulders and slid it onto his own back as she steadied Penny and helped him adjust the straps to fit his larger frame. "Thanks," she said. "I really appreciate this."

"I'm Penny's father." He frowned. He still didn't like how tired Holly looked, and it pushed him past his hurt feelings about the way she'd rejected him. "Tell you what," he said. "You take the dogs back to wherever they belong and then go home and take a shower, rest a little. When you've had enough of a break, walk down to the beach. Penny and I will be there."

"Well…" She bit her lip. "I have to walk two more dogs, but I wouldn't mind doing it without Penny on my back."

"Then grab a little time for yourself after you're done walking dogs. You can't take care of Penny very well if you don't take care of yourself."

"True," she admitted. "All right."

He felt an absurd sense of triumph at having convinced her to let him help her by caring for his own child. His friends back in Atlanta wouldn't have believed it.

"Doesn't seem like beach weather," she said, looking up at the cloudy sky. "There's an extra sweater and blanket in the bag, and some snacks, but you bring her right home if she gets upset or cold, okay?"

"Of course, but she won't." He smiled to reassure her and risked a little flirtation. "I'm a baby whisperer, remember?"

"Oh, right." She lifted an eyebrow and laughed, her gaze connecting with his. "Okay."

Now he was on a quest. He strode toward home, Penny on his back, clicking Liam's number on his phone. "Listen, I know you're working," he said when Liam answered. "But I need a favor. Can you get me a permit for a bonfire?"

There was a silence. Then his brother asked, "Are you back to that?"

"To what?"

"You know."

Until that moment, it hadn't occurred to Cash that he'd often used bonfires to put the moves on a lady. "Not the same thing at all," he said. "This is for Penny and Holly."

"Uh-huh." Liam's neutral tone said he was reserving judgment. "I'm headed to the courthouse now. I'll take a picture of your permit and send it to you."

He took Penny back to his apartment, changed her diaper and put her into the high chair he'd borrowed for her. He sprinkled some kind of baby crunchies on the tray to keep her occupied while he gathered his supplies.

She seemed cheerful and wide-awake, so he loaded her into the backpack again and headed to Safe Haven's downtown. Situated on the water, the downtown had a fish-processing plant at one end and a small beach at the other, with a boardwalk, shops and restaurants in between.

He picked up the sandwiches and drinks he'd ordered and walked down the boardwalk through the afternoon light. He heard harmonica music, a little mournful, and scanned the storefronts, decorated with wreaths and Christmas trees and gift displays. Sure enough, there was Rip Martin, a town fixture, leaning against one of the brick buildings, looking out toward the water as he played. "Hey, Rip," he said when he reached the man, and fished a twenty out of his wallet to put in the hat Rip had set up beside him for donations.

"Thank you kindly," Rip said, then launched into something bluesy.

Cash hummed along as he continued on down toward the beach. Penny babbled nonsense in his ear, and when he turned his head, she grabbed his nose, then yanked on his hair. She was heavy, too. How did a petite woman like Holly manage to carry her around on her back all day, every day?

In front of him, the empty beach stretched out. He'd always loved walking on it. Some of his biggest dreams and plans had been formulated while pacing this beach, working off the restless energy that came from being a kid who wanted more than he had.

Now, though, he was in a weird, poignant mood. He wasn't here as an angry, displaced kid, or as a player out to put moves on a lady.

He was here as a dad.

He didn't know how to be one, didn't know what it all meant. He only knew that when he reached up to touch Penny's leg or tilted his head back to smile at her, his heart turned to mush.

He shook off the girlie emotions and chose a sheltered area protected from the wind by a dune, and then gathered some driftwood and pine to burn. Bending down to work on the fire was tough with a backpack—though he was sure it was nothing compared to leashing up a bunch of dogs, which Holly did every day—so he spread the big blanket he'd brought and set Penny on it with a couple of toys.

The gulls squawked overhead, and Penny laughed at them. When a few late fishermen cruised by on their way to dock, her head whipped to watch them.

Cash inhaled the salty ocean air as he started the fire. He uncorked the wine he'd brought to let it breathe. Found a few shells and showed them to Penny, talked nonsense to her.

Maybe he was crazy, thinking Holly would want to chill and spend a little time with him rather than grabbing Penny and taking her home. But he'd sensed a softening in her attitude toward him. And some force inside him, stronger than hurt feelings, stronger than pride, pushed him to make the effort to close the distance that had grown between them.

He was just leaning back on his elbows, wondering if Holly would actually come, when there she was, walking toward him with the sun behind her. She wore ripped, faded jeans and a sweater, and her blond hair blew around her.

She wasn't classically beautiful; her eyes were set a little wide and her nose turned up. Right now, though, Cash had never seen anyone more appealing.

Was it just because she was caring for Penny with him, or was it something more? She was sexy, for sure, but he was getting this weird she's-the-woman-for-me vibe, which made absolutely no sense.

He tried to shake it off. The last thing either of them needed was for him to fall in love with her.

Fall in love? He, Cash O'Dwyer, didn't do that.

Or maybe he did. Because when Holly's eyes lit up, looking at Penny and the wine and the bag of sandwiches, he thought that maybe he'd like to cause her to have that look again, and again, and again. It filled something deep inside him, a hole he hadn't known was there.

"Penny looks sleepy," she said, kneeling down beside the baby and pulling her into her arms. "I missed you, sweetie," she whispered, looking down at Penny with eyes full of love.

Cash's heart went all soft again.

But he had to toughen up, had to talk seriously to her and not about his weird romantic feelings. He got out the sandwiches and poured them some wine and tended the fire. Holly cuddled Penny and rocked her until her eyes started to close. Putting her down gently, Holly covered her with a blanket.

He handed Holly a sandwich and set a glass of wine in the sand beside her, digging it in so it wouldn't spill.

"Clever," she said, smiling. "You're a man who's had a beach picnic or two in his day."

His face heated as if she could see the string of girls he'd brought here. "I don't want you to work anymore," he said abruptly.

She froze in the act of unwrapping her sandwich and stared at him. "What do you mean?"

"Look, it's hurting you and it's hurting Penny. You can't keep lugging her around like that, having her cry, and you can't adequately tend to her, with jerks like Mitch Mitchell yelling at you both."

Her eyes got shiny and she looked away, and Cash had been around enough upset women to realize she was going to cry. "Hey, hey," he said. "I didn't mean it as a criticism. You've been doing the best you can."

"I *thought* I was doing pretty well, until today."

"You are. You've started a business from nothing in just a few weeks, while raising a baby. If I could, I'd give you a prize. But the child support is supposed to make things a lot easier for you. You don't need to work. Or at least, you don't need to work this hard."

"The child support is for Penny," she said, her voice stubborn. "Cash, no one's ever supported me. I'm not that kind of person."

"You never tried to raise a child before."

"I can do it!" She got up on her knees and backed away a little bit from him and Penny both. "I don't want to be obligated to you, Cash."

"You wouldn't be obligated." Suddenly the irony of the situation struck him. Here he was begging a woman to accept his support, when he'd evaded commitment for years, had gently pushed away all the hangers-on who wanted his money.

"Look," she said, her eyes softening, "I don't mean to be ungracious. I appreciate the generous support payments, I really do. I just wouldn't feel right using it to support me. Like I said, it's for Penny."

He drew in a breath and let it out slowly. She was stubborn and independent, and he admired both qualities. But the image of her standing in the street with dogs barking and Penny crying—and Mitch yelling—wouldn't leave him. "You don't like accepting help," he said. "Nothing wrong with that when it's just you. But Penny is suffering for it."

She bit her lip as a flash of something—worry, pain—crossed her face. Then she seemed to take hold of herself and lifted her chin. "Do you really think so? Seriously, Cash. Set aside your preconceptions about what a baby's life ought to be like. Is it so wrong, me basically taking her to work with me?"

Cash had his mouth open to argue, and then he processed her words and stopped. She could be right. Moreover, he recognized something in her— that core of strength beneath what hadn't been an easy life—and his heart and mind shifted toward her.

She was a woman, yes, and a beautiful one. But she was fundamentally like him, too. He knew her, that part of her at least; he *got* her. Got her in a way he'd never gotten a woman before.

He'd think later about why he'd always pushed women into the object box, looked at them as conquests rather than people. For now, he was on a blanket with a beautiful woman. A beautiful *person*.

"You're right," he said. "Some of what I'm worrying about is probably some imaginary, sexist image of how mothers should be."

"Thank you," she said, her teeth chattering.

He pulled the extra blanket from his backpack and draped it around her shoulders, not squeezing in an extra cuddle like he might have in times past, even though he wanted to more than he ever had. This new accord between them felt too fragile for any of his old moves.

"Perfect," she said, pulling it tighter around her. When he sat back down, she tilted her head to one side. "Don't you have a blanket for yourself?"

He shook his head and faked a sad face. "Are you offering to share?"

She studied him for a moment, eyes speculative, and then nodded, holding out one side of the blanket.

He couldn't turn that down, could he? He scooted over next to her and put an arm around her, feeling the sparrow thinness of her shoulders, smelling her honeysuckle hair. They huddled together, and between the fire and the body heat, Cash was warm. Almost hot.

She might not know it, but she was affected by him. Her lips softened and her eyes darkened, and she shifted the slightest bit closer. He watched her chest rise and fall a little faster beneath her sweater and his thoughts went wild.

To distract himself from his physical reaction to her closeness, he pulled back his arm from around her shoulders. He grabbed their sandwiches and the wine bottle and pulled them closer, easier to get at. Something else to focus on, but it wasn't enough. He drew in a calming, cool-down breath and cast about for a topic of conversation. "So tell me something about you, when you were younger."

"Like what?" She took a sip of wine. "Tiff was the exciting one. I just kept my head down and got through."

They ate their sandwiches for a couple of minutes while he processed that comment. "How come you're so independent?"

She shrugged and wiped her mouth. "All the school moves meant I couldn't count on friends. And Mom had a lot of boyfriends, one after the other, so we learned pretty quickly not to get close to them."

"Sounds lonely." But it also sounded familiar. Cash hadn't found people so dependable, either.

They ate and chatted a little more, but when they'd both finished their sandwiches, he was still thinking about her being lonely as a kid, and the connection to her major independent streak today. He had the same streak, but it didn't come out quite the same. He did a lot of his best work with other people.

What he'd had different was his brothers. "Were you and Tiff close?"

She frowned, tilted a flattened hand from side to side. "At home, we were inseparable. Shared a room, stuck together when Mom was in a rocky spell, figured out how to cook something from nothing. But out in the world—" She broke off.

He let himself put a friendly arm back around her. "Out in the world, it was different?"

She nodded. "I kept to myself, but Tiff was always good at making friends fast. Lively, funny, warm…" She trailed off. "Well, you remember."

He did, and now that he knew Holly better, he could see the similarities between her and Tiff. Holly was funny, had the same sense of humor. And while it took a while for her to show it, she was also a very warm person.

But there were a lot of differences, most of them much to Holly's advantage. Tiff had been friendly and fun, but also a lot more worldly. He found Holly's innocence appealing. She wouldn't ever try to take advantage of someone; just look how she'd reacted when he'd suggested he give her more money.

No good would come from comparing Tiff and Holly, not now. "It got Tiff into trouble, being so friendly, I guess." He was surprised to find his throat felt a little tight. Had he been part of the trouble? He guessed he had, but then again… He reached out to cup Penny's head, adjust her blanket. When such perfection had come out of his and Tiff's brief relationship, you couldn't call it anything but right.

Penny turned, sighed and then settled back to sleep.

Holly smiled. "She's such a good baby."

"She is." Cash felt…tender. Different from how he'd ever felt before about a woman. He was attracted, sure, but he almost felt he wanted to shelter her from his own physical desires.

Holly shifted a little closer, and he got the sense that she was having some tender feelings, too.

When she looked up at him, eyes darkening, he knew it. Automatically, he leaned toward her and brushed her lips with his.

Her sharp inhale told him she liked it, and the way she looked up at him through half-closed lashes confirmed it.

So maybe her rebuff of him at the parenting class hadn't been the final word.

He really wanted to pull her into his arms, and there was every chance that if he did, she'd let it happen. He even leaned a little closer, and she closed her eyes. Yep. This could definitely go in that direction.

Don't.

He didn't know where that voice came from. Seemed like somewhere deep inside, but if so, he was unacquainted with it.

But he wanted to be a good father, better than his own dad. He didn't want to do things he'd regret, like Pudge had said. And for all her courage and strength, Holly seemed pretty innocent when it came to men.

On the other hand…she'd shifted closer. She was definitely willing. He'd be an idiot not to take advantage of what was right in front of him.

Don't.

He sighed regretfully. "It's getting cold out. We should probably go back."

Her eyes fluttered open, and two tiny wrinkles appeared between her eyebrows.

He moved away from her, tucked the blanket around her shoulder and patted her arm in as impersonal a way as he could manage. Then he started stuffing sandwich wrappings and wine into the backpack.

After a minute, she joined him, then picked up Penny so he could fold the blanket. But something about her movements was sort of…muted.

She was hurt.

So he'd restrained himself from taking advantage of Holly, moving things in a direction he wasn't sure they should go. For all the best reasons, and it hadn't been easy because he was more attracted to her than he'd ever been to any woman in his life.

And instead of feeling like a good guy, he felt like a chump.

CHAPTER NINE

THE KNOCK ON the screen door made Rita jump. "I'm not ready!" she called, feeling panicked.

It was an unseasonably warm day, and she had all the windows open. The new things she'd bought for Taffy the yellow dog were all out, her water bowl filled, kibble neatly in a clear plastic bin.

But she'd looked around her place and realized that it wasn't in the least dog-proofed: that her shoes were out on a rack by the door, dish towels were hanging on the oven handle and there were small knickknacks on an end table that could choke an untrained, mouthy dog. The awareness came from somewhere deep inside her, because she didn't remember baby-proofing for her own kids, let alone puppy-proofing for a dog.

What she remembered, what she felt in her body, was that laser-like vision that took in a room at a glance and saw every potential hazard as if it was framed in fire.

Unfortunately, that preternatural mom-vision hadn't come back to her until five minutes before Taffy was to arrive.

"It's just us," Norma called through the door. "Can we come in?"

"Sure," Rita called back, relieved. "Who's with you?" She had a small hope that it was Cash, but she doubted it; he seemed ever-so-slightly more friendly in his waves and greetings, but he still didn't voluntarily seek her out.

A male throat cleared. "It's me, Stephen."

Aka the Silver Fox. Rita opened the door and looked at Norma, quirking her eyebrow a little to ask "why is he here?"

Norma rolled her eyes as if to say "wasn't my idea." "I'm here to offer moral support."

"And I insisted on coming along," Stephen said with a twinkle in his eye Rita hadn't seen before. "I love dogs," he added sheepishly.

"Do you have one?" Rita spotted an electric cord that was exposed and chewable and moved the floor lamp closer to the couch, then tucked the cord behind it.

"No." Stephen went to the other end of the couch and did the same thing Rita was doing with that floor lamp. "But I grew up with standard poodles, and I always wanted to get another one. I'm hoping to convince her—" he nodded over at Norma "—to adopt Snowball."

"Why didn't you get a poodle if you always wanted one?" Norma's voice was impatient. "I always say better to make a mistake than to live with regrets."

"Ah." Stephen nodded. "A wise philosophy. But my wife didn't care for dogs."

"Mistake to get one, then." And that idea, too, came from a deep place inside Rita. Had she gotten the yellow dog Cash insisted they used to have against her husband's will? Had that been a part of the problem between them?

"I don't see a wife in the picture now," Norma said. "What's stopping you from doing what you want? In fact, why don't *you* adopt Snowball?"

Stephen looked at her, surprised. "I don't know. It never occurred to me."

"Never occurred to you to follow your dreams?" Norma sounded disgusted.

Rita frowned at her friend. "Don't be so hard on him. Not everyone has the—the recklessness to just jump in and think later."

"I travel, too," Stephen said hastily. "I guess that's why I never thought I could get a dog. No one's at home to take care of it during my business trips."

"I'll take care of Snowball when you travel, for Pete's sake," Norma said.

A smile spread across Rita's face. She'd been searching fruitlessly for a way to get Norma and Stephen together. She knew, from how gruff Norma was being, that she was starting to like Stephen; that was how Norma was.

Snowball might just be the cupid she'd been look-ing for.

"Yoo-hoo, anyone home?" Holly called through the screen door, accompanied by a lot of excited barking.

When Rita hurried to the door to let in her new companion, she saw Cash behind Holly, holding Penny.

Maybe Taffy would be a unifier, too.

Taffy burst into the apartment and pulled might-ily on the leash, trying to see everything and start exploring.

Rita took one last look around but couldn't see any more hazards, though undoubtedly Taffy would discover some she hadn't noticed. And that, too, was something she just knew in her bones. "Okay, let her free," she said, and Holly unhooked the leash.

Taffy ran madly around the perimeter of the room, sniffing out the new environment.

"Her owner kept her in a crate most of the time," Holly explained. "She's going to love getting more attention and being able to explore."

"Sit down, everyone. I'm sorry my hostessing is so weak. Who wants some sweet tea?"

"I'll get it," Norma said. "You enjoy your dog."

So Norma poured tea while Rita, Stephen, Holly, Penny and Cash watched the little dog run around. Rita felt mesmerized by her, and she sat cross-legged on the floor, delighting each time the dog rushed over to greet her before zooming away again.

"I love her already." She looked up at Holly. "Thank you so much for suggesting I adopt her." She looked at Cash, a little curious about why he'd come. She thought it had to do with Holly, because those two were obviously interested in each other. But instead of paying attention to Holly, Cash was staring at the yellow dog. "Is she a lot like the dog we had?" she asked quietly.

Cash nodded, then looked at Rita. "You don't remember at all?"

She shook her head, surprised to find tears pushing at the backs of her eyes. "I wish I did. I wish I remembered a whole lot more than the dog." She glanced up at Stephen. "Amnesia," she said by way of explanation, and he looked startled, but nodded.

She looked back at Cash. "I wish my old brain would remember you, your childhood, but it doesn't. It breaks my heart."

Taffy trotted over, climbed into Rita's lap and jumped up to lick her face.

"Aww, she knows you're sad," Holly said.

"She's a sweetheart." Rita rubbed the dog's ears and sides until she ran off to sniff around more. She found her water dish and slurped some up, then pounced on a squeaky toy.

"She loves to tug," Holly said, demonstrating. "It's a good way to use up some of her extra energy." She wrinkled her nose at Rita. "She has a lot of that. I hope you're ready."

There was another knock on the door. "Hey, you home?"

Jimmy. And for once, she didn't feel excited to see him, because she knew he wasn't excited about Taffy. But how could he resist her once he saw her? She got up and opened the door, gave him a quick hug and kiss. "Come meet my new family member," she said.

"I didn't know today was dog day," he said, waving to everyone and greeting them. "Why didn't you tell me?" he asked her in a quieter voice.

"Because you as much as told me you didn't want to know," Rita said. Deliberately, she turned away from any guilt trip he was going to offer. She didn't need that. And she didn't need a man making decisions about how she ought to live her life.

"You'll be able to go to the dog park with her," Holly said. "She loves other dogs."

Stephen cleared his throat. "Bring her over to see Snowball," he said.

Rita and Holly both squealed at the same time. "You're getting her?" Rita asked.

He looked at Norma. "If you'll really help," he said.

She nodded, a smile tugging at the corner of her mouth. "I'll help. I'm in favor of people following their dreams."

"I'll totally bring Taffy over to visit," Rita said.

A movement from the corner of her eye caught her attention. Jimmy, crossing his arms and glaring at Stephen. He'd gotten jealous of Stephen once before, when Rita was attempting to set up Stephen with Norma. She'd thought he was over it.

While Stephen, Holly and Norma figured out the details of getting Snowball set up in Stephen's home, and Cash played tug with Taffy, adeptly holding Penny on one knee while he did it, Jimmy beckoned Rita over. "What are you going to do with her while you're working?" His voice was every bit as sulky as a teenager's.

"Do you think I haven't thought of that?" Rita heard the sharpness in her own voice and tried to dial it back. Maybe Jimmy was just concerned. "I'm going to have a crate for her," she said more gently. "She's been crated for long hours before, so my shifts will be less than what she's used to."

"And you'll have to leave right after and hurry home," Jimmy said.

"At least at first, yes," she said. She studied him. "Are you jealous of a dog?"

Jimmy laughed, but it sounded forced. "Maybe a little," he admitted.

She put an arm around him. "You're still my favorite." She leaned into him, squeezed.

"I should bring in the rest of her stuff," Holly said.

"Let me help you." Rita disentangled herself from Jimmy.

Cash stood up. "You stay here with the pup. I'll help."

"Me, too," Stephen said.

Rita was thrilled that Cash had offered to help. And her heart was warmed by having her friends around her; Norma, yes, but also Holly and Stephen, both new friends. And Jimmy, of course. But he was now shrugging back into his jacket.

"Are you taking off already?" Rita looked up from where she was kneeling, giving Taffy a belly rub. "Don't go. Stick around."

"No thanks," he said. "You've got a lot going on right now. I'd just be in the way."

Rita sighed, wishing she didn't have to manage Jimmy's emotions and could just enjoy the excitement of getting a new dog. But that was what relationships were about, and her relationship with Jimmy was important to her. She tried to explain. "It's not like that, it's just...this is a thing I really want to do. I don't even quite know why, but I know it's important to me." She looked at him steadily now. "I hope you can be supportive."

He shrugged. "Sure," he said.

He didn't sound sure.

And as the others came in carrying the crate and a dog bed and toys, talking excitedly, Jimmy let himself out. And Rita felt a double pang: annoyance and fear.

Was she ruining the wonderful thing she had in the present because of a dog who seemed to have leaped right out of her past?

"IF YOU EVER need dog-walking in the future, give me a call," Holly said into her phone later that afternoon. She was back in her apartment and getting better than she wanted to be at this conversation.

It was her third cancellation since the difficulty with Mitch Mitchell yesterday. She put down her phone and turned to look at the crafting materials spread all over her little kitchen table. She was decorating flowerpots and planting them with bulbs that would bloom over the winter, an inexpensive gift that she hoped would make her new friends smile. She would have gone an even cheaper route with the Christmas presents if she'd realized just how tight money was going to be.

She did a double take when she saw Penny's face on the other side of the coffee table. "You pulled up! Good—" She broke off as she saw Penny stuff a paper-white bulb into her mouth. "No, no, no!" she cried as she rushed over and pulled Penny away from the table and stuck her fingers in the baby's mouth to pull out the bulb. What else had she consumed during Holly's two-minute phone conversation?

Having Penny gain mobility was a mixed blessing.

Penny started to cry, either startled at Holly's sudden grabbing of her or upset because she wanted to keep chewing, and Holly hugged her close and scolded herself. Of course she was glad, one hundred percent glad, that Penny was getting more mobile. She shifted Penny to one arm, making soothing noises, and tried to move all her supplies away from the edge of the coffee table.

Knots tightened in her stomach, and she realized that she hadn't eaten since breakfast, but it was more than that. She was scared, plain scared. How was she going to make it in this town if customers kept canceling? Was she going to have to cave in and not work and let Cash support her, basically, by using his child-support checks as her only source of income?

She found Penny a couple of toys and set her down in the Pack 'n' Play, where she continued to fuss a little. Holly needed to fix them both some food. But in the kitchen, she saw the small box of Christmas decorations she'd pulled from one of her moving boxes earlier today, and a smile crossed her face even as tears sprung to her eyes.

Oh, Tiff, I wish you were here to look through these with me.

They'd toted the little box of Christmas ornaments and knickknacks from place to place in their childhood, both of them hungry for a little bit of tradition that their mother hadn't been able to make happen. After looking back in on Penny, who'd settled with a rubber doll to chew on, she sank down at the table and opened the lid.

Somehow Tiff had ended up with this scrap of memories from their childhood, so Holly hadn't looked through the box in years. She was ashamed to realize that she didn't know whether Tiff had managed to put up ornaments in recent years or not.

Why hadn't she made more effort to spend holidays with her sister? Yeah, Tiff had claimed to be busy with friends, but Holly should have tried to join in or arranged to see Tiff before or after.

Just another way she'd let down her sister.

She pulled out a small Nativity scene inside a hutch with a southwestern theme, a remnant of a six-month spell they'd spent in Arizona. Christmases had generally been on them, but that year, Mom had had a boyfriend who'd made an effort and bought them each a present. Next, she found cardboard angels they'd made in some Sunday-school class they'd attended for a couple of months, with their own photographed faces glued on top. Typically, Tiff had crafted some devil horns and glued them behind her own head, arguing that it was a hair bow when the Sunday-school teacher had scolded her.

Holly's throat tightened and she flipped quickly through the rest of the items in the box. At the bottom, she found an unfamiliar book. She opened it and sucked in a breath at Tiff's handwriting. It was a blank book, a journal. And true to form, Tiff had written exactly one entry, on January 1. Most likely, she'd put away Christmas decorations and accidentally shoved the journal in with them.

The date was almost two years ago. Tiff must have recently found out she was pregnant.

Joke's on you, Orin. I got the last laugh.

Yeah, you got me to hook up with him. And yeah, he was as rich as you said.

But your son's also a good guy, and those aren't easy to come by.

Our plan worked. I'm carrying his kid. But you'll never know that. You'd just use her— it's a little girl—to get what you want. You'd milk Cash of money, and that would make Cash hate her.

And you know what? I'd rather have him be a father to Penny than get rich off him, like we planned.

Luckily, they put you away. She'll be safe from you, my Penny. Little joke, right? He's Cash and she's a smaller version of that, a penny.

I'm not doing any more drugs and I'm not hanging out with any more lowlifes like you. I'm taking care of my baby. If I can't—if I'm

not strong enough—Holly will do it. And
maybe Cash can help.

She won't poison it by letting Cash know
you had anything to do with our getting together. She'll keep it pure. Sweet, like she is.
But strong, like me.

You stay where you belong, in prison, Orin
O'Dwyer. And stay out of my life, and Penny's.

And maybe, God willing, I'll get to surprise
Holly with something she'd really, really love:
a sweet, beautiful niece.

Holly felt out of breath, her eyes blurring and
her mind reeling.

Tiff had put so much faith in her, and that was
touching.

But the rest of it?

Tiff had conspired to get pregnant by Cash.
Egged on by a man named Orin, who was—if this
journal entry was to be believed—Cash's father.

She closed her eyes. *Oh, Tiff, how could you?*

Her head spun. She'd known about Tiff's relationship with a guy named Orin. He'd been Tiff's dealer.

What she hadn't known was that he'd talked Tiff
into connecting with Cash—his biological son—out
of wanting some of Cash's wealth.

She lifted Penny from the Pack 'n' Play and
pulled her up into her lap, needing the comfort. Tiff
had left a sealed letter for Holly, along with the will,

telling her to seek out Cash, that he was the baby's father and had plenty of money to help with Penny's expenses. But she'd been clear that she wanted Holly to be the one to raise her baby.

The journal entry put a terrible new spin on things.

Tiff had done something awful, under the influence of her addiction. She'd tricked Cash, who was a good man.

And she'd intended to let him know he was Penny's father without telling him that his own father had encouraged her to make the connection so he could use it to extort money from his wealthy son.

What would Cash think if he found out? How would he feel about Penny?

And what about this man Orin? Would he try to find Penny and somehow use her? No, he was in prison. Thank heavens.

She hugged Penny tight. "I'll take care of you, keep you safe," she whispered into the baby's soft hair. "Just like your mama wanted me to."

The tap on her door took her by surprise, and she hastily wiped her eyes and went to answer it.

There was Cash, looking at her expectantly, smiling at Penny. "I'm here for my sweetheart," he said.

"You're here for… Ooohhh." Heat suffused her face as she remembered the baby-care schedule they'd planned for today. "I'm sorry, everything's gotten switched around and I forgot. I'll get her ready in a flash."

"No rush." He came inside, all easy and relaxed, and held out his arms for Penny. "C'mere, sweetie."

As he took Penny, love for her written all over his face, determination filled Holly's heart.

She'd been a little miffed that Cash hadn't gotten into kissing her when they'd been together at the beach. But now, his lack of romantic interest turned out to be a blessing, even though it kind of hurt her feelings.

Tiff had wanted Holly to raise the baby and to keep the truth about why she'd connected with Cash away from him. How would she do that if she got involved?

For Cash to care for Penny and help with her was a good thing. Just a glance around her messy apartment, a thought about her financial worries, confirmed that she couldn't do it all alone.

But that didn't mean it was okay to get involved with Cash on a personal, let alone romantic, level. They could be cordial and work together with regard to raising Penny, but after Christmas Cash would move back to Atlanta and everything would settle into a normal routine.

That was how it had to be, especially now that she'd learned what Tiff had done. If she let that information slip, if Cash somehow found out about it, then Penny's connection with him would be in jeopardy.

Watching his eyes warm as he set down Penny on the floor and then stretched out beside her, graceful as a cat, Holly's heart tugged dangerously. Christmas couldn't come soon enough.

"If you want me to just watch her here, I can," he offered. "Don't you have another dog to walk?"

"No." Her stomach roiled as she thought about her financial situation. "I was supposed to, but that client was a friend of Mitch's. She decided she didn't want a dog walker after all."

His eyebrows shot up. "Seriously? He's been talking trash about you?"

She nodded, her stomach knotting tighter. "Third cancellation today."

"I'll talk to him."

She shook her head. "I think the damage is already done. Even if Mitch stops spreading tales about me, those he's already talked to aren't going to keep it to themselves."

He frowned. "Maybe God's trying to tell you something. You're working too hard. I'd like to see you just stay home and take care of Penny, anyway."

"I can't do that!" She shook her head, feeling hopeless. "If all else fails, I'll have to get a regular job." With the child support he'd offered, she could afford to put Penny in childcare, but her heart broke at the thought. Penny still needed to get close and attached to Holly, not go off and stay with a stranger.

Cash was sitting up now, absently shaking a rattle, his hand on Penny's back. "That wouldn't be good for her. Look, let's double the child-support number we worked out. Triple it. Whatever would let you stay home and take care of her."

She stared at him. Apparently there was no limit to his money or his generosity, and a big part of her—a *tired* part of her—wanted to take him up on it.

But she glanced back over at Tiff's journal, and red warning lights seemed to flash off of it.

The more entangled she got with Cash—and the more she depended on him—the likelier it was that she'd let slip something about Tiff's connection with his father. She couldn't do that. "No," she said. "I need to work. I'll figure something out."

"If I just had her and you weren't in the picture, I'd hire a nanny," he said. "How is this different?"

"It's different!" she said. "I'm her aunt! I'm trying to be her mother. I'm *not* a nanny."

He held up a hand. "You're right. Of course. I shouldn't have said that."

At least the guy apologized well, even when the problem wasn't entirely his fault.

Penny stared at her, wide-eyed.

"I'm sorry," she said. "It's—it's been a rough day. And the holidays can be hard."

"I get that." He stood and picked up Penny, and for a minute she thought he was going to come over and give her a hug.

For a minute, she thought she'd let him.

But he veered away and ended up looking at the table full of craft supplies. "What's all this?"

"I'm making Christmas gifts, or trying to. Didn't get much done today." She frowned at the mess and the irony. She finally had people she wanted to give presents to, and she was too worried about money to buy already-made gifts.

"You're doing handmade gifts on top of everything else? Holly, that's just too much. Just buy presents."

He was so clueless. "I can't afford it."

"I pay you enough child support to buy some Christmas presents!"

She sucked in a breath. He was right and he was wrong. "That money's not for me to buy expensive Christmas presents for my new friends, and it's not necessary. I like making gifts. Anyway, I'm the thrifty type."

"But I could—"

She held up a hand.

"I know, you could just take me Christmas shopping. But I don't want that."

"Scary you're starting to read my mind. You're a stubborn lady, you know?"

Their eyes met and held and something arced between them. He seemed to be looking at her with respect. Which, given the complete disparity between their financial positions, was a little ridiculous, but there it was.

"Holly, are you home?" It was Norma's voice.

Holly snapped out of the romantic mood and just in time. She hurried to open the door. "Hey, Norma, what's up?"

"I need some help. There's a thing at the women's center. We're going to surprise the parenting class with a photo booth, and Rita was going to help with it, but she's a little preoccupied with the dog." She looked past Holly. "Cash! Perfect, I was coming to see you next. Listen, I have a bunch of supplies—scrap wood and building stuff—I need loaded into a truck and then taken into the center tomorrow afternoon. It's all out at Pudge LeFrost's place. And then we need to put it together and plan how the event will work."

"You want Cash, then, not me." Holly was mostly relieved, a little disappointed.

"I want both of you. Him to haul stuff, and you to figure out how to set it up. That plant arrangement you delivered to me was gorgeous, and I can tell you're crafty."

"I have to take care of Penny." Holly was glad to have a good excuse.

"No, you don't. I'll take care of her if you two will work a few hours on this project. Believe me, it'll turn out better. And you'll get a break. Go out for a meal or shopping after, whatever. You need time off from parenting." She winked at them. "It takes a village, right?"

Holly wanted to withstand the force of Norma's personality, but she couldn't think how. Especially when Cash was nodding, and then said, "Sure, sounds fun."

"What do you think, Holly?" Norma smiled at her. "It'll really be a big help."

"Umm…sure, okay." What else could she say?

So all of a sudden she was spending tomorrow working on a project with a man who was so danger-ously attractive—and dangerous to her and Penny—that her stomach was doing flips.

At least, she was pretty sure the flips were about the danger. Whatever else they were about didn't bear thinking about.

CHAPTER TEN

CASH PULLED HIS brother's truck into the gravel area in front of Ma Dixie's place and turned to look at Holly. "You okay?"

She'd been quiet for the twenty-minute drive out here. Not quiet like she was mad at him, but thoughtful. "I'm fine," she said. "Well, a little uncomfortable leaving Penny with Norma, but I know in my head she'll be fine."

"You haven't left her much." It was a statement more than a question.

"Almost never." She smiled over at him. "Keeping her with me while I walk dogs isn't just an economy measure. I want her with me. It's good for both of us."

"True." His respect for her kept growing. She hadn't chosen to have a child, but she'd embraced mothering Penny as if the child was her own. "Do you want to call Norma, check on her?"

She shook her head, laughing a little. "I want to, but I'm not going to. I have to get over my new-mommy nerves."

"I understand them." He got out and came around

to open her door. "Although I'm sure Norma will smother her with attention and watch her like a hawk." He held up a hand to help her down.

She glanced into his eyes for a moment and then took his hand. Her own was small, but not soft.

He had the strangest urge not to let it go.

Unfortunately, or fortunately, his brothers pulled up in Sean's truck, apparently here for a visit. "Good," Cash said, turning away from Holly with reluctance. "Since you're here, you can help me load up the truck."

"Bad timing," Liam said to Sean.

"Have you talked to Pudge?" Sean asked. They were all worried about him.

The man himself came around the side of the house at that moment, breathing hard. "No," he said, puffing, "he hasn't. But I understand he's going to take some building supplies off my hands." He beckoned them over to a stack of boards beside the house and picked up a couple of them.

Ma Dixie appeared on the porch. "Pudge! You're not supposed to—" She glanced toward the three brothers. "Don't let him do any heavy lifting. Doctor's orders."

Pudge waved a hand and looked away from all of them. He was used to doing for himself, and activity restrictions had to be hard on him.

But Cash could read the worry on Ma's lined face. "I'll pull up a chair and you can supervise," he said to Pudge, and dragged a double wooden bench into a sunny spot.

"I ain't a cripple." But the large man did sit down.

"Thank you," Ma said, and beckoned to Holly. "Come on inside where it's warm. There's plenty of muscle out here."

"Sounds good," she said, and followed Ma into the house without a backward look at Cash.

With his brothers' help, he made quick work of loading up the truck, and then they all gathered around to talk with Pudge. The older man wore his trademark overalls and a thick wool shirt, and he looked a lot better than he had when Cash had last seen him, at the car dealership. Cash knelt so he wasn't towering over the older man.

"Any more medical procedures?" Sean asked, a little too abruptly. Ma had been his foster parent, and Pudge had been in the picture for most of that time; he was something of a father figure to Sean. To all of them, really, and it didn't feel great to have him ailing.

"Nothing much." Pudge got very busy looking for something in his overall pocket, avoiding their eyes.

The brothers exchanged glances.

"Tell us what's going on with you," Liam said finally. "We want to know. And you know if you don't tell us, our wives will get the truth out of Ma."

Pudge rolled his eyes. "I can imagine. Women." He sighed. "It's nothing surprising. Complications from my diabetes. Some circulation troubles in my legs, and they're taking a closer look at my heart."

His words made Cash's insides twist. He looked out over the marshland, inhaling its rich, fertile fragrance, listening to the chorus of frogs and birds to calm himself down. "You know we'll help out with anything that needs done around here, right? You don't have to kill yourself keeping the place up."

Pudge lifted an eyebrow. "Does that mean you're sticking around?"

The question caught him off guard, and he let it hang in the air without answering. When he saw his brothers' curious expressions, he got self-conscious. "I'm staying until Christmas," he said. "After that, I need to go back to Atlanta to keep things together there."

"Is Holly joining you?"

"No." He looked at Liam, who'd asked the question. "Why would she?"

"Oh, I don't know. Maybe because she's got custody of your child?"

Cash spread his hands. "Look, I'm doing what I can. Trying to talk her into taking more child support so she can stay home with the baby more. But nobody thinks I should be a hands-on parent."

Sean and Liam and Pudge all looked at each other.

"I do," Sean said.

"I do," Liam said.

"Me, too," Pudge added.

Cash blew out a breath and looked away from the three of them. They should know why he couldn't do it; they knew their father's blood ran in his veins, that he carried the strongest resemblance to Orin, both physically and emotionally. He wasn't going to spell it out to them. "I'm going inside to check on Holly," he said.

"Hang on a minute," Sean said. "What's going on with you and Holly, anyway?"

He turned back. "What do you mean?"

"She's real pretty," Liam offered. "Seems like a good person. Any interest in…?" He trailed off and raised an eyebrow.

"He'd be crazy *not* to be interested," Sean said. "Good women don't fall into his line of vision every day."

"Clue for me was, he's trying to talk her into accepting more money. Most women, they're trying to get more money out of a man." Pudge leaned back on the bench. "Grab me one of those cigars, would you?"

"You shouldn't, should you?" But Liam was already holding it out.

"Long as he doesn't inhale, it's fine." Sean had been trained as a medic in the Middle East and was their go-to for all things medical.

They were settling in for a longer chat, and Cash didn't want to be the subject of it. Or if he was, he didn't want to know about it. He left them to their smoking and went into the cabin.

The place was half-decorated for Christmas, with boxes of lights and ornaments spread around the living-room floor. Cash frowned. He'd always seen the place fully decorated, often by Thanksgiving or soon after. But Christmas wasn't too far away, and Ma hadn't finished decorating. Strange. Even a little worrisome.

From a corner of the room, he heard laughter. There was a smallish live Christmas tree, and Holly was scooting out from under it. "You're sure it's straight? I felt like it was tipping over."

"It's as straight as it needs to be," Ma said. "Oh, hey, son, you're just in time to help us."

Ma always called him "son," but today it struck him forcefully: Rita *never* did. Could be she just had a different habit of speech, having spent so much time in the north. Or it could be she didn't feel like he *was* her son.

Or maybe he'd been so standoffish that she was afraid to. He certainly didn't call her "Mom."

As he pulled decorations out of boxes and handed them to the women to put on the tree and mantel, he thought about Rita and the dog. She'd been upset that she didn't remember their dog from their growing-up years, but she'd appeared sincerely heartbroken that she didn't remember Cash.

His heart softened, just a little, toward her. It

must be pretty rough to have no idea about your own kids.

You knew nothing about Penny until she was a year old.

That realization hit him hard, but he argued back against it. He hadn't even known of her existence until a few weeks ago.

Rita didn't know about you, either.

It was true. He tended to blame Rita, thinking that she should have remembered him, but if amnesia truly erased your memory, then what could you do about it? It was the same as him not knowing about Penny: it wasn't his fault.

Even though he blamed himself.

Maybe if he stopped blaming Rita, he could stop blaming himself.

Holly was hanging ornaments, stepping back after each one to gauge its effect on the overall tree. Ma's approach with the garland was more of a random toss, which she quickly finished. Then she started unwrapping figures from a Nativity scene, which she did much more reverently. Carefully, she set them on the mantel.

Cash remembered coming out to Ma Dixie's place at Christmastime growing up. The contrast with his own foster family's home had been extreme. There, six themed Christmas trees were spread throughout the house, decorated perfectly by the commercial operation that brought them out each year and took them away after the holidays. That same company had wrapped garlands around the staircase and strung lights outside the house.

It had all been grand. He remembered being shocked and impressed his first year with the family, because it had been so different from the humble holidays back in Alabama. But he hadn't been allowed to invite his brothers over; too much noise and mess, his foster mother had always said. If he wanted to see them, he had to find a ride out to Ma Dixie's, which he had done frequently.

Here, Christmas really felt like Christmas.

He opened another box of ornaments, pulled out an angel made of hard plastic and handed it to Holly to place on the tree.

"Is this your tree topper, Ma?" Holly asked, holding it up.

"Yes, it is. I usually have Pudge put it up, but... could you do it, Cash, honey?"

He did, easily reaching the top of the small tree. "Is Pudge okay?" he asked Ma. "Is that why the place isn't decorated yet, that he's too sick to help?"

Ma arranged the last figures in the Nativity scene and sank down onto the couch. "That's part of it. Mostly, it's me feeling blue. I'm not used to Christmas with no kids around."

Holly tilted her head to one side. "Did you have a lot of kids?"

"Dozens," Ma said with a wide smile. "That's the beauty of being a foster parent."

"Oh," Holly said as she sank down onto an ottoman beside Ma. "Do you…not foster anymore?"

Ma sighed. "I really can't with Pudge having all these doctor appointments. I guess maybe we're getting too old for it." She looked wistfully at the tree. "I just, you know, always enjoyed having the little ones around."

Holly looked thoughtful. "Is that why you wanted to take care of Penny? Not to help me out, but to have a little one around?"

"That's part of it," Ma said, "but don't you worry about it. I understand being picky where your child is concerned."

"It's not pickiness," Holly said. "If I were being picky, who better than an experienced foster parent like you?" She reached out and rubbed Ma's arm back and forth, two or three times, an affectionate gesture that made Ma smile.

Cash came over and sat at Holly's side, leaning against the ottoman. His heart, like that of the Grinch in the movie playing muted on the television, seemed to be expanding.

He'd taken plenty of women to high-end Christmas parties and fancy restaurants. But sitting here in Ma Dixie's house, talking with her about holidays and kids and family problems, decorating the tree with her, felt different. Like coming home.

Like coming home, with Holly beside him.

He put that feeling together with the questions his brother and Pudge had been asking. He was getting the horrifying notion that he might be falling in love with Holly. But he wasn't the falling-in-love type, nor the settling-down type. And Holly wasn't the type for a short, superficial fling.

So what exactly was he going to do with all these feelings?

RITA WAS ANNOYED, tremendously so, way more than the occasion warranted. And a lot of it had to do with the handsome, infuriating man who'd just driven her and Taffy out to Pudge LeFrost's place.

It was a cool day, overcast and in the fifties. Jimmy wore a heavy winter coat; Rita wore a sweater. And she knew he was about to make another comment about it.

"You sure you'll be warm enough?" he said right on cue, turning off the truck.

Taffy leaped out of her arms and flung herself on Jimmy, trying to lick his face. Apparently, she'd figured out the person who liked her the least and was determined to grovel until she changed his mind.

Rita wasn't groveling. "I told you this wasn't necessary," she said as Jimmy attempted to block the excited dog with his arms and turn his face away. "I could just as well have trained her myself, at home. You wouldn't have even had to be involved."

"I *want* to be involved. I just wish you'd involved me before you made the decision to get a dog."

Rita blew out a breath, reeled the dog back toward her and opened the truck door to climb out.

A truck loaded with building supplies was parked on the other side of the driveway. Great. She was pretty sure it meant her least enthusiastic son, Cash, was here. They'd seen Liam and Sean driving away just as they'd turned onto the road that led out here; she hadn't figured on Cash still being here as a visitor.

The moment she climbed out, sure enough, there was her middle son, looking out the door. He walked over, giving her a slight wave.

He shook Jimmy's hand in a way that was distinctly warmer. Of course.

Ma Dixie came out onto the porch, and her broad face broke into a smile. "More of my favorite people," she said. "And who's that precious creature? I didn't know you had a new pup."

That was Ma; she saw the best in everyone, even Taffy, who was straining at her leash and barking frantically, practically ripping Rita's arm from the socket. "This is Taffy," she said, kneeling down to gently restrain the dog. "Hey, okay, it's okay, settle," she crooned. It was gratifying when Taffy at least stopped barking long enough to lick her face a couple of times.

"Bring her inside," Ma said, and when Rita protested that the dog wasn't perfectly house-trained, she waved a dismissive hand. "Honey, there's been more dogs and boys in this house than you have fingers and toes. If it's not been destroyed yet, it'll stand for a little dog like that."

"Thanks, Ma." Rita couldn't help flashing a glance at Jimmy. If only he could be as welcoming as Ma was.

But, of course, Ma was a saint among women, and most people—Rita included—couldn't live up to her sense of hospitality and generosity.

She urged Taffy up the steps, Jimmy and Cash following behind, talking about carpentry or some such manly thing. When she reached the porch, she realized that Holly was there, too. "Hey, honey," she said, reaching out and giving her and Ma both a quick hug.

Holly looked mildly surprised, which made Rita remember that she was from the north and a little shy. She'd get used to Southern friendliness soon, just as Rita herself had.

"Did you see Penny before you left?" Holly's voice was anxious. "It was so nice of Norma to come over and babysit. I hope Penny's being good for her."

"There's nothing she could do that Norma couldn't handle," Rita said. "They're having a blast together. I never heard Norma sing so many silly songs, and her voice is terrible. But Penny just laughs and laughs."

"Oh, good."

"I told you she'd be fine." Cash came up behind Holly and patted her on the back. His hand lingered a little longer than it needed to.

Interesting.

The other thing that was interesting was that Rita was feeling fully connected to this community, so much so that she felt like she wanted to welcome Holly to it and show her the ropes. It wasn't that long ago that Rita had come here as a stranger, looking for information about her past.

Well, she'd found it, or some of it. She just wished she could remember the background of the people she'd found, her own sons. Wished she could remember birthing them, and nursing them, and loving them as kids.

She glanced around the small living room, decorated for Christmas, with boxes indicating that the decorating had maybe just happened. "Are Rocky and his mom still visiting?" The teenager and his troubled mother had lived with Ma and Pudge briefly, recovering from some issues connected to Rocky's abusive stepfather. They'd been back to visit over Thanksgiving, and Rita had enjoyed seeing them at the crab boil.

"They're back in Colorado," Ma said. "Was hoping they'd come visit again for Christmas, but money's tight. They promised they'd get back here in the spring."

Cash lifted an eyebrow. "Another success of the Ma-and-Pudge project," he said wryly.

Ma smiled. "I hope so. I'm in the rehab business, helping people who have problems. Wouldn't mind getting another family or a few babies in here to stay, but…" She spread her hands and glanced toward the back of the house. "Now isn't the time."

Cash put an arm around the older woman. "You just had a visit from three of your rehab projects—me, Liam and Sean."

Shame heated Rita's face. The reason the boys had needed rehabilitation was her own neglect and bad choices.

Just now, for whatever reason, the thought of the past and those choices brought horror and dread to her heart. Sometimes her amnesia worked that way: it seemed to lift just enough to let in a few emotions, and usually they weren't good ones. She knelt and stroked Taffy, the wiggly warm body a comfort.

"Listen," Ma said, and Rita realized she was watching her, reading her thoughts, "it's nothing to feel bad about, that your boys had to go into foster care. Everyone has problems from time to time."

"Yeah," Jimmy said, "like Taffy." He touched the dog with his foot.

Taffy cringed.

"Hey!" Rita glared at Jimmy. "Don't scare her."

Jimmy lifted his hands, palms out. "Sorry."

A door in the back of the house opened, and

Pudge came shuffling out. His face lit when he saw Rita, Jimmy and the dog. "Hey, glad you're here," he said. "So this is the brand-new pup you want to train?"

"Yes, this is Taffy." And she *didn't* want to be seeing a trainer so soon. She'd rather get to know Taffy herself, but she'd felt like she had to make a move toward doing something Jimmy wanted her to do, since he was so disgruntled about her getting Taffy without consulting him.

Pudge sat down on a sturdy chair and leaned forward to run his hands over the dog, simultaneously checking her over and calming her. "It's early to start her training, if you just got her the other day," he said. "Not that there's anything wrong with that."

"I had a few people tell me—" She glanced over at Jimmy. "Warn me, really, that I should start training her right away. And I know you're the best."

Jimmy took a step back. "Hey, hey, I only suggested it," he said quietly. "If you don't want to train her now, don't."

"Now you tell me," she snapped back, keeping her voice low to avoid offending Pudge. "When we're already here."

Once again, she was aware that her annoyance—anger, really—with Jimmy was out of proportion. But she couldn't shake the feeling that he was untrustworthy. Weird, since he'd always seemed rock solid to her.

He tilted his head to one side, frowning. "Is this about me, or about the past?"

"I don't *remember* the past, remember?"

Pudge cleared his throat. "Why don't you try some basic commands with her, see what she knows?"

"Sure." Her face felt warm, her heart rate a little too fast, but she took some breaths to calm herself and then focused on the dog. "Taffy, sit," she said, gesturing to her.

The dog sat and looked at her expectantly.

"Uh-oh, I don't have any treats. Do you have something I can use?"

"I'll get you some." It was Cash; she'd almost forgotten he was in the room. He disappeared into the kitchen and came back just as she put Taffy into a "down." He handed her a bag of dog biscuits.

"Good girl!" She broke off a piece of biscuit and gave it to Taffy. Then she held another small piece in the palm of her hand. "Touch," she said, encouraging the dog to bump her hand with her muzzle.

The moves with the dog calmed her; animals were amazing that way. She tried several more commands, discovering that Taffy could "sit pretty" on her hind legs, but completely ignored the important "come" command.

When she looked up, she saw the others in the room watching her and Taffy as if they were putting on a show.

"You've trained dogs before?" Pudge asked.

She shook her head. "My late husband and I had a couple of dogs, but they were mostly for hunting. I didn't work with them—he did."

Pudge's expression was thoughtful. "You know all the gestures and moves of a trainer. From the way you move your hands to the way you hold your body and use eye contact."

Cash leaned forward. "I remember more dogs than just the yellow one at the house," he said.

An image flashed into Rita's mind, complete and vivid: a backyard fenced with split rail, lined by chain-link. Green grass with some worn-down spots. A small group of people, each with a dog, standing in a little circle facing her while she spoke like she knew what she was talking about.

A feeling came along with the image: happiness. She looked at Cash. "Could I have been a dog trainer? Taught classes in our backyard?"

He nodded slowly. "Me and Sean had to stay inside but we could watch cartoons when you were working." He made a little "huh" sound. "That's what Sean always said—'Mommy's working.' He was in charge. I don't think Liam was born yet."

That came back, too, then: kneeling down in front of her two small boys, telling them they had to help Mommy by staying inside and being quiet while she worked.

When she tried to grasp onto more details—like

where her husband had been during that time—it all got kind of blurry around the edges.

Her head pounded so badly that she looked around, grabbed the arm of a chair and sank into it. Pudge had reached down and lifted Taffy into his lap. Ma, Jimmy and Holly were watching her.

Cash came over and sat beside her. "You okay?" he asked, his voice rough-edged.

She looked at him and tears came to her eyes. "I remembered you as a kid," she said, her voice catching a little. "Caught a glimpse in my mind's eye. Just a glimpse, but still, it's something."

He nodded. When she reached out and gripped his hand, he didn't pull it away.

"If you trained dogs, had people to the house for classes," Jimmy said, "how does that fit with your husband being an abuser?"

She blew out a breath. "I don't know. Do you?" she asked, looking at Cash.

He let go of her hand and shook his head. "I mostly remember it being just us at the house, aside from the classes. We couldn't have kids over after school."

"What about Sean?" Holly asked. "He's older, right? Would he remember more?"

"Sean blocked some stuff out," Ma said. "But it wouldn't hurt to ask."

"Liam could look at records from your old town,"

Jimmy offered. "Maybe you had to register as a trainer, or advertise."

"Get your own dog a license," Pudge said.

"Yeah. Wow." Rita leaned forward and clapped her hands softly, and Taffy ran to her. She picked up the dog and buried her face in soft fur. "Thanks, girl," she murmured. "Thanks for giving me back a piece of my past."

But along with the happiness of remembering lurked a thread of fear. What else might she remember? And how awful would it be?

CHAPTER ELEVEN

HOLLY STOOD NEXT to Cash in the recreation room of the women's center, looking at the jumble of boards and props and Christmas decorations before them. Some they'd brought in from the truckload they'd gotten at Pudge's; others they'd pulled out of a closet under the direction of Yasmin's new secretary, Pearlie.

"So," Cash said, staring blankly at the materials before them, "a photo booth? Any idea exactly what Norma means by that?"

Holly was busy trying not to stare at *him*. What was it about a guy with rolled-up sleeves, and muscles that strained the shoulders of his shirts?

And how did Cash have that kind of muscles, anyway? His work in the business world must be sedentary, but he was the restless, never-sit-still type. He probably paced while talking on the phone and jogged through airports. Worked off his extra energy at the gym.

She was dangerously close to falling under his spell. Which could never happen. Especially not with what she'd learned about Tiff and Cash's father.

She forced herself to get businesslike. "It's just a background where you can take cute Christmas pictures," she said briskly. "You make it real festive so a family can get a nice picture. Then the organization, or the family, can put a cute filter on it."

"Like when my nieces and nephews got their pictures taken with Santa." He nodded and rubbed his hands together. "You tell me what you want it to look like, and with my amazing carpentry skills, I'll build it." He wiggled his eyebrows for emphasis.

She laughed. "Do you even *have* amazing carpentry skills? In addition to being a business whiz and…everything?" She clamped her mouth shut just in time. She'd been about to say "in addition to being the most handsome and sexy guy in Safe Haven."

He was, but no need to let him know she thought so.

"Actually, no." He held up his phone. "What I do have is the internet. And my brother Sean, who's an actual carpenter, on speed dial."

"Good enough."

So she found a few example photos, and Cash started hammering boards together while Holly worked on untangling long strands of red velvet ribbon and evergreen garland. She found herself exquisitely conscious of him: his striking blue eyes, his easy smile, his catlike grace.

Her feelings weren't his fault, and she needed to get over them. The solution was to be a friend—a kind friend—and nothing more. "That was a lot, what Rita figured out today," she said. "How do you feel about it? If you don't mind my asking," she added quickly. Maybe he wanted to be private about it.

"Very weird." He paused in his hammering. "I hadn't thought about those people coming over with dogs in ages. I must've been pretty young, under five, because Liam wasn't around."

"Were things good in your family then?"

He shrugged. "When you're a kid, everything seems fine if you have food and clothes and toys. And a mom who takes care of you." He looked thoughtful. "Which Rita did, I think. Sean, who's closest to her and remembers the most, says she was a great mom, took us places and read to us, stuff like that."

"But you don't remember that."

"Bits and pieces," he said, and shrugged. "I think, like Ma Dixie said about Sean, I've blocked some things."

"Hey, more supplies!" Pearlie came in, carrying a big box. "Yasmin called and let me know we should use these, too."

Cash, with his Southern manners, had risen to his feet the moment the older woman had come in, and he took the box out of her hands and set it beside the one Holly was working on. "You should have called me in to carry that."

"Now, now, Cash O'Dwyer, there's no need to exert that trademark charm on me. Or to coddle me, even though I'm old enough to be your grandma."

"Trademark charm?" Holly was amused.

"Oh, my, yes. He's notorious in these parts."

Cash looked skeptical. "Is that right?"

"Yes, sir." Pearlie nodded vigorously. "It's all good, though. You're good boys." She took Cash's hand and held it. "Don't you forget that, or let anyone tell you different."

Some emotion flashed across Cash's face and was gone so quickly Holly wasn't sure she'd seen it. Vulnerability, maybe? Longing?

But surely the confident, wealthy Cash O'Dwyer wasn't vulnerable, didn't long for the approval of a local women's-center secretary.

"Y'all let me know if you need any help. Otherwise, I'll be out in the office, getting Yasmin caught up on her paperwork. It's crazy, all the permits and reports we need to do to get the expansion of this place underway." Her phone buzzed in her pocket, and she took it out, spun and hurried out.

"I didn't know Yasmin had found a secretary," Cash said. "I was going to suggest you apply. It's part-time and flexible. You might even be able to bring Penny to work."

Reality swept back down around Holly—a reality she'd been able to forget for a few hours. "If it's that casual and part-time," she said, "it probably wouldn't make me the money I need."

"Which is why you need to accept *my* offer of more child support," Cash said. "That way, you can spend more time with Penny. Like you want to."

"No," she said without heat. "I need to find a job or... I'm really hoping I can find a way to make the dog-walking business work. I have no competition, and surely most people won't listen to that Mitch guy. My other clients have been superpositive."

Except for the ones who had quit, of course.

She started twisting garland around the frame Cash had put together. "We'll wrap some empty boxes so it looks like presents, and maybe we'll find a pretty old chair out in the church parlor. And... h-e-eyyy." She snapped her fingers. "I just got an idea of how to get the word out about my business."

"Yeah?" Cash pounded a loose board into place and looked up at her, nails bristling from his mouth. "How?"

"I could offer to do dog photos here. Like, bring the dogs I walk and take pictures and share them on social media. Tag the town, so local people start hearing about me."

Cash took the nails out of his mouth and grinned. "I do admire your entrepreneurial spirit," he said.

"If you wanted to help, you could be Santa," she teased. "Although you don't exactly have the figure for it."

"I'd help, with pillows for stuffing," he said. "Or even better, you could get Pudge to help. I've seen him dress up as Santa a bunch of times. And he'd be good with the dogs."

"That would be perfect!" Holly clapped her hands together, and then had another, more sobering thought. "Although…is he in good enough health?"

Cash frowned. "I can't get a bead on that. They're not telling us everything. And, anyway…" He broke off, looked at her, looked away.

"What?"

"You'd have to let yourself depend on him. Ask him for help. I'm starting to figure out that you don't like that."

That he'd noticed that about her, paid attention, made her face go hot. "True, but if it's Pudge…"

"What? He isn't a threat?"

She looked away, hoping he wouldn't notice her blush. "Right." Not as much of one, anyway. There was something about the good-natured older man that got through her defenses.

"Am I a threat?"

The question hung between them. She stole one glance at him and then focused on the paper she was twisting into a star.

Because Cash was definitely a threat, more and more every time they were together. She was seeing beneath the suave surface now. Seeing the part of him that genuinely wanted to help others, that related to country people like Ma and Pudge, that would build a photo booth for a women's center even when his phone kept buzzing, undoubtedly harkening business opportunities, responsibilities and deals.

She felt rather than saw him scoot closer. "I don't mean to be a threat, Holly," he said. "And I'm no kind of good risk, but I'm starting to feel—"

"Oh, that's beautiful!" Pearlie's voice saved them from whatever revelation might have been forthcoming, and Holly should've been grateful, but she wasn't. "Someone needs to test it out. Why don't the two of you get up there and I'll take a few shots so you can check the lighting and spacing and such."

"You game for that?" Cash asked.

When she nodded, he stood gracefully and then held out a hand to help her up. They'd brought in an old-fashioned love seat, and when they sat down together on it, there was no way to be except close. Close enough that she could smell his cologne and the good manly scent of him, close enough that she could feel the warmth of his leg next to hers.

"Now, don't sit so far apart," Pearlie coached.

Was the woman joking? They couldn't be much closer.

"Put your arm around her. That's how the families will sit when we do the photo booth for the class."

"You're not playing matchmaker, are you?" Cash asked.

"Would I do that?" Her smile was wide and innocent. "Here, give me your phones and I'll do some pictures on them as well."

They both set up their cameras and handed them over, and the little bit of tension was broken.

Broken, that is, until Cash put his arm around her.

She didn't make a conscious decision to nestle in. Her body decided for her. He pulled her closer, tucking her beneath his arm.

And Holly, who never relied on anyone, felt the strongest urge to just rest in his arms and let him take charge, take care of her.

"That's perfect. Yeah. Like that. Now look this way." Pearlie was snapping pictures as she spoke, changing phone cameras like a pro. When she finally paused, she looked at a couple of the shots and brought the phones over to them. "See what you think."

There was a noise in the outer hall then, and Pearlie checked the time and snapped her fingers. "I have a vendor coming this afternoon. This must be him." She handed them their phones and hurried off, shutting the door behind her.

They looked at the pictures, and Holly's heart turned over. They looked like a happy couple. A couple in love. Something she'd never expected to have and never known she wanted.

Something she shouldn't want. She clicked off her phone and slid it into her pocket.

Cash put away his phone, too, doing all of it with one hand because his other arm was around her. Every minute she expected him to take it away, to move away, but he didn't.

Instead, he pulled her the tiniest bit closer.

Her breath caught and her heart started pounding faster. She should get up. She should really extract herself and get up. Because otherwise…

"I should get up," Cash murmured, close to her ear. "But this feels too good."

Her heart thumped harder.

"At least, it does to me." His breath tickled her temple. "How about you?"

She swallowed. "It feels good," she admitted, her voice a little hoarse.

He lifted a hand and ran a finger along her jaw-line, and instinctively she glanced up at him, only to find him looking directly into her eyes. She hadn't been this close to him before, and the blueness of his eyes was disconcerting.

Gorgeously disconcerting.

"Holly…" He broke off.

"Yeah?"

He shook his head a little, laughed. His fingers played with her hair now. "You look very kissable," he said.

"Oh, do I?" Her own voice sounded breathless.

She had so little experience with men, with kissing. Whereas Cash... She started to pull back, but he leaned in at the same time and the effect was that she pulled him to her.

He lowered his lips to hers and kissed her.

His kiss was glorious, the sun and moon and stars all together. She tasted him a little, felt the slight scratch of that unshaven beard. He shifted to pull her closer, took her arm and gently moved it from where it sat in her lap, then wrapped it lightly around him. All of it with complete confidence and expertise, and it was so different from the few fumbling kisses she'd experienced before that she just sighed and let it happen.

Sensations rushed through her, making her muscles clench with awareness. If she wanted a man to introduce her to the ways of love, Cash would be a masterful teacher.

But it was the tenderness that got to her. With his experience, he might have pushed to deepen the kiss too fast, let his hands roam, especially since she wasn't resisting at all. Instead, he kept it so very gentle. His hand came up to skim her cheek, just lightly, and then stroked her hair.

She was melting, right down to the bones.

He lifted his face from hers, barely. She could still feel his breath against her lips. "That's the best kiss I ever had," he half whispered, half growled.

She pulled back and sucked in a breath, and

with it, reality. They were in the women's center where anyone could walk in. In fact, Pearlie's voice sounded from somewhere, an indistinct murmur.

And this was Cash O'Dwyer, who couldn't possibly be telling the truth about this being the best kiss he'd had, because he must have had hundreds, thousands. He was lying, not in a horrible way, but in a fake, flattering way that meant he had something up his sleeve.

Even if he didn't, she needed to get a grip on herself. Getting involved with Cash, even in the superficial way he'd undoubtedly want, would be a big mistake because of Penny. Not only the background—Tiff's motives that he didn't and shouldn't ever know about—but also the fact that it looked like she and Cash would be dealing with each other while Penny grew up.

Making that dealing uncomfortable by adding a romantic history to it would be a big and damaging mistake.

She wasn't just making an excuse because she was afraid of getting close to a man. She *wasn't*.

She drew in another breath and scooted away as far as she could on the bench, regretting the chill that replaced that warm, close feeling. "Hey, uh, we shouldn't."

His face tilted a little, and his forehead wrinkled as if her words puzzled him. His blue eyes looked almost…vulnerable.

But that wasn't possible, was it? Cash had been in similar situations with dozens, probably hundreds of women, and with his personality and looks and money, he'd surely been able to call the shots.

"Shouldn't what? Kiss under the mistletoe?"

"There's not..." She looked up. Sure enough, hung on the evergreen garland she'd strung above them was one of those mistletoe balls. Who had put it there? Cash? Pearlie? Or had it already been hooked to the garland, and she just hadn't noticed it?

It changed things a little. Maybe this had just been a meaningless mistletoe kiss. She scooted farther away and forced out a chuckle. "Right. Well. Wow, look at the time." She pulled out her phone as she said it and saw that, in fact, it *was* time to go.

Even though the picture of her and Cash that flashed on the screen somehow gutted her.

"I've got to get back to Penny," she said, because he was oddly silent. "Can you run me home or...? I can get a ride with Pearlie, if you can't." She got off that horrible, treacherous love seat and started gathering her things, then slid into her coat.

He cleared his throat and stood. "Right. Sure. Let's get you home." He looked around. "I'll run you there and then come back and straighten up, get the rest of this stuff back to Pudge."

"Do you mind? Do you want me to help?" Oh, this was awkward. Which just went to show what a mistake it had been to kiss him.

Even though her lips still tingled from it, and her body yearned to press itself to his side.

"No, that's okay. I don't mind. You ready?" He was putting on his coat as he spoke, then started toward the door.

"Sure." But she wasn't. Wasn't ready for the awkward car ride home. Wasn't ready to dive back into her busy, lonely life.

She didn't have a choice, though. She straightened her spine and scolded herself and headed out of that magical place as if walking away from Cash O'Dwyer's embrace wasn't the hardest thing she'd ever done.

THE NEXT DAY was Sunday. Cash felt a little strange dressing up in a suit and walking into the back of the small church in Safe Haven that most of his family attended. He wasn't a regular churchgoer. Not that he had anything against it, but he didn't often make the time to attend.

Time was, his brothers had been the same way. Like a lot of people, though, their views had changed when they'd become parents.

This morning, his nieces were in the Christmas pageant. Hope was, appropriately, an angel, while Hayley was the Virgin Mary. He'd agreed long ago to come, wouldn't miss it.

He'd intended to ask Holly to come and bring

Penny. But after that disastrous kiss yesterday, he hadn't done so.

He blew out a breath and slumped back into the seat of the Tesla. Looking at the church, he really didn't want to go, not anymore. He wasn't like his brothers. He wasn't a family man looking to raise his kids in the church, giving them a port in life's storms.

He was just a guy who'd accidentally fathered a child. A sperm donor with a wallet.

Around him, cars were pulling in and doors were slamming, people greeting each other with extra good cheer. Yeah. Christmas, church, community, family—all of it was what people wanted, what he wanted when it came down to it.

But nobody got everything they wanted.

The church bells rang out and he got out of his car and headed toward the door. He would go in the back, sit where he could escape easily. Somehow, he just didn't feel like talking to anybody.

He walked in the door and there she was.

Holly stood talking to some guy. She was wearing a short skirt, holding Penny.

His blood boiled.

He started forward.

"Easy, bro, that's the pastor," Liam said from behind him. He had Yasmin on one arm and was holding little Gino in the other. "Come sit with us, unless you have a better offer."

"I don't." Why hadn't Holly let him know she was coming? Why hadn't she called him to help her with Penny?

"Hurry up, it's crowded." Yasmin shifted out from under Liam's arm and walked ahead. When she found half a pew, she gestured to them to hurry up.

As soon as they'd sidled into the pew, the music started and then Norma was there, whispering for them to scoot down. Right behind her was Rita.

And then came Holly and Penny.

There was a little argument in the aisle. Rita and Norma tried to go back out so Holly and Penny could sit beside Cash.

She shook her head and smiled and waited until the older ladies had gone in, then she sat on the end.

Cash sat looking at his knees. Rejection stung. Rejection in front of his family and friends stung worse.

The children's skit wasn't the whole church service, just the opening act, and Cash wondered how hard it would be to slip out after watching his nieces steal the show.

Then the pastor started making announcements, and the first hymn was "Angels We Have Heard on High." On the long "Glo-o-o-oria" refrain, Liam looked over at him and grinned, and Cash remembered they'd hammed up that song pretty well when their foster parents had arranged for them to all meet up at Christmas-Eve services. On the second verse's chorus, Sean turned around and gave them a thumbs-up, his mouth formed into a round, laughing O, and Anna elbowed him in the side.

As soon as the song was over, the children marched in, a ragtag parade of shepherds, angels and a couple of mysterious-looking beings draped in sheets, with four human legs each and papier-mâché donkey heads on top. Giggles emitted from the donkeys, and "shhh" from a very irritated angel.

Cash's insides settled as tradition and the Christmas story made him rise above his own hurt feelings. This church would always have kids, and they'd always behave mischievously, and hopefully, they'd grow up to bring their own kids. Like Sean was doing; like Liam was.

Even, Cash realized with some sense of shock, like *he* was.

First time he'd been to a kids' church pageant as an adult, of course. He remembered his dad avoiding any school shows or events he and his brothers were involved in. "That garbage is for women," he'd said once when their mother had told him it would mean a lot if he'd come to the boys' talent show.

In his head he knew that was wrong. His brothers, new to fatherhood, enthusiastically attended everything their kids did.

But somewhere inside, Cash had always figured that, because he was like his dad in some ways, he'd end up sharing all his attitudes and he would have no interest in kids' activities or shows.

But that wasn't true. It had taken Hope and Hayley thirty seconds, max, to persuade him to come.

The pageant started with bible readings, read aloud and acted out. Cash was proud that both Hope and Hayley got to read verses and barely stumbled; he had to restrain his impulse to clap after each one. Things got a little dicey when the kid cast as Joseph tripped over a shepherd's crook and fell into the manger, knocking the baby doll representing Jesus onto the floor. Most of the adults in his aisle—Rita, Norma, Liam—shook with repressed laughter. Yasmin bent next to little Gino, who was frowning with concern.

Again he was proud when Hayley helped Joseph get up and go back to his place—scolding him a little on the way—while Hope picked up the baby doll and placed it tenderly back in the manger. The Sunday-school teacher who was in charge gestured to the pianist and then led the kids in a vigorous rendition of "Away in a Manger," and then it was over and everyone did applaud. Cash even let out a "bravo" and then looked around sheepishly, but he saw only pride and joy in the people around him, no posturing or judgment.

Man, did he love his adopted hometown.

He glanced down the aisle at Holly and Penny as the service went on. Holly listened to the bible read-

ings and then the sermon with rapt attention. Cash's
jealousy surged again, until the minister mentioned
his wife in a loving way. After that, he was glad
Holly was getting a moment to sit quietly and re-
flect. It couldn't be a common occurrence in her
life, not these days with the responsibility she'd assumed for Penny.

He probably should help her out more, at least
while he was here in town.

When Penny got fussy, he slipped past Norma
and Rita, then scooped Penny out of a surprised
Holly's lap. "You stay here. We'll be in the nursery
downstairs. Or somewhere close by."

She opened her mouth as if she wanted to protest
and then closed it again. When he started to head
down the aisle, she called quietly after him, and he
figured she'd changed her mind. But she was just
holding out the diaper bag. He grabbed it, feeling
sheepish to have forgotten it, and went down the
aisle.

He found the nursery but didn't want to put Penny
in it. She was settling down now, but there was no
telling how she'd react to an unknown caregiver.
Besides, he felt proud to be able to calm her, loved
the sweet weight of her in his arms, the way she
cuddled into him.

He found an empty classroom full of bright toys
and with a comfortable-looking rug on the floor. He
was just sitting down with Penny when Sean came

in with HoHo, looking harassed. "Can you watch him for a few? Apparently Hayley spilled punch on her dress and is all upset, and I don't want to bother Anna. She needs a break."

"Sure, no problem," Cash said, and Sean plunked down the baby and his diaper bag and disappeared.

So here he was, Cash O'Dwyer, CEO of a multimillion-dollar investment group, up to his ears in childcare.

And he didn't even mind. He dug around in the diaper bags and found both babies some little crackers, and when the need became obvious, he changed Penny's diaper. He found a couple of toys the two babies could bang at and suck on, and kept them busy and entertained that way.

Then HoHo flipped over into an expert crawl, sped over to a chair and pulled himself up. Cash found him a push toy and he toddled merrily after it, laughing at the bells and blinking lights.

Penny just sat there.

Cash tried to entice her to move, but she seemed uninterested, even with the example of HoHo's rapid movement.

HoHo rammed his push toy into a wall, crashed down onto his rear end and began to wail. Cash hurried over, picked him up and joggled him on his hip until he settled.

A deep sense of peace came over him. He was managing kids and particularly his own kid, and doing an okay job of it. So maybe he wasn't such a horrible person after all.

He turned back to set HoHo beside Penny. Halfway there, he stopped and stared.

Penny was crawling, all right…backward. In fact, she was backing herself right under a table and chair set, pushing herself with her arms as if her legs didn't even work.

Cash put down HoHo and then swooped over to pick up Penny before she got stuck. Once he'd gotten her out and handed her a binky to keep the imminent meltdown from happening, he studied her legs. They were so small and thin, especially compared to chubby HoHo's. Was there something wrong with her physically, in addition to the delays they'd discussed with the pediatrician? They'd had a preliminary assessment from the early-intervention team, who'd been reassuring. But the way Penny had been crawling was downright weird.

He couldn't help it; he texted Holly. Come to room next to nursery.

Then he set down Penny a few feet away from HoHo, facing him. "Come on, sweetie, this way." Hadn't she crawled forward before?

But although she pushed up with her arms and rocked back and forth, in the end she scooted backward again. She was staring at HoHo as if she wanted to come toward him but couldn't.

Her face screwed up in a cry just as Holly burst

through the door. "What's wrong?" she asked, hurrying toward Penny and picking her up. "Is everything okay, sweetie?" She sat on the edge of a chair to study her.

Dog that he was, Cash couldn't help but notice her great legs, clad in tights and boots, her short denim skirt and sweater further revealing her sweet figure. He tore his focus away from her looks and refocused on his daughter. "Did you know she crawls backward, not forward?"

"Yeah, I've been noticing that."

He stared at her. "You noticed, and didn't tell me? Aren't you worried?"

"Yeah, I noticed, but…I don't know, I think it's kind of common for babies to crawl in weird ways. Usually when they're younger, but Penny has those delays."

He went over and knelt beside the two of them, holding out Penny's leg for Holly to look at. "Look how skinny she is. She needs more exercise for her legs."

"I guess that's what her backward crawling is doing, right?" She rolled a bouncy ball past Penny, who stared at it with rapt attention.

She didn't seem in the least bit upset or worried, and that made Cash mad.

"I don't want you hauling her around in a carrier anymore. Her legs are atrophying!"

Holly dipped her chin, raised her eyebrows and

stared at him. "Are you accusing me of causing her physical delays?"

"No, but having her immobilized for most of the day isn't helping her." He'd identified a problem and he wanted to solve it. That was what he did; that was how he'd survived and thrived in the business world. "You need to quit walking dogs and get her more stimulation. Maybe we could start her in one of those classes for babies, where they do gymnastics or—"

"Cash, she's a year old! We can't start her in gymnastics!"

Penny stared at Holly, and she rubbed the baby's back and lowered her voice. "And we asked the developmentalist about her coming along when I was walking dogs, remember? She said it's good for Penny to have the stimulation."

"It's obviously not, though." He swung up HoHo for her to compare. "Look at his size compared to Penny's, and he's only a month older."

She drew in a breath and let it out slowly, as if she was struggling to find patience. "That's normal. She's a girl, and Tiff was petite. And don't forget, we're going to have therapists visiting a few times a week once the paperwork goes through."

He shook his head, still in problem-solving mode. Penny was his daughter, and she wasn't going to suffer from lack of parental knowledge and support. He hadn't intended to become a parent, but it had happened, and despite his flaws, he was going to do his best to raise her right. "She needs more. Better food and more exercise."

"I'm doing the best I can!" Holly's eyes filled with tears, but she didn't say anything more as they packed up the babies and headed out into the throng of people just released from church.

Oh, well. Women cried. He'd make it right as soon as he handed off HoHo.

Once they reached the parking lot, though, Cash got caught up talking to Sean. Then Hope and Hayley came running up to him, and he had to congratulate them on a job well-done, commiserate about the clumsy Joseph and commend them for how they'd handled the glitch in the show.

When he turned to look for Penny and Holly, they were gone.

Oh. So he'd made Holly more upset than he'd realized.

"What's wrong, Cash?" Sean's wife, Anna, laid a hand on his arm. "You okay?"

He turned to her. Anna had raised her twins to age five basically on her own, defending them from an abusive father. If anyone knew how to parent in trying circumstances, it was her. "I'm worried about Penny," he said. "She's crawling backward, and she's way skinnier than HoHo. But Holly doesn't seem to take it seriously."

"Lots of babies crawl backward. No big deal."

She glanced over at HoHo, wiggling in Sean's arms. "And the pediatrician wants us to watch what HoHo eats. He's almost too chubby."

"Really? I think he's cute. Perfect."

She smiled and leaned into him, putting an arm around his waist. "Thank you. I think he's perfect, too. But whenever someone questions his size— or anything about him—I start doubting myself. Worrying it's my fault, wondering what I should be doing differently."

"Yeah. Guess I'm doing that, too."

She studied him. "You and Holly can be a lot of support to each other. I know Sean's great when I start worrying about HoHo or about the girls. Balances out my worrying."

"That's good." But he'd done the reverse with Holly. When she hadn't taken his worries seriously, he'd started blaming and accusing her. No wonder she'd fled.

He sighed as he turned toward his car. Obviously, he had a lot to learn, not only about being a father, but also about being half of a parenting team.

CHAPTER TWELVE

On Monday, Holly pushed open the door of the Safe Haven Public Library and held it while she lifted Penny out of her stroller and attempted to fold it with one hand. The diaper bag flopped to the ground.

It sure would be nice to have someone to help.

The thought seemed like self-betrayal. *You don't need any help*, she told herself as she finally managed to get the stroller into its folded-up position. She leaned it against the wall of the library just inside the door, shifted outside for her diaper bag and finally made it inside.

Despite the cool December day, she was sweating.

But coming to the library was preferable to sitting in her apartment, stewing over Cash O'Dwyer and Penny's motor skills. Besides, it was good for Penny to get out.

Just like when she'd done the baby lap-sit, the fragrance of old books took her back to childhood days, when she and Tiff had hung out in the various public libraries near the places they'd lived. Tiff had soon tired of them and found other places to spend her time, but Holly had loved the combination of a peaceful environment and exciting books. No matter whether their home situation was good, bad or neutral—they'd experienced all three, sometimes in breathtakingly fast succession—she'd found the library a safe and stable place, often used it as a second home.

She could hear people talking softly near the circulation desk, but mostly the place was quiet. Hmm. Not necessarily baby-friendly. Would Penny be too loud for this place?

It was very possible, but for now, she held on to Holly's shoulder and stared wide-eyed at the tall Christmas tree decorated with messy, handmade book ornaments of various sorts, probably the product of some children's activity. Tinsel was draped around the edges of the room, also drawing Penny's curious gaze.

Holly was more attracted to the display of Christmas books, cozy mysteries and romances with cute covers that promised a fun escape.

You're not here for an escape, you're here for information.

Although she did want to escape from thoughts of the kiss she'd shared with Cash at the women's center, the kiss that had shaken her to the core. Even now, thinking about it, her stomach did flip-flops and her skin broke out in a light sweat.

Not only was Cash handsome and kind, but he was also an amazing kisser.

But she'd pushed him away for good reason, and it was just self-torture to second-guess that decision. Look how overbearing he'd gotten about Penny's size and way of crawling. He'd as much as told her it was her fault.

His words had planted a question in her mind, though, one she hoped to answer here.

She wandered through the well-organized displays of bestsellers and magazines, thinking about Cash. His pushiness at the church was annoying, but she couldn't fault him for his concern. Would actually like to have him around more, so she could bounce ideas off him and share the burden of helping Penny achieve her developmental milestones.

And kiss him some more.

But no. No way. Now that she was learning more about Cash's family and the Safe Haven community, she found it was even harder to reconcile what Tiff had done.

She couldn't betray her sister and jeopardize Penny's future by revealing that Tiff had gotten pregnant on purpose to get something out of Cash. But she couldn't get close to Cash while hiding that kind of a secret.

She'd seen people acting selfishly and manipulating other people in her childhood and even among the rich people she'd dog-sat for in New

York. Among many of those folks, Tiff's deception wouldn't have drawn a second glance.

But people didn't do that sort of thing here. Not that small-town residents were perfect—just look at Mitch Mitchell—but there was a sort of self-policing mechanism at work in a place like Safe Haven. The fact that neighbors knew each other's business meant that you couldn't act too far out of line and get away with it. Case in point: word that Mitch was wrong and that she was a good dog walker had spread quickly around town. Two of her lost clients had already come back.

She made her way over to the bank of computers and quickly figured out the cataloging system, keeping Penny entertained in her lap with goldfish crackers. She'd pick out a book or two and get going before Penny started to fuss.

But when she went over to look up the books she'd found, she ended up browsing through the whole child-development section. There was a world of information here, and she wanted to study all of it, now. She'd always done well in school, had taken a couple of community-college courses in New York and planned to keep going when she could. She loved to learn.

She pulled some books off the shelves and started to skim through the first one, but Penny wasn't having it. She thrashed and babbled, and when Holly wouldn't set her free to crawl around, she began to cry in earnest.

"Shhh, sweetie, shhh." She bounced Penny, to no avail. "Okay, okay, we'll leave. Just let me get these books checked out, if they'll give me a library card—or maybe not—"

"Can I help you?"

"Oh!" Startled, Holly turned to see the woman who'd scolded Mitch Mitchell when he'd yelled at her in front of his shop. She seemed to have materialized out of nowhere.

Holly struggled to contain Penny and hold out a hand. "Hi, Miss Vi. I'm so sorry we were loud. I... we'll be on our way."

"That's one sound that doesn't ever get shushed in this library," the woman said. "I run this place, and I'm all in favor of getting kids started here early."

The absence of judgment calmed Holly, and she remembered then how positive Miss Vi had been about mothers who worked. "Thank you. I appreciate that. Penny loved the baby lap-sit program, and I—we—will definitely get her more involved with the library as she gets older."

"Good. Now, can I take your books up to the counter for you?" Without waiting for an answer, Miss Vi took the stack of books Holly had been holding and started walking toward the front desk, slowing to let Holly and Penny catch up, soundless in her orthopedic shoes.

They'd just reached the desk when a twentysomething woman in workout clothes and expensive-looking furry boots rushed up to them. "Oh, my gosh, wait here. I have a whole bag of baby clothes for you." She turned and headed toward the library's exit. "I'm Chelsea, by the way. Don't go anywhere."

Holly stared after her, bemused. "I don't even know her," she murmured.

"No, but she may know you. That's how small towns are." Miss Vi cracked a slight smile. "Especially when you're raising Cash O'Dwyer's baby. Here's the form to fill out for a library card."

Holly took the form and pen the librarian was holding out to her. "I'm confused. What's that got to do with a bag of baby clothes?"

Miss Vi was opening the books she'd carried to the counter for Holly, preparing to check them out. "Half the women in this town have a crush on Cash. It helps that he's wealthy and not around much to reveal his feet of clay." She smiled wryly. "Some of them may have figured out that the way to his heart is through his baby."

Holly didn't care for that idea at all. No, she couldn't have Cash's heart for herself, but she didn't want to watch a bunch of other women compete for it.

Not my business. She filled out the form while Miss Vi played peekaboo with Penny, making her laugh.

"Hi, Holly, Penny, Miss Vi." Anna O'Dwyer came over, smiling widely. "I was hoping to run into you. I brought you a Christmas gift." She rummaged in her giant bag, shifting HoHo to her other hip. "I mean, I'm sure we'll get together for Christmas, but this is for beforehand." She located a gift bag and pulled it out. "It's a Christmas outfit for Penny. You should hold it up and see if it looks like it'll fit. I have no perspective, since I'm already buying twenty-four-month clothes for this behemoth."

Discomfort gnawed at Holly's stomach, warring with a strong desire to see whatever cute Christmas outfit Anna had bought for Penny. Both women looked at her expectantly, and so she set down Penny on the carpeted floor beside HoHo and pulled out the outfit, a red-on-white striped dress with white-on-red striped stretchy pants to go underneath. "See," Anna said, "I like things that they can wear even after Christmas, so it's not got reindeers or anything like that. But it's festive. I always wanted to buy stuff like that for my twins when they were tiny, but I couldn't, so…you'll just have to indulge me. Do you think it'll fit?"

"Wow, it's adorable." Holly held it up and looked at the size tag. "It should fit perfectly. Thank you so much."

"You're welcome. Uh-oh." Anna looked down at HoHo, then knelt and picked him up. "When his eyes get droopy like that I have about ten minutes until nap time, and I'd like to get him home for that. Great to see you." And she was off.

Chelsea came back, hauling a big bag. "Here are the clothes," she said, thrusting the bag into Holly's arms. "All designer, and barely worn. Be sure and tell Cash they're from Chelsea." She turned and rushed off toward an adorable little girl who was headed out the door on her own.

"Told you so," Miss Vi said, sounding amused. "Overwhelmed yet?"

"A little bit," Holly admitted. "I guess I thought of the library as a quiet place, but everyone in town seems to be here today."

"It's the library open house," Miss Vi explained. "We have activities going on all day, and most of the town stops in for cider or to check out a Christmas book or pick up a gift for their kids."

"That's great. For the library to be such a central part of the community."

"That's how we like it in Safe Haven." Miss Vi took a laminated library card from a machine behind the counter and handed it to Holly. "There you go. I hope we haven't scared you away."

"Not at all. I guess…I'm not used to this. I'm the independent type, and I just moved here from living in New York."

"Nothing wrong with being independent," Miss Vi said as she stacked up Holly's books. "Anna was *very* independent when she moved here."

"You're kidding." She thought of Anna surrounded by her loving family: her kids and Sean, Sean's brother Liam and his wife, Yasmin. And Cash, whenever he was in town. Anna seemed deeply enmeshed in family and community. Holly had almost felt jealous.

But, of course, Anna had come in vulnerable, guiltless. While she, Holly, was participating in a deception.

"Need help getting your things to your car? I'll hold my granddaughter." It was Rita, and before Holly could even respond, she'd swept Penny out of her arms. "You go load up the car and I'll bring Penny out in a minute."

What could she say but "thank you" without seeming ungracious? There was no reason for Rita to remember that Holly didn't own a car. And she was grateful for the help, didn't know how she'd have gotten books and clothes, diaper bag and baby all out of here on her own.

Didn't, in fact, know how she was going to carry it all home, but she wasn't going to impose on any of these generous, too-knowing Safe Haven residents, so she jammed the clothes and books into the stroller and a bag she could hang on the back once Penny was strapped inside.

She needed to focus on finalizing plans for the dog photos with Santa she was setting up. Pudge had agreed to play Santa, and they'd arranged to make it happen tomorrow night. She'd spent Sunday afternoon putting up flyers and posting online, and she'd already heard from seven dog owners who definitely wanted to attend. Today she was going to make calls to all her clients, current and former, to see if they'd like a complimentary photo with Santa.

Thinking about her business and ways to grow it calmed her down, distracted her from the friendly intrusiveness of the Safe Haven community.

She had to admit, the people here were kind, and she was grateful. But the feeling of connectedness, with its hint of dependency, was way out of her comfort zone.

ON WEDNESDAY, Rita knelt beside Taffy on the front porch of Ma Dixie's place, trying to calm the dog while Norma rang the doorbell and then knocked at the door.

Taffy broke free of Rita's grip and took off for the side of the porch, and only Rita's frantic grab of the leash kept her close. Tugged to the ground on one hip, her shoulder aching, Rita had a moment of wishing she'd listened to Jimmy and let him talk her out of taking on a dog with issues.

Then Taffy checked back in with her, jumping up to lick her face, banging hard into her cheekbone. It hurt, but her heart melted. Taffy was a sweet dog who'd had almost no training or stimulation. The or-

dinary world, smelling of marsh and fish and squir-
rels, almost overwhelmed her with terror and joy.

"Taffy needs a lot of help," she told Norma as she
regained control of the dog, shortening her leash and
putting a hand in front of her chest to restrain her.
"And Pudge is really excited about training her."
She lowered her voice. "He's been sick, but he still
needs to feel useful."

"Coming, coming." Ma Dixie's voice from inside the little house sounded frazzled, and when the
woman answered the door, her face was flushed, her
grey hair coming out of its usual neat bun. Her eyes
went from Norma to Rita to Taffy, on her hind legs
and pawing at the air. "Oh, my lands, you've come
to work with Pudge, haven't you? And he's not even
here. Come on in."

"We can come back another…" Rita's words
trailed off as Ma shook her head and held the door
open for Norma and Rita. Taffy had an attack of
shyness and hung back, but Ma reached down and
wiggled her fingers, and Taffy finally darted forward to lick them.

"Pudge is having some trouble with his medi-
cations," she explained as she took their coats and
hung them on a row of hooks beside the door. "He
had a good time playing Santa for the dogs last
night, but he stayed too long. Missed taking one
of his pills, so he took two when he got home even
though I told him not to… Anyway, he felt poorly

this morning. Cash ran him in to his doctor for some tests while I stayed here to do my Christmas baking. Speaking of... Oh, no!" She turned and hurried from the room.

Norma and Rita followed and watched as she quickly pulled a tray of some kind of nut bar from the oven, sniffed it and then set it on the table on top of a couple of hot plates. "Just in time," she said.

Rita looked around at the pans and bowls and trays, a mess the likes of which she'd rarely seen at Ma's house, even when it was full of kids and guests. "We can help you finish up," she said.

"If we don't figure out something to do with that dog, we'll be more of a hindrance than a help." Norma frowned at Taffy, who was flinging herself at the counter, where a dozen eggs and a stick of butter perched precariously.

Ma wiped her hands on a dish towel. "We'll put her out in the big pen with a nice soup bone to chew on. Pudge will get a kick out of seeing her when he gets home." A shadow crossed her face for a moment and was quickly gone.

Rita glanced at Norma, wondering if she'd seen it. From the tilt of her head and the slight frown she wore as she studied Ma, Rita was guessing she had.

She quickly settled Taffy in the outdoor pen and came back in to find Ma pouring coffee for her and Norma at the kitchen table. "We're only staying if you'll put us to work," she warned. "We don't want to add to your burdens. We want to lighten them."

"Honey, just having the company of some adult women I like is help enough." Ma smiled. "But I'm too smart to turn down your offer. One of you can grease this pan and then put in a layer of graham crackers, all matched up like bricks." She shoved the materials toward Norma. "And the other one can slice up these pecan-sandie logs. I think they've been cooling long enough." She opened the ancient refrigerator and pulled out four long rolls of dough wrapped in waxed paper, then handed them to Rita along with a cutting board and a knife.

"Just how many cookies do you bake?" Norma asked as she worked on lining the pan with graham crackers.

Ma smiled. "Never enough. Christmas is when most of my fosters come back to say hello. Lots of times they bring kids of their own. I'm behind on my preparations this year." Again the shadow crossed her face.

Rita glanced at Norma, then back at Ma. "How's Pudge doing?" she asked as she sliced cookies and set them in neat rows on a cookie sheet.

Ma's hands stilled for a moment, then resumed their stirring of something that smelled rich and caramel-like. "He'll be all right. He always is." She smiled with her mouth, but not her eyes. "How's that man of yours?" she asked, smiling at Rita for real this time. "Gotten used to the idea of you having a dog in your life?"

"Nope." Rita shrugged. "Guess I should have consulted him, but…"

"But you're not his wife, or his slave," Norma said.

"You get to make your own decisions," Ma added. "What about you?" she asked Norma. "I heard something about you taking up with a neighbor man."

Norma snorted. "Stephen. You can't really say we've taken up together when he runs so hot and cold."

"And you don't?" Rita asked, keeping her voice mild.

Norma glared.

"Appreciate your men, that's all I can say." Ma poured a thin trickle of vanilla into the pot on the stove, then pulled a pan of pecans out of the oven and slid them onto a cutting board. She rocked a big knife over them, chopping them, and then stirred them into the pot. "Got that base ready for me?" she asked Norma.

"Sure thing." Norma pushed the pan toward Ma and she poured the creamy mixture over the top, spreading it out with a spoon until it coated the graham crackers.

Rita sliced the last of the pecan sandies, reflecting on what Ma had said. It was true; she needed to appreciate Jimmy. Although he was annoying her with his reaction to Taffy, it was just possible that her issues were her own, that he was the one with a normal concept of how independent you should be when you were in a relationship.

They worked, chatting companionably, for another hour and then Cash and Pudge arrived home, the big man looking wan and pale. He forced a smile for Rita and apologized for not notifying her he'd be gone, and then Cash quickly helped him back to bed. Cash emerged and Ma went back into the bedroom and shut the door.

"How is he?" Rita asked her son.

Cash shrugged. "He wouldn't tell me and he wouldn't let me go back in to see the doctor with him. I don't know." He moved his shoulders as if they were tight, looked out the window and then did a double take. "You brought Taffy! Mind if I go out and see her?"

"Help yourself," she said, although she'd have preferred Cash stay inside and talk with her.

But as she watched him jog out to the pen, release Taffy and throw a stick for the ecstatic pup, she had another flashback.

She remembered Cash throwing sticks for another dog, when he was much smaller.

Her memory was coming back. Which should have been a good thing, a thrill.

Only this time, the sweet picture of a boy and his dog was tinged with terror, a looming bad presence.

Orin.

CASH KNOCKED ON the door of Holly's apartment Wednesday night, and while he waited for her to answer, he found himself straightening his collar and checking his teeth in his phone's reverse camera. He hadn't been this nervous picking up a woman in years.

And it wasn't even a date, or at least, it wasn't supposed to be. It was the parenting class's Christmas party, the one for which they'd prepared the photo booth last week.

Just the thought of that experience made Cash sweat. He shouldn't have kissed her, he guessed, but he'd wanted her badly. Still did, and for more than kissing. She was a beautiful woman with an unconscious sensuality that gave a man all kinds of ideas. But she was also kind, and good, and fun to be with.

He'd have called her wife material if he'd wanted a wife.

The door opened, and there was Holly. The color in her cheeks was high, and well it should be because she looked hot. She wore a green sweater-type dress that showed her sweet curves. Her hair was down, not in its usual ponytail, and was styled in waves that made him want to touch them, they looked so soft. She was just of average height, but her legs looked a mile long in high boots.

His mouth went dry as more sweat broke out on the back of his neck. "You look great," he blurted out.

"Thanks." She gave a half smile he couldn't interpret, and he felt awkward, like he'd said something inappropriate. "I'll get Penny. She's not quite ready so…you may as well come on in."

"I know I'm a little early. I'm sorry." He followed her inside, sat down on the edge of the couch and drummed his fingers, and then stood again when she came out of the back bedroom with Penny. "I just thought we should be on the early side since, you know, we made the photo booth and all—"

"I remember," she interrupted.

What was that expression on her face? Was that a smile tugging at the corners of her mouth and laughter behind her big grey eyes, or was he imagining things?

She was fussing with Penny now, adjusting something on the shoulder of her dress. "This outfit is so cute, and it's adjustable so it can kind of, like, grow with her. But it's hard to get these buttons done up right."

Penny struggled and twisted, causing Holly to lose what progress she'd made. She said something under her breath and started over.

"Let me help." He hurried over, knelt down and held Penny still while Holly worked on the buttons. "It seems like she's getting more active and energetic all the time. Speaking of which…I'm sorry I acted like you were neglecting her needs, that day she was crawling backward. You do a terrific job with her."

"Thanks!" As she worked on the buttons, she flashed him a smile that took away his breath.

She smelled incredible. Cash really, really wanted to pull her into his arms.

"Anna got her this dress." Apparently oblivious to his desires, she nodded down at the red-and-white confection. "So cute, and you can tell it's really well made. She must have spent a fortune on it."

"It's pretty." Cash could hardly focus on what she was saying, he was struggling so hard not to reveal his intense attraction to her. This close, the fragrance of her perfume was mingling with some flowery shampoo she used, and when her hair swung his way, he drew in a slow, delicious breath.

She glanced up at him. Had she noticed?

But no, she looked back down at Penny and was now putting a little pair of moccasins on her. And oh, man, she was wearing makeup. That was what made her eyes look so huge. Unlike most men, he didn't mind a little makeup on a woman, especially if she knew how to use it.

Holly did.

"Oh, and that reminds me," she said as she finished with the outfit and rose smoothly to her feet, leaving Cash feeling a slight chill. "This woman named Chelsea gave me a bag of clothes for Penny. She wanted me to make sure you knew it was from her." She waved a hand at a shopping bag standing in the corner of the room. "I haven't had time to go through it yet. And even though I've got Penny set up in her own bedroom now, it's tiny and space is tight. Maybe you'd like to keep those clothes at your place?"

He was still having trouble focusing. "Where'd you say they came from?"

"From *Chelsea*," she said with emphasis, as if he was a little slow. "Miss Vi thought she probably was someone you'd dated before, or someone who wants to date you."

"Chelsea...oh, that Chelsea. Wonder why she gave you clothes." He shrugged. "Are you ready?"

"Heartbreaker." She shook her head, smiling a little. Then she handed him her coat.

He helped her into it, wondering about Holly. She didn't act experienced with men, didn't act interested for the most part—although that kiss had been an exception, at least for a minute—but she expected a man to treat her right, to help her with her coat and hold the door.

He liked that. She had confidence, and now that she was settled into Safe Haven, it was showing more and more.

Ten minutes later, they walked into the women's center, Holly holding Penny and Cash holding the diaper bag. Sure enough, they were the first ones there, except for Norma and her friend Stephen, who were moving tables and putting up crepe-paper decorations. The big poodle they seemed to be raising together, Snowball, was lying glumly on the floor in the corner of the room, head on paws, looking ashamed of her antler headpiece and bedazzled green coat.

"I'll go help," Holly said, turning toward them.

"Holly." Cash didn't know what made him put a hand on her arm. "Don't."

She lifted an eyebrow. "Pardon me?"

Now how was he going to justify *that* request? Should he tell the truth: that he wanted her by his side? Even though she'd as much as told him she didn't want to be there?

A look at her skeptical, quizzical face suggested not. "You work too much. We put together the photo booth." *Lord help him, he'd almost called it the kissing booth.* "Just sit down and relax."

"You sound like Tiff," she said, and a bleak expression flashed across her face. She pulled out a chair at one of the long tables and sat, Penny on her lap but struggling to get down.

He sat beside them, grabbed a blanket out of the diaper bag and spread it on the floor, then set Penny on it. "Did Tiff tell you you needed to relax more?" he asked as he dug in the diaper bag for toys that could keep Penny entertained.

She nodded. "All the time. She was definitely the happy-go-lucky one." She looked at Penny, then reached down and placed a hand on her back as if she needed the comfort. "Which was great, until it wasn't."

Cash blew out a sigh. He knew what she meant. The Tiff he'd known had seemed fun-loving and carefree, definitely not the type to read child-raising books and go to a parenting group like Holly was doing. "I don't know if I told you this," he said, "or if I told you enough, but I'm sorry for what happened. With her, you know, getting pregnant."

"It takes two. Tiff knew what she was doing."

"True. But it must have been pretty surprising for her to find out she was expecting, especially since she was on birth control and everything."

Something changed in Holly's face and he tried to interpret it, rewinding what he'd just said. "She *was* on birth control, wasn't she?"

Holly bit her lip. "I don't… I just don't know. We weren't the kind of sisters who shared all the details, unfortunately, and when she was pregnant and giving birth, we were estranged."

"She *told* me she was." Cash was sure of it, even though the conversation had taken place at a bar, where they'd both had a couple drinks more than they should have. He prided himself on always having that conversation before things got too heated.

Holly nodded and got very busy rubbing a spot of something green on Penny's sleeve.

She was acting weird, and Cash's gut twisted just a little. He'd had a situation once before where a woman had claimed to be on birth control and wasn't, and had threatened a paternity suit on him. Just someone else trying to get at his money. Fortunately, or so he'd thought at the time, she'd miscarried, or said she had; in fact, he wasn't sure the pregnancy had ever been real.

Now that he had Penny, his perspective had changed entirely. He wasn't a crazy bachelor who just wanted freedom at all costs. He'd held his own flesh-and-blood child, taken care of her, come to love her.

If that long-ago fling had conceived a child with him and miscarried it…it could have been another Penny.

He swallowed hard, then picked up his daughter and held her close against his chest.

Her life was precious. He'd fight to the death to protect her.

And the idea of casually, carelessly hooking up with women held zero appeal for him now. The potential of an unplanned pregnancy was so real, as real as the sweet child in his arms.

Not just that, but how would he like a man to treat *his* daughter the way he'd treated women over the years? Oh, he'd never been unkind, never made promises he couldn't keep. But had he been loving and honorable and chivalrous, the way he'd want a man to be around Penny?

He looked up and realized Holly was watching him and Penny, a tender look in her eyes.

His lack of desire for casual flings just might have something to do with her, too. He didn't want to treat her that way, and he had the feeling she wouldn't stand for it, anyway.

But he *did* want her, more and more all the time.

People were starting to drift in, so any chance of pursuing the conversation about Tiff went away. Which was okay. He'd come to realize how different Holly was from her sister. Even if Tiff had deceived him about birth control—which didn't make sense, since she'd been the last person to want a baby—it had nothing to do with Holly.

"Look, Cash," she said, leaning closer so they wouldn't be overheard, "Tiff made some mistakes, a lot of them actually. But her heart was in the right place. Whatever she did wrong had to do with the people she was running with." Her expression darkened. "One in particular."

Her voice shook when she said it, and he opened his mouth to ask more, but suddenly Christmas music blared out loudly, along with squeaky feedback from the old-fashioned sound system.

"Turn it down, Stephen!" Norma called across the room.

Penny started to cry, and a couple of other babies joined in.

He stood, Penny still in his arms, and held out a hand to Holly. "Should we mingle?"

"Yeah. Good idea."

As they walked over toward the other members of the class, he touched her back to guide her, and she didn't move away.

The Christmas decorations and music, the small group of couples with kids they'd started to get close to—it felt like some mushy holiday movie to Cash, and he was usually too cynical for that sort of thing. But as people greeted them and exclaimed over Penny's cute outfit, as he watched Holly laugh at someone's joke and accept a cup of hot chocolate from Norma, a deep sense of rightness settled into his soul.

All the years he'd spent chasing money, all his business successes, had felt nothing near as good as this moment. In his town, with his daughter, with his friends. With Holly.

They chatted and ate small plates of decadent food and admired all the other children. Holly got talked into attending a meeting of a local entrepreneurs group. Santa came, and half the kids, including Penny, freaked out at the sight of the big bearded man in the red suit, so Holly and Cash weren't alone in soothing a screaming baby. Penny calmed down, and they got a picture in the photo booth that, when he saw it, made his breath catch because they looked like a real family.

Cash wanted it to be a real family. His family.

His phone was buzzing insistently in his pocket, and finally Holly told him he should just go ahead and take it. He checked and saw that the call came from an unknown number. "I don't need to—" he began, and then realized he had a bunch of work messages, too.

"Go on. We're fine." She smiled up at him. "You know you want to."

Thing was, he didn't want to. He wanted to stay right here with Holly and Penny, but it was probably smart to get a little distance before he ended up sinking down on one knee and proposing to her.

He shot a group message to all his business texts and then clicked into the voice mail that had come from the call.

The message he heard chilled him. Deeply, like his very bones had turned to ice. "Hey, um, Cash," it said. "Give me a call at this number as soon as you can." There was a long pause, and then… "It's your father."

HOLLY HELPED PENNY eat a couple of the crunchy cookies specially made for babies—no peanuts, no eggs, no possible allergens of any sort—and then wiped her face. She accepted a second piece of amazing chocolate-pecan fudge that one of the other mothers had made, and enjoyed the jazzy, hip Christmas playlist in the background. As she talked to the couples from the parenting class, she realized she was starting to consider them as friends. Liam and Yasmin came in, and *they* almost felt like family.

Heady stuff for a girl who'd never belonged anywhere.

She tried to stay focused on Penny and the other party guests, but it was impossible to keep from glancing over at Cash every couple of minutes. He'd gone out into the hallway but was still visible through the open door.

He was so handsome, real movie-star material, with his dark hair and blue eyes and sexy build, all wrapped up in a cashmere sweater and Italian leather shoes. Talking on his phone, he looked like an important rich guy, just as he had when she'd first encountered him. But she knew him so much better now, and she knew that beneath the suave exterior was the heart of a small-town boy.

"Are you and Cash married?" one of the women asked. Her daughter, Bianca, was three years old and wore leg braces that barely slowed her down. Now, Bianca's mom caught her by the shoulders and helped her turn back toward them. Bianca caught sight of Penny, grabbed the toy out of her hand and started jingling it in Penny's face.

"Gentle, Bianca," the mom said. "Sorry. It's like impossible to have a conversation. And I was probably being too nosy, anyway, asking about you and Cash."

Her words made Holly blush for some reason. "No, we're not married," she said.

"See? I knew it. You guys are way too conscious of each other to be married."

Norma approached in time to hear the remark. "That's how husbands and wives should be—attentive," she said.

"We're not even dating!" Holly said and then looked away. She could tell that both women wanted her to confide about her feelings for Cash, but those were too new for her to even consider revealing to people she barely knew.

Fortunately, Cash strode back toward them just then. He greeted the other two women and took Penny from her arms.

He was still acting the devoted father, but his face had changed completely, from warm and open to hard and closed. As soon as the others' attention was diverted by an announcement of some door prizes, she leaned closer to him. "Is something wrong?"

"No, why?"

"You look upset."

He shrugged, looked away.

"Bad business news?" she persisted.

"What? No, no."

Obviously he didn't want to talk about it. She

should accept that and let it go. Prying would mean
she wanted to get closer, to be more in his life.

I do want that.

The thought made her heart flutter. She'd never
wanted to be deeply involved before. She'd actually
avoided involvement. Was this real?

A deep, shaky-but-settling feeling in her chest
suggested that maybe, just maybe, it was real.

She plunged in again. "Cash, if you're having
trouble, I'd like to know about it. We're friends." She
tugged him toward two side-by-side folding chairs
in a corner of the room, where there was no one
nearby to overhear.

"Is that what we are?" he asked, his voice that of
a practiced flirt. "Friends?"

She put a hand on his arm. "Don't, Cash. Don't
cover it over with...that." She waved a hand at him.

"With what?"

"That fake romantic stuff."

"It's not fake, Holly."

Her heart pounded, but she ignored it. "Okay,
it's not fake, but you're covering up something real.
What's bothering you?"

He met her eyes, studied her, then shook his head.
"Holly, Holly, Holly. What's going on between us?"

"You're avoiding telling me why that phone call
upset you so much." She caught his hand and smiled
at him to soften her words.

He looked like he was about to tell her, but a

commotion at the doorway made them both look in that direction. It was Sean, speaking urgently to the woman who'd been checking people in. She pointed in their direction, and as soon as he saw them, he started beckoning to them.

They hurried over, Cash still holding Penny.

"What's wrong?" Cash asked.

"It's Pudge," Sean said. "He's in the hospital, and it's not looking good."

CHAPTER THIRTEEN

RITA WALKED INTO the hospital waiting room, already freaking out.

Hospitals weren't her favorite places in the best of times. In fact, they made her feel sick, not so much physically as mentally.

She remembered her own surgeries after T-Bone had found her, the roaring confusion and aching head as she'd come to understand that she'd lost the memories of her entire life up to that point.

Her other hospital experience had been T-Bone's last days, the sadness and grief made confusing by her anger that he had withheld the truth about where hc'd found her until the very end. So she'd had a double loss in that hospital in Maine: the loss of the man she'd come to love, and the loss of the years she might have spent trying to find her past, her children.

Now, walking into the waiting room outside the intensive care unit, she wasn't exactly shocked that the tension in the air was thick. Sean was kneeling beside Ma Dixie, who had her face in her hands and was unsuccessfully trying to conceal the fact that she was sobbing. Liam, Yasmin and Anna were talking to a nurse.

Cash was pacing, his face tight with tension; Holly sat watching him, Penny on her lap, sleeping.

"What are *you* doing here?" Cash stopped pacing and frowned at her.

Well, okay then. She gave him a pass on politeness, because she knew that he was close to Ma and closer still to Pudge. "Got a couple of phone calls asking me to come," she said, keeping her tone easy. "I hope I can be of some use, even if it's just running out for coffee or taking Penny home."

"Sure. Sorry." He turned away. It was as if he was angry at Rita for the fact that Pudge was sick.

Holly beckoned to Rita, and she went over and sat beside the younger woman.

"I'm sorry he's acting awful," Holly said. "This was a shock, and he was already upset about some phone call he got right before we rushed over here."

"Hard to keep up all your social graces when you're hurting."

"He'll be glad you came when he settles down and realizes that we need some help. Ma Dixie is a wreck, and the boys need you."

The thought of her sons needing her, of being able to help them, warmed Rita's chest. She hadn't been able to help them when they were younger, and she'd built up a serious lack of mothering somewhere deep inside. Any way she could fill that gap just made her happy.

"How's Pudge doing? What happened?"

"As far as I can tell," Holly said, stroking Penny's hair, "he just keeled over in the kitchen out at their place. Of course, Ma couldn't move him. She was afraid she'd lose him before the ambulance could get there, but they were able to revive him and bring him in."

"His heart?" Rita asked.

Holly nodded. "Probably so, although they're not saying for sure."

The small group talking to the nurse broke up, and Yasmin came over. "Everyone always said he was a heart attack waiting to happen," she said, her expression bleak. "Now, it's happened."

Ma Dixie was sitting alone, wiping her eyes on her sleeve, so Rita went to sit down beside her. At the same moment, Cash sat down on her other side.

"I sure am sorry you're facing this," Rita said, handing her a box of tissues from the end table. "I've been in your shoes. I'm here to help with anything you need, back at home, or wherever."

"Thank you, honey. I love that man." Ma's chin trembled, and Rita's own chest hurt, remembering her last days with T-Bone. She put an arm around Ma and gave her shoulders a squeeze.

Cash drew in an audible breath. "Look, Ma, I

hate to bring this up," he said, "but should his next of kin be notified?"

Ma's head swung around to face Cash. "He told you about that, did he?"

Cash nodded.

"I think you're the only one of the boys who knows, then," she said. Her lips flattened. "Yes, they should be notified. I have the phone numbers back at the house."

Realizing this was a domestic drama that didn't concern her, Rita started to stand, but Ma put a hand on hers, pulling her back down. "You said you were willing to run errands? I might have one for you."

"Of course. Anything."

Ma looked from Rita to Cash. "His kids never did one thing for him," she said, "but I reckon it's their right to know, to have one last chance to make amends," she said. She turned to Rita. "There's an envelope clipped up top of the refrigerator that has the phone number of Pudge's wife and children," she said, meeting Rita's eyes with a kind of defiance, daring her to judge.

"His... Oh." Rita kept her face still, concealing her surprise. She wouldn't have pegged Pudge and Ma for an illicit relationship. There must be a lot more to the story, but now wasn't the time to probe or discuss it. "Do you want me to bring it to you?"

"No," Ma said. "I don't want to talk to that woman, or those children, either. If you could just tell them that their father, Pudge LeFrost, might not make it…" She broke off and buried her face in her hands again.

"Of course." Rita squeezed the other woman's shaking shoulders.

"I can take care of it," Cash said.

"No," Ma choked out to Rita. "Cash shouldn't have to deal with that. Will you do it for me?"

"Ma, I can—"

"She's right. I'll handle it." Rita had had little enough opportunity to protect one of her boys from something ugly. Doing it satisfied something deep inside, even though Cash was in his thirties and didn't really need protection.

"Check with the doctors first," Ma said.

"Of course." She knelt in front of Ma. "If his prognosis improves, do you want me to hold off calling them?"

Ma nodded and squeezed her hand. "Thank you," she said. "Just use your own judgment. I'm in no state to make a decision."

"I will." Rita left Ma to be comforted by Cash. Now she had to make a call that involved eating some crow, but there was no help for it. She scrolled through her contacts and tapped on Jimmy's number.

"So you finally decided to call," he said. His voice wasn't friendly.

Not a good start. "I need a favor." She glanced

around the room and reminded herself that this wasn't about her or looking good and righteous in front of her boyfriend. "Look, I'm at the hospital because Pudge LeFrost is quite ill. I have to do some things for the family, and I need help with Taffy."

"How's Pudge? What happened?" All sarcasm was gone from Jimmy's voice.

She looked up and saw a couple of scrubs-clad doctors approach the small cluster at the door. There was a quick conversation and then they all headed over to Ma. The woman who appeared to be the head doctor sat down and took Ma's hand, and Rita's heart sank. But she was smiling, and Ma listened and didn't break down. No bad news yet.

"I think they're getting more information right now," she said into the phone, "but it's serious. His heart."

"Aw, man." Jimmy was silent a few seconds. "If you get the chance, give my regards to Ma Dixie. I'll do anything I can to help." He hesitated. "And you're right to be there when the family needs you. I'll take care of Taffy."

"Thank you." Relief swam through her because Jimmy was so willing to help. Quickly she gave instructions on feeding and walking the dog. She wanted to make a joke about how they might bond, but decided she'd better leave well enough alone. Jimmy was a good man at heart and knew how to look beyond his own petty concerns and emotions. She was grateful for that.

She started to gather her things, figuring she should probably go out to Pudge and Ma Dixie's before the sun went down since their place was rather remote. She would get the phone numbers and hold on to them until more information was available.

She glanced back at the group, unsure of whether it was her place to listen in on what the doctors were saying, or ask questions. Probably best to just go and run this errand.

But as she walked out the door, Cash came up beside her. "Can you talk a minute?" he asked.

"Of course. Did you find out anything about how Pudge is doing?" She figured it wasn't terrible news. Ma and the doctors were still talking, and they all looked serious, but not *he's-dying* serious.

"It's a waiting game for now. He came through surgery and the damage doesn't seem to be extensive. But his overall health isn't great." Cash looked away, then looked back at her. "Listen, I'm sorry I was short with you before. I'm a little upset, but there's no excuse for me being rude to you."

Rita blinked and patted his arm. Another surprise today, this one good: Cash was acting civil. "You're forgiven. It's a stressful time."

"How do you *do* that?" He was looking at her closely, studying her as if he'd never seen her before.

"Do what, honey?"

"Forgive so easily. Keep coming back."

She didn't have to give that a second thought. "It's easy," she said. "It's what mothers do."

THE NEXT AFTERNOON, Cash headed south. He knew he was driving like an idiot, especially with the heavy rain that had blown in, but he felt like his whole life was about to wash into the swamp.

Pudge had made it through the night and was hanging on, but not by much more than a thread. Seeing him pale and still in that hospital bed had done something to Cash. Especially when he considered that Pudge might die, and that his kids might never have the chance to see what a great guy he was. Or to make up for neglecting him, or to settle their grievances.

It made the fact that he was driving to see his own father now doubly strange. He remembered the bad side of his dad, definitely. You'd had to be careful around him; he was as likely to beat up their mother as say a civil word. He'd given Cash a few licks as well, though not as much as Sean, who had tried his best to take the blows for his younger brothers.

Liam and Sean flat-out hated their father. As a kid, at least, Cash's feelings had been more mixed. Memories he'd long forgotten welled back up. He remembered when Orin had come home from work excited, telling about how he'd sold three cars that day or, later, how he'd rolled back the odometers on some vehicles and made successful deals. That last had made Mom frown, but she'd taken the bills he'd handed her from a big roll of money.

Odometer fraud. As an adult, he realized that it was illegal, a felony even. No wonder their mother had frowned.

Cash hadn't known that as a kid, though. He'd just admired the money, had high-fived his father. It was one of the few times his father had slung an arm around him, smiled and laughed.

"That's my Cash," his father had said, "living up to his name." He'd pulled off a twenty and handed it over, untold riches to a kid.

As he'd gotten older, Cash had followed in his father's footsteps. He'd gone around the neighborhood collecting broken appliances, cleaned them up, charmed the local old guys into helping him fix them and then sold them. He used the money to buy the kind of stuff an eleven-year-old wanted—fancy sneakers and shirts, an expensive handheld video game.

"Where'd you get the money for that?" his father had asked when he'd seen the game, looking suspiciously at their mom. She'd gotten a scared look on her face, like she didn't know what story to tell. She always tried to protect them, but in this instance, she hadn't known how.

He'd jumped in and told the truth, expecting to get a beating for it and maybe be made to return the game. But to his surprise, his dad had laughed uproariously and fist-bumped him. "That's my boy," he'd said. The next day he'd taken Cash down to the bar and bragged about what he'd done.

The approval had felt good. Another time, he'd bought a bunch of glow sticks cheap and sold them to people at the Fourth-of-July celebration, enticing the kids and making them beg their parents. That time, he'd shown his father his earnings and then regretted it, because Orin had been down a few and "borrowed" most of Cash's stash. Instead of paying him back, he'd brought Cash some poorly fitting clothes and shoes, which Cash now realized had almost surely been stolen.

The way Cash had tried to impress his father made him ashamed, now that he was older and knew the awful things Orin had done. By putting together what Sean remembered and what Rita had told them, gleaned from the long-haul trucker who'd picked her up on the side of the road, he knew Orin had beaten her badly and left her for dead.

Cash hated to think it of his father, but it was believable, given what he remembered about how Orin had treated their mother.

He sighed and looked out at the salt marshes on either side of the road—they stretched out flat, with waving gold-green grasses, cut through with meandering creeks. Way off in the distance, on the left, the ocean rolled. Birds soared overhead, sometimes swooping to partake of the marsh's delicacies.

The land, the low country, comforted his brother Sean. For Liam, it was the town of Safe Haven that meant the most to him; his mission in life was to keep it safe.

As for Cash, he'd always felt like his thing was money. It was what comforted him. Now that he had Penny, though, now that his brothers had settled down and he'd developed this strange longing for Holly, he didn't know what his goals were, what to work toward.

In the midst of that confusion, his father had called, claiming to be sick and wanting to see Cash. He'd chosen to call Cash out of the three brothers. Which made a certain amount of sense, because Cash was the one who was most like Orin, and probably least likely to judge. Maybe Orin, like Pudge, regretted the past and wanted to open some doors.

The whole situation had him thinking about Rita a lot, too. How she'd shown up at the hospital, had put up with his own rudeness and just quietly helped people, not intruding, not acting like she was in charge, but ready to help.

That's what mothers do, she had said to him.

Cash supposed he needed to grow up and stop blaming her for something that had happened long ago. If anyone was to blame, it was the man he was headed to see.

He spotted his exit, put the blinker on the Tesla and turned off. Orin was staying a few miles off the highway in a little town at the very southern border of South Carolina. Out in the boonies. Well, he'd liked that rural environment when they were growing up so it made sense that was where he was living now.

Ten minutes later, he pulled up in front of a blue, single-wide mobile home straight out of the 1950s. Probably really was that old, judging from the rust stains along the base. A tumbledown shed stood beside it, and long-needled pines waved their branches overhead. Off to one side, he could make out a house; the other side was a tangle of vegetation.

So this was what his dad had come to. The big wads of money had never been a regular thing, but it looked like what supply there'd been had dried up.

He got out of the car, walked through the rain to the front door and climbed sagging wooden steps. His heart was thumping double-time, triple-time, and he was sweating through his shirt.

He hadn't told anyone he was coming here. He'd considered telling his brothers, but he knew they'd insist on joining him, probably to beat up Orin for what he'd done to their mother. Understandable, but it wouldn't fix anything. Besides, his brothers were needed back at home, needed by Ma Dixie and by their children.

There was every chance that Orin was still a

skunk, and if so, Cash wanted to limit the damage. His family didn't need to know the man had tried to get back in touch. It was a book that could quietly be closed if things didn't look right.

But there was another reason Cash wanted to see his father: in his heart, he was hoping the visit would reveal something to him, something about himself. If his father had changed, as he had sounded like on the phone, then maybe Cash could change, too. If Orin regretted what he'd done and had turned over a new leaf, gotten more interested in people he loved and less focused on money, then there was hope for Cash. Hope for him as a father and a family man.

He hadn't seen his father for fifteen years at least, and he'd been a kid back then. A sick sensation of fear rose in his throat, his body bringing back the terror that used to accompany his father's return home.

In his memories of his father, he'd forgotten about that terror. Maybe this wasn't such a good idea after all.

He actually took a step back, but the door opened.

And there was his father.

The man who'd given Cash his name and the worst of his traits looked out from the same dark blue eyes that Cash saw in the mirror every day. His hair was overlong and greasy, and the shirt he wore wasn't any too clean, but he was a good-looking man for all that—strong, fit, clean-shaven.

"Glad to see you, son," he said.

Son. The word shook Cash to the core. He could never remember his father calling him that before, couldn't remember anyone calling him that except Ma Dixie. His foster family hadn't been demonstrative types.

Rendered speechless, he simply studied his father. Orin did look sick, his color pasty, his eyes bloodshot. He reached out a hand, and after a moment's pause, Cash did, too. Their handshake evolved into a slight man-hug, but the smell of Orin—sweat covered by cheap cologne—practically made Cash reel, and he stepped back quickly as memories threatened to overwhelm him.

He remembered ducking away from his father, dodging blows, running outside or upstairs, anywhere to get away from those cutting words and swinging fists.

And whoa, that definitely overcame any admiration he'd been feeling for his father's occasional financial wizardry, any sense of them being from the same mold.

"Come on in." Orin turned, beckoning for Cash to follow.

He remembered that his father had normally smelled like alcohol, but he hadn't noticed that particular smell today. Maybe he'd stopped drinking, gotten less volatile. Also, Cash now had a couple of inches and a few pounds of muscle on his father. It was ridiculous to still feel intimidated.

He squared his shoulders and followed Orin into a living area that looked clean, though a faint odor of old food and soured laundry suggested that looks weren't everything.

"Have a seat. Beer?"

"Um, sure."

He took the can his father offered, cracked it open and drank deeply.

"Thought you might be too highfalutin for my brand," Orin said. Again, Cash got a sudden memory of Orin's tactics: always poking and prodding at people, looking for a weakness he could exploit.

Cash shook his head and took another swig. Liquid courage.

There's nothing to be afraid of.

But old feelings died hard. And it was awkward. What did you say to your father after fifteen years? After he'd beaten your mother nearly to death?

He cleared his throat. "How's your health? You said you were having problems?"

"Yeah." Orin looked at the floor, then over at the kitchen, then into the back of the trailer. "Truth is, I'm having a little money trouble."

Cash had half expected that, but his gut still twisted. "Do you need help with medical bills, paperwork? I can take a look—"

"I need fifty thousand. In cash."

Cash stared at Orin. "What? Why cash?" That didn't sound right for paying medical bills.

The man shrugged. "Just…life." Again, he looked at the walls, the other rooms, the floor. Anywhere but at Cash.

A heavy stone settled on Cash's shoulders. The weight of it made him realize he'd had some kind of hopes for this meeting. Hope that the old man wanted to make some kind of connection.

He should have known that wouldn't happen. People mostly liked Cash for his money. Why should his father be any different?

Because he's your father.

Cash was a father now, and he loved his daughter unconditionally. That was what fathers did. Or should do.

Orin hadn't taken the trouble to locate his sons until he needed money. He hadn't tried to explain what had happened in the past, why he'd treated them all so badly. Where did he get off asking for a loan—or a gift, actually, since he hadn't mentioned paying it back—after all he'd done?

Cash swallowed enough of his bitterness that he could speak in a level tone of voice. "I'm not going to be able to give you that much money."

"Why not? You've got it." Orin's mouth twisted into a sneer, and Cash remembered the expression, how it preceded an insult or worse. Sure enough, the next word out of his father's mouth was an ugly one.

All of a sudden, Rita's face flashed into Cash's mind. She'd shown up for him, over and over. Asked for nothing, even though she was obviously far from wealthy. Just kept trying to help with Penny, talk to him, connect.

And Cash had turned her away, repeatedly.

Which was nothing compared to what Orin had done to her, and sudden rage flashed over Cash. "One," he said, "you almost killed my mother. Two—"

"Wait," Orin said. "*Almost* killed? You...followed up with her?"

Cash glared at him and didn't answer. "Two, I have a kid now. I don't want any kind of connection with someone like you. You can just delete my number from your phone and forget I ever came here, because you're getting nothing from me."

"Whoa, whoa, whoa." Orin lifted his hands, palms out. "I'm sorry. I went about this all wrong. You have a *kid*? How old? Boy or girl?"

"Are you not hearing what I'm saying? I don't want you involved in my life. No need for you to know."

"But that's my grandchild." Orin squeezed his eyes shut and then blinked rapidly, almost as if he was trying not to cry. "I... Look, I know I don't deserve it, I haven't been much of a father..."

"That's an understatement if I ever heard one." Cash shook his head and turned toward the door. "I shouldn't have come. You just want money out of me, and I have no obligation to help you after what you did to our mother, our family."

"Do you have a picture? Of your child?"

"You don't deserve to see her." He started walking. When the cool, damp air from outside hit him, he breathed deep. He really wanted to get out of this place, to be somewhere healthy.

He wanted to be with Holly, he realized. Couldn't wait to get back to her, her honesty, her clean wholesome nature, her sweetness. Holly was the only person in the world who could make him feel complete and decent again.

Orin grabbed his shoulder and spun him back. "Does your daughter look anything like *this*?"

He scooped a picture off an end table and held it toward Cash.

Cash was about to shove the photo aside, probably to slug it out with Orin, when his eyes focused in on the photo Orin was jamming into his face. Tiff?

What was Orin doing with a picture of Tiff?

He stared at his father, fists clenched at his sides. "How do you know her?"

Orin laughed, an ugly sound. "Old friend," he said. "I'm guessing your kid is about…a year old? Little more?"

Cash stared, his thoughts reeling.

Orin shook his head. "That trashy thing never told me you knocked her up." He crossed his arms and seemed to ponder. "Which is strange, since Tiff and I were like this." He held up two fingers, close together, and waggled his eyebrows so there was no doubt as to his meaning.

Cash clenched his fists to keep from punching his father and shook his head, trying to clear it. "If you know Tiff— No. That's too much of a coincidence, that she'd end up getting involved with your son."

Orin snorted. "For a rich businessman, you're naive. Did you think she liked you for your charm and good looks?"

Well, yeah. He kind of had thought that.

"If I hadn't gone to prison, it would've worked," Orin said.

"What would've worked?"

"Tell me, how'd you meet Tiff?"

Cash looked down. "At a bar."

"Did you hit on her, or she on you?"

"I don't remember." But he did. She'd approached him, hit on him.

Which meant... "Why'd you ask that? Did you send her my way? Why?" But the reason was coming to him.

Orin and Tiff must have conspired together, trying to find a way to get at his money.

Orin's eyes narrowed. "You want the whole story, you give me fifty thousand."

Cash stared at him. "You think you can blackmail me based on *that*? You're losing it, old man." He spun out into the rain and strode to his car, ignoring the taunts and shouts of the pitiful man behind him.

The pitiful man who was his father.

His father, who knew Tiff. Had known her, well, before Cash had ever met her. Tiff had approached Cash in that bar, hit on him. Seduced him, although things had gotten mutual fast.

They'd shared a very lovely week, but they hadn't revealed much personal information. They'd been too busy going at it like rabbits.

But not to worry, Tiff had said, because she was on birth control.

Only she wasn't.

That conversation with Holly flashed back into his mind. He'd seen something in her face when he'd asked about birth control. She'd hedged in answering him.

Had she *known* Tiff wasn't really using birth control? Had she conspired with Tiff—and, sickening as the thought was, with Orin—to entrap Cash?

But if so, why hadn't Orin seemed to know the trap had worked and he and Tiff had made a baby?

He was driving now, faster and faster through the pounding rain, the aftertaste of his father's bad beer sour in his mouth. He was still not sure he understood what his father had told him. He definitely didn't understand all the reasons and connections.

But one thing he was starting to realize: Holly just might know about his father. She just might know that Tiff had tricked him into getting her pregnant with Penny.

Holly was benefiting from that now, living well with the baby. Was she laughing inside at his offers to support her, to throw more and more money at the situation?

She must think him to be such a fool.

Cash took a curve too fast, skidded a little off the road and then straightened the wheel. Carefully, he pulled off.

He had to think about how to handle this, what to say. But he couldn't think. He just wanted to hurt someone back.

CHAPTER FOURTEEN

HOLLY HUMMED AS she walked around her apartment, lighting candles. She wasn't even worried about the approaching tropical storm. Thanks to the advice of Rita and Norma, she'd bought a bunch of hurricane candles at the hardware store in case the electricity went out.

She was pleasantly tired from walking six dogs today, and relieved, too. Business wasn't exactly booming, not yet, but it had picked back up after the success of the photos-with-Santa event.

Thinking of that made her think of Pudge, and she shot up a quick prayer for the kind and generous man.

It was raining hard, but she and Penny didn't need to go anywhere. She'd snuggle up with her baby under the small Christmas tree she'd bought, read her some stories. Maybe she'd let her fall asleep out here in the front room and take her to her bedroom later.

The loud banging on her door took her by surprise. She peeked out, then opened it wide. "Cash!

You look like a drowning person. Let me get you some towels."

"Da! Da!" Penny held up her arms in Cash's direction.

"He'll pick you up in a minute, sweetie, he has to take off that wet coat first." She grabbed a couple of towels off the shelf and brought them out. He took them and dried his head and face, then shed his coat and hung it on the hook beside the door.

He turned back to face her, and only then did she notice his lowered eyebrows, the vertical lines between them, the downturned mouth.

He hadn't said anything yet, either. And he wasn't making a move to pick up Penny.

He was more than unhappy; he looked angry. "What's wrong?" she asked. "Is everything okay?"

"How long have you known my father?" He spit out the words.

Holly lost her breath. For a moment she stared at him while she processed the question.

His father. Orin. He'd discovered the connection.

"I don't know him," she said slowly. "Why do you think I do?" Inside, her stomach churned.

His expression darkened. "Because Tiff did," he said.

She sucked in a breath and let it out again. Nodded. "It's true, she did. But I wasn't very involved in her life at that point. I never met him."

He stared at her out of hollow eyes. "I don't understand the scam, not exactly. But that you were part of it…" He trailed off, shook his head back and forth rapidly, looked away from her. "Wow."

"I wasn't part of it. I just found out about it."

"Yeah. Right."

"Come sit down and let me explain," she urged him, instinctively reaching for his arm.

He jerked away. "I'll stand."

His cold tone combined with the physical withdrawal felt like a blow to the chest. But for Penny's sake, she had to stay calm and do damage control. Had to try to find a way to keep Cash from pushing away his child.

That he was going to push away Holly was a given, and her heart cried with loss.

She studied his face, eyebrows drawn together, lip slightly curled. If only she'd found a way to tell him the truth. But she hadn't, because she'd feared this very reaction. She had to think. "Cash, it's urgent that you tell me how you found this out. Has your father been in touch with you?"

He nodded slowly, looking away. It was as if he couldn't stand the sight of her.

Her heart ached with the sadness of that, but she had to think of Penny first. "He's not a good man, Cash. Not from the little I heard from Tiff. You need to—"

"Don't you think I know that?" he shouted. "Don't you think I know the scum I came from?"

He clamped his jaw and took a breath, like he was trying to compose himself. "The idea that you were connected with that…"

Penny had started to fuss, and Holly hurried to pick her up. "Shh, it's okay." Poor Penny wasn't used to hearing people yell and it disturbed her. Holly meant to keep it that way. Penny wasn't going to have a childhood like she and Tiff had had, where angry men were a part of the landscape.

The only good thing was, she *was* used to this. She didn't like shouting matches, but they didn't scare her.

Cash opened his mouth like he was going to go on berating her. "I—"

"Keep your voice down. Please? You're upsetting her."

His mouth snapped shut.

"And listen. What I was going to say is, you need to stay far, far away from him, and don't let him know where Penny and me are staying. Even though he's in prison, he scares me."

He stared at her, his eyes still black and hollow. "That's it? That's all you're going to say?" He paused, then added, "And by the way, he's not in prison anymore."

"What?" Panic raced through her.

"Don't worry, he's in no shape to do anything to you. What I want to know is…" He swallowed hard.

"What I want to know is, why didn't you tell me?" He spoke over Penny's continued wails.

That got to her, because she could hear the hurt behind his words. Vulnerability affected her a lot more than anger did.

She sat down on the couch and swayed back and forth, trying to comfort Penny. "I kept the truth from you because that was what Tiff wanted. She felt like if you knew, you wouldn't want anything to do with Penny, and she really wanted Penny to have a good life."

"Don't you think I would've liked to know that she got together with me because my dad told her to? That she was using me, trying to get money out of me?"

"Did she ever ask you for money? She wasn't even in touch with you after that one week, was she?"

"No, but she had my baby!" The words burst out of him. "And then you brought her here, and look around, you're doing well because I'm providing for you. What's not to like about that? You can walk a few dogs, live the good life, because I was a sucker!"

She squeezed her eyes shut, partly to get rid of the sight of his angry face, partly to hold back tears. She'd always prided herself on being independent. She'd been determined to start her life here on her own terms, working, being Penny's primary support. And yes, she'd needed money from Cash, child support, but she hadn't wanted to depend on him too far or take advantage.

You wanted to be his girlfriend, to make a family with him.

She couldn't avoid the reality that she'd thought about it, and could anyone really blame her? He'd kissed her, he'd treated her with chivalry and respect. She'd thought they were getting close. The romantic vibes between them had been strong.

Now, he was looking at her with something very close to hatred. She wanted to fold up in a little ball and sob like a child, but she stiffened her spine. She had to be strong. "Look, I understand that you're angry. I should have found a way to tell you—"

"Ya think?" Sarcasm weighted down his voice.

Outside, a bigger surge of rain beat against the windows, making them rattle. She rocked Penny gently, took a few yoga breaths. She couldn't transmit her own anxiety to the baby. "If you'd like to sit down and discuss it, you can. But only if you can keep your voice down and be rational."

He stared at her. "You're one cool customer. I thought you were something else entirely. I thought we were starting to build something."

A half sob rose up inside her, but she stifled it. He'd thought they were building something? He'd *wanted* that? She'd hoped that was the case, but until now, she hadn't known it for sure.

Now, when it was too late. What had she thrown away with her deception?

"I have to wonder how long you've been planning this. What did you get out of stringing me along, making me think you cared?"

His words punched at her like physical blows. "I didn't want to deceive you, Cash. I... Tiff didn't want you to know her connection with Orin, because—"

"Because she knew it would make me *sick*?" His fists clenched at his sides. "Do you know how it felt to find out she was sleeping with Orin? My own father?"

"Oh, Cash, she wasn't sleeping with him. I don't think so. She wouldn't..." Holly trailed off. She didn't think Tiff would stoop that low, but she couldn't swear that she was right.

"She did. He made that very clear."

Holly's heart cracked into pieces. "I don't think she would have done that," she whispered.

"I didn't think *you* would lie to me." He blew out a breath, shook his head. "People are pretty disappointing when you get down to it."

His tone was dreary, final, and she missed his warmth and laughter, was only now appreciating how upbeat he normally was. Loss wrapped around her like a heavy, leaden shroud, and yet she knew it was nothing compared to how she'd feel later, once this had all had the chance to sink in.

Penny's fussing had mostly subsided but she still

moved restlessly, letting out the occasional whimper. Holly's heart broke for her. She'd lost so much already through no fault of her own; she couldn't lose her daddy, too. She stood, cuddling Penny close, and approached him. "Could you hold her while I—"

"No," he said, and turned away.

"Cash! You can't take out your feelings on an innocent—"

"What do you know about innocence?" He spun back to face her. "You're the craftiest, sneakiest little liar I ever…" He trailed off. "There's no point in talking about this." He pulled out his phone. "Let's figure out a custody schedule. I'm going back to Atlanta, but I'll take her one weekend a month like I originally planned."

"That's not enough!" For a baby, it was practically nothing. "What about the parenting class?"

"I'm not going through those motions anymore. Who are we trying to kid, that we can do a good job with Penny?"

"You're giving up on her?"

He gave Holly a level glare that chilled her. "I haven't decided how I'm going to go. I might just try to get full custody of her. But for now, I'll plan on…" He frowned at his phone, presumably at his calendar. "The first weekend of every month. Any objections?"

So many objections. "She'll be upset," she said. "She's used to seeing you almost every day."

He narrowed his eyes at her. "What's wrong, you're afraid if I leave town you'll lose my financial support?"

"No! That's not it at all."

"Right." He clicked off his phone and dug in his pocket. "Here. This should keep you going until my lawyer gets in touch." He pulled out a huge wad of money and, without even looking at it, threw it down on the table. "See you next month. Or better yet, we can get Rita to help us do the transfer. That way, I won't have to look at your lying face."

Then he turned around and walked out into the storm.

Carefully, Holly set Penny down. And then she doubled over, because the pain inside was so sharp.

Eventually Penny's renewed crying got to her, and she picked her back up and comforted her, settled her in for the night. Then she went back out to the front room and sat listening to the storm.

Leave. Get out. Run away.

It was what she'd always done. Human connections didn't pay off.

But Safe Haven seemed different.

She squeezed her eyes shut and rocked while her heart slowly broke. Cash hated her. He actually hated her.

It had been a mistake to get involved, to think there was a chance she could belong.

FRIDAY MORNING, Rita got out of her car in front of Norma's condo complex, waved to her friend and surveyed the storm damage with her hands on her hips.

"You made it! Girl, I'm grateful." Norma tossed an armload of brown palm fronds into a dumpster and then turned toward Rita. "Don't hug me, I'm a mess."

"Brought my work gloves. What do you need me to do?"

"We're just picking up debris from this parking lot so people can get in and park. I took the easy job." She gestured down toward the beach. "Most of the men are hauling the bigger stuff away."

"Not Stephen, I see." He was at the other end of the lot, alone, hauling branches to a temporary dumpster that had been placed down there.

"I don't want to talk about him." Norma's lips tightened. "Where's Taffy? Thought you were going to bring her."

"Jimmy's still taking care of her." Rita smiled. "He was pretty reluctant when I called from the hospital, but when I asked if he could keep her another day, he sounded a little more positive. I think she's working her magic on him."

"Then she's a better dog than Snowball," Norma

muttered. She was pulling a heavy branch toward the dumpster, and Rita moved to help her, sloshing through the water, glad she'd dug up her duck boots.

"Heave it on count of three," Norma said, breathing hard. "One, two, three." They lifted the branch together and threw it in. "Whew, I'm getting hot. Let's collect little stuff for a while." She pulled large garbage bags from a box beside the dumpster and handed one to Rita. "How's Pudge doing, anyway? Last I heard, he was still in intensive care."

Rita had called the hospital as soon as she'd gotten up. "He's hanging in there. It takes a while to recover from surgery like that, especially for such a big man."

"Did his kids come?"

"Nope." Rita scooped up wet palm fronds and tossed them into the bag, hard. "They said to call if he passed. Which seemed to me to be more about making sure they inherited his money than about caring for their dad."

Norma puffed out a breath. "Couple of times I've met Pudge, he seemed like a good guy. Wonder why they're carrying so much resentment?"

"You're the therapist."

"Yeah," Norma said, "and professionally, I get that what happened to you as kids, any neglect or perceived shortcoming, looms pretty large. But it's also the case that losing a parent who's estranged can cast a long shadow in a person's life."

Rita was stuck on some of Norma's words: *any neglect or perceived shortcoming looms pretty large*. Involuntarily, she glanced up at the building's top floor, where Cash had his apartment, now converted into a business center.

Cash was trying to get over his resentment toward her; she could see that and she appreciated it. But underneath, he still blamed her for abandoning him and his brothers.

Talking with Pudge's snotty kids had made her realize how irrational such resentments could be. But that didn't make her feel a whole lot better. She didn't remember Cash as a kid, not except for a few glimmers, but she felt a mother's love for him, somehow. The fact that he treated her in a cool, distant way made her heart hurt.

She turned to refocus on her work, helping Norma to right an overturned planter. "What's made you hostile toward Stephen again? I thought you two were going to go out."

Norma's lips tightened. "We did."

"And?"

Norma sorted through the plants, tossing broken ones, replanting those that might make it. "I asked him to dance."

"That's great!"

"He said no."

"Oh." Rita frowned. "Maybe he just doesn't like to?"

"Or maybe he meant the evening to be just friends. Maybe he's not attracted to me. He really clammed up after that and we left pretty soon after. He barely spoke to me all the way home." She shrugged. "Doesn't matter. I told you men aren't worth getting your hopes up for."

"You also told me not to give up on Jimmy, that grown-ups have to work through things," Rita said. "Why don't you ask him what happened, what his attitude was all about?"

"Nope. I'm done with him."

"Norma! You give everyone else a million chances, especially as a therapist. Why can't you cut him a little slack?"

"Because he hurt my feelings." Norma smiled as if she was making a joke, but it was a forced effort.

"Maybe he wants to apologize," Rita said. "He's coming over this way."

Norma glanced back and stiffened. "I don't want to talk to him."

"Be a grown-up," Rita said, and grabbed her friend's arm to make sure she didn't bolt. "Hey, Stephen. How's it going?"

"All right." He smiled stiffly at her, then looked at Norma. "Wondered if you have a minute to talk."

"Not really." Norma crossed her arms and looked out toward the ocean as if intent on counting the gulls and pelicans flying low over the water.

"I'd like to explain about last night."

Norma took her time looking back at him. "So explain."

He glanced at Rita.

"I'm leaving," she said.

Norma clutched her arm. "Anything you want to say, you can say in front of her."

"Norma…" Rita backed up, but Norma's grip on her arm grew tighter. Like a claw.

Like she was terrified.

Wow. Rita stepped closer to her friend and put an arm around her. It had been years since Norma had gotten this close to romance, and from the way her throat was working and her back was sweating, Rita guessed that the bored look on her face was a complete facade.

"All right." Stephen's slight British accent sounded stronger. "I wanted you to know that the reason I don't dance has nothing to do with you."

"Right." Norma rolled her eyes, but Rita could feel her shoulders tightening.

"There is nothing I'd like more than to take you in my arms," he said, "but I just don't have the skills to dance."

"Hmmph." Norma turned away from him. "We done here? I've got work to do."

"Why don't you have the skills?" Rita asked him. While Norma was barely looking at Stephen, Rita could read both sincerity and pain in his eyes.

"I've recently…" He broke off, took a breath and

then spoke up again. "I've recently been diagnosed with Parkinson's. It explains some difficulties I'd been having with gait and balance. Walking, I manage quite well, but dancing is out of the question. I'd hoped…" He broke off. "Well. It doesn't matter now. I just wanted you to know that it was nothing to do with you."

Norma was looking at him now. "You hoped what?"

"I hoped there was a chance for us, but when I saw how important something like dancing is to you… Well. You deserve a man who can give you everything, a whole man. That's all."

He turned and walked away, and Rita saw what she'd never noticed before, a slight shuffle to his step.

"I thought it was me," Norma said. "That nobody would want to— Stephen!"

"Go after him," Rita urged, and Norma did.

Rita watched as Norma caught up and spoke urgently to Stephen. He shook his head and continued on, but she grabbed his hand, spoke some more, and then hugged him. Then they looked into each other's eyes for a long moment. When they hugged again and then walked off together, talking, Rita's eyes blurred.

No one deserved love more than Norma. Maybe, just maybe, she was going to find it.

Rita had just found a push broom to brush muck

and sand off a walkway when she heard a voice from above. "Rita? Is that you?"

She looked up and saw her son leaning out over the third-floor railing. "Cash?"

"What are you doing here?" He trotted down the stairs.

"Just giving Norma a hand with the cleanup. What are *you* doing here this early? Hard at work?"

He looked away. "I slept here."

"Why?" She'd gone back to sweeping, but when he didn't answer, she stopped and looked at him. "You're upset."

"Yeah." He looked down. "Holly and I had a fight."

"That's normal," she said. "Why don't you take her flowers or something?"

"No," he said. "I'm moving back to Atlanta. Leaving right away."

She leaned her broom back against the wall and faced him. "Away from Holly and your child? Why?"

"She…" He trailed off, looked out toward the ocean, pressed his lips together. Then he looked back at Rita. "She kept something from me, something pretty major."

Rita frowned. "Holly doesn't seem like she'd mislead you on purpose."

"I didn't think so, either."

"How good is your source?"

He looked at her a moment and frowned. "I don't know exactly," he said. "It's my father. Orin."

LATE FRIDAY MORNING, Holly woke up from a beautiful dream. Cash *wasn't* angry at her anymore. He'd come back and looked in on Holly, then he'd gone to Penny's room and picked her up and soothed her crying.

Holly drifted back into sleep with a smile on her face. Woke up feeling warm and happy.

Only gradually did she realize that Cash's presence in the apartment had been a hopeful delusion.

He couldn't have forgiven her. He surely still hated her for what she'd done.

She tossed, restless. She'd gone over and over it in her mind, and she still couldn't figure out what she could have done differently. Oh, she could have told Cash the honest truth when she'd discovered that journal entry, but she'd been terrified that he would cut them off, emotionally if not financially. And Penny needed a daddy.

Cash's actions now made it seem like Tiff had been right: once Cash knew the truth, he'd lose all interest in his child. He hadn't even touched Penny, let alone comforted her crying. He'd thrown down that big wad of money and left.

How could he think she only wanted him for his money? The truth was, she'd fallen in love with him. With his humor and his kindness and his protective nature. With the way he cared for Penny. With the way he cared for *her*.

Only he didn't, not anymore. It hadn't been stable and real, because it hadn't lasted.

The flicker of anger she felt burned out quickly, though. Despite all the risk of it, she should have told him the truth. Shouldn't have kept herself isolated and kept the secret. She should have realized she needed him and needed him to know everything. Once there was a baby in the picture, that highly independent lifestyle had to go by the wayside.

If she ever saw Cash again, she'd tell him that.

Feeling too warm, she pushed off the covers and opened her eyes, blinking. It was later than she'd thought, way later, and the sun was heating up the room.

Weird that Penny hadn't woken up. But she'd been worn out by crying, herself.

Feeling a hundred years old, Holly got out of bed and dressed and washed her face. Nothing like having a baby to keep you from wallowing in sadness.

She opened the door to Penny's room, glad it was bright and cheerful, glad she could provide a good place for her child. No matter what happened between her and Cash—especially if he was going to cut way down on his visits with Penny—Holly had to stay strong and be a good mother. "Good morning, sunshine," she said, forcing cheer into her voice.

Penny wasn't stirring, so she walked over to the crib. A giant fist clamped around her chest as her mouth went dry as straw.

Penny wasn't there.

CHAPTER FIFTEEN

CASH GUNNED THE Tesla as he headed south toward Atlanta. It was a shiny, perfect December day in the South, although evidence of the recent tropical storm was visible along the roadsides: trees and electrical wires down, standing water in low-lying areas, pieces of debris.

Amazing how a big storm could pass. Today, it was hard to believe the winds and rain had been so strong as to wreak this destruction.

His phone buzzed for the umpteenth time, but he ignored it. His own storm had passed, mostly, too, leaving him sad and empty.

He missed Penny fiercely, didn't know if he could follow through with his idea of only seeing her once a month. In the short time he'd known her, she'd taken over a huge part of his heart. He liked to think that he was important to her, too, but he couldn't swear to it. Penny had lots of people who loved her—Rita, his brothers and Holly. She'd be fine with minimal contact with Cash.

Holly. He couldn't shut her out of his mind. The look on her face when he'd thrown the money at her and walked toward the door… Well, it would have been priceless if he'd been only angry. But he was hurt, too, almost grieving a loss. Hard when something you were excited about turned to dust.

His phone buzzed again, and since he was basically alone on this stretch of highway, he put the car on autopilot and glanced down at the screen. The same two numbers that had been trying to reach him all morning: a no-caller-ID, and Holly.

Maybe it was cowardice, but he wasn't going to call her. A man was only so strong. If she cried, or sweet-talked, he might turn around and go back. It had been hard enough to leave.

But he couldn't stay in Safe Haven feeling like a chump, knowing Holly had purposely deceived him, even entered into a relationship of sorts with him when she knew the basis of it was pure lies.

When the phone buzzed once more, his heart leaped, but then he saw it was the no-caller-ID number. He hated his own hope that it was Holly calling again, hated the temptation to give in and talk to her. He took the call just to distract himself.

"This Cash O'Dwyer?" The voice was unfamiliar: deeply Southern, young and male.

"Yep." He slowed down.

"Good." There was the sound of something rustling. Then a baby's cry.

It sounded like Penny.

His heart skipped a beat. "Who's this?" he asked as he eased the car onto the berm and stopped.

"My name ain't important. But this li'l baby goes by the name of Penny."

Cash's heart stopped. "Where are you?"

"That ain't important, either." The man gave a low chuckle. "What's important is the money you're going to give me if you want to see your baby again."

Rage and terror exploded inside Cash's head, but he fought down his emotions. "Yes. What do you want?" His phone had a record feature and he clicked it on.

"Oh, let's just say…fifty thousand dollars."

It was the same amount Orin had asked for. Alarm bells were going off wildly inside Cash's head. "How do you know me?"

Again came the chuckle, which now sounded distinctly evil. There was no more sound of Penny. "It ain't you I know."

Orin. Without a doubt, this man was working for Orin, and Cash's hands gripped the steering wheel tightly, his whole body taut with fury. "Let me talk to my father."

There was the sound of voices away from the phone, conferring. It gave Cash a moment to scroll back through his calls and see the multiple ones from Holly with new insight. She must be looking for Penny; she must know Penny was gone. Unless she was in on it with Orin? Was that possible?

"Hello, son," Orin said.

"You better get me my child back and don't you dare touch a hair on her head. Where are you?"

"That don't sound so respectful," Orin said. "Don't know if I want to talk to you." There was more conferring, and then the call clicked off.

Cash checked for other vehicles, did a squealing U-turn and flew back toward Safe Haven. When he got a little command over his emotions, so that his fingers weren't shaking so badly, he clicked into one of Holly's calls to return it, but she didn't answer. Then he tried to redial Orin. That was fruitless at first, but on the second try, his father picked up.

This time, Cash could clearly hear Penny crying and it felt like his heart was going to burst out of his chest. "What do you want? Where can we meet?"

"Not so fast. I don't want to meet." Orin paused, and then the other guy came on the line again. "All you got to do is transfer the money. I'm gonna text you the number to send it to. You can wire it or do a prepaid bank card."

Cash snorted as he took a curve too fast. The Tesla's tires scraped over the median and the screen flashed a warning, and he let up on the gas pedal a little. "I'm not sending you guys money until I have Penny back."

"Seems to me you're not the one setting the terms." There was a pause, and then Penny howled.

The sound gutted Cash, but he knew enough

about negotiation that he was able to keep his voice steady. "Nope. I have the money, and I'll get it to you, but in person. You have to bring Penny to me. Unharmed." Sweat was dripping down his back with the effort to keep his voice steady.

He could hear the two men murmuring quietly. He took the turn into Safe Haven fast, but there were people on the sidewalks and he hit the brakes, slowing to a less dangerous pace. Unbelievable that people were walking and talking and laughing, buying groceries or going to lunch, when his child was in the hands of a known abuser.

Holly. He had to get to Holly.

Orin got back on the phone. "All right," he said. "We'll bring the baby to the diner where Choctaw Highway crosses Haven Pike." Voices conferred again. "You come to the east side and stay there. Bring the money. We'll bring the baby to the west side and leave her there. You can see her, but you can't pick her up until we have that money in our hands." There was another loud cry from Penny, and the call ended abruptly.

His heart pounded and his mind reeled with fear. What would Orin do to Penny? After all, he'd beaten their mother to within an inch of her life, and she'd been a grown, strong woman.

His only hope was that Orin knew he wouldn't get his money if he didn't produce a happy, healthy baby.

His mind churned with questions. Was Holly involved in this? Was it some elaborate scam? Had the whole thing been a conspiracy from start to finish?

The very idea made him nearly double over in pain. But no. He couldn't fathom it. He could believe, barely, that Holly had known about Tiff's deception. But he couldn't believe she'd coldly participate in a deception of her own making, or that she'd collaborate with Orin. He knew for sure she didn't have a drug problem, which had to be the only reason Tiff had gotten involved with the skunk who was Cash's father.

He detoured off the road and pulled into the bank parking lot. It would take a little explaining to put his hands on as much cash as Orin wanted, but he knew the people in the bank and he knew he could do it. He'd start the process now and then consult Liam.

Liam. He'd never been so glad to have a police officer in the family.

While he waited for old Mrs. Roosevelt to finish a drawn-out conversation with the teller about her granddaughter's successes in law school, he sent texts to Liam and Holly. Let them know that he was on his way to Holly's, that Orin had contacted him and that he was working on complying with Orin's demands. Most importantly, that he'd heard Penny and she'd sounded upset, but safe.

If he hadn't driven off like that last night, headed for his old condo and then for Atlanta, would Penny have been kidnapped? Was it his fault, more evidence of him being a pathetic father?

Was he just following in Orin's footsteps?

He wrestled with the pain of that notion while he explained his needs to the bank teller, got bumped up to the manager and convinced him to do some rule-bending to produce the funds Cash needed by the time Cash came back for them later.

As he walked out of the bank, thoughts of Holly and Penny and the time they'd spent together played out like movies in his mind. He questioned the notion that he was following in his father's footsteps. He wasn't Orin and this was Orin's fault, not his. Cash was an entirely different person. He made mistakes, and plenty of them, but Orin was evil.

He hoped his feelings for Penny meant he could be a great father. He'd taken steps in that direction, at least.

And he wanted to be a great father, wanted it desperately, for the rest of Penny's life. Not a once-a-month, throw-money-at-it father, but a hands-on, loving one.

He wasn't much for prayer, but he sent up a fervent one: *please, God, keep her safe and let me be a real father to her.*

HOLLY OPENED THE door of her apartment to three couples from the parenting class. Their presence bewildered her. How had they found out? Why had they come?

Her legs felt shaky, like they could barely support her, but she couldn't stay still, couldn't focus on the hugs and kind words. There was barely room for everyone here: Liam and Yasmin, Sean and Anna, Norma and Stephen, Rita and Jimmy. Ma Dixie. Liam had gotten the word out to all local officers and, unofficially, to a couple of state cops he knew. Yasmin filled in the new visitors about what had happened—apparently, she was the one who'd contacted them—and the search they'd begin just as soon as Liam gave the go-ahead.

"Why is it that we can't do an amber alert?" she asked Liam again, because she was panicking, and not thinking straight, and she hadn't been able to listen to him before.

Liam got a call and his phone was dinging with texts. He held up one finger, telling her to wait, and spoke quietly into the phone.

Anna touched her arm. "It's because they think the baby's father took her."

Holly stared at her blankly, and then the words computed. "Cash? They think Cash has Penny?"

"*We* don't think so," Anna said, and beside her, Sean nodded agreement. "But the cops will. It's the most likely scenario. And since he's not an actual risk to the child, they won't do the alert."

"Could he have taken her?" That was Yasmin,

joining in. "You said you two were fighting. Was it severe enough that he'd take Penny and run?"

Holly pressed her fingers to her temples and tried to think, tried to quell the panic fluttering inside her chest like a bird under attack. "He was really angry," she said. "Angry at me, but his impulse seemed to be to back away from Penny, not take her." She bit her lip. "I wish he *did* take her. I'd know she was safe." No matter how angry Cash was, he'd treat Penny with love and care. That was the kind of man he was.

There was a pounding at the door, and Holly opened it.

And there was Cash, looking like he'd been attacked by vampires. His hair, normally neat, stood nearly on end and his face was white and haggard. "Did you get my texts? Orin has Penny," he said without preamble. "He contacted me. He wants money, and if he gets it, supposedly he'll return her to us safe."

Holly sagged against the wall, and Sean steadied her on one side, Anna on the other.

Penny was alive, and only now would Holly admit to herself that she'd feared the worst, thought her dead. She wrapped her arms around herself as a new set of fears replaced the old ones. By all accounts, Orin was a terrible man. What would he do to Penny?

"We need to make a plan," Cash said, "because even though he says he'll give her back unharmed, I worry that he won't." He looked over at the parenting-class members, waved his thanks. "He's my father, and he's unstable and volatile. I'm afraid he'll try to keep her to get even more money out of us."

"Good point," Liam said.

Holly was trying to keep it together, but her chin wouldn't stop trembling, and the words burst out. "I can't stand thinking of her scared, without me there. Or of him hurting her."

Immediately, Yasmin, Anna and one of the parenting-class moms came over, making soothing noises, telling her it would be okay. She let them try to comfort her, but she couldn't relax; she had to listen to the plans being made. Had to help Penny however she could.

"If she's upset and scared," one of the dads said, "she'll scream and cry and make him glad to get rid of her. At least, that's what our Troy would do."

Liam and Sean looked at each other. "You know..." Sean began.

"No. Uh-uh. We don't want to make him more upset," Liam said.

Cash looked from one brother to the other, his expression bewildered. "What are you guys talking about?"

She felt his anxiety and longed to go to him, but she couldn't. She didn't know his attitude toward her. There was no reason it should have changed for the better; it might have changed for the worse, because he might be blaming her.

"I know," Troy's dad said. "Remember in the parenting class, we talked about creating an environment where our kids could succeed? Calm, good food, lots of rest? Well, what about creating an environment where she—and that jerk—can't succeed?"

"You want to deliberately upset the baby so she's so hard to deal with, he wants to give her back." Liam shook his head. "Evil."

"Penny does have a pretty piercing cry when she's upset," Cash said. "But how do we make that happen?"

"HoHo cries if he's hungry, or hot, or tired."

That was it. The thought of Penny uncomfortable, frightened and without her or Cash to help made Holly break down. She couldn't hold back the sobs.

"It's okay, honey, it'll be okay. I know just how you feel." Anna was stroking her hair, and Holly remembered that her two girls had once gone missing, in the hands of their criminal father.

Everyone still talked about how brave Anna had been. Likewise, Holly had to hold it together. She looked across the room and met Cash's eyes, while her own streamed with tears. "Isn't there something we can *do*?"

Liam shook his head. "I know how frustrating this is, but to go out searching for her, when someone has taken her away in a car, is just a waste of time. Better if we all stay together until we've got more information."

She knew Cash was frustrated with doing nothing, too. She wanted him to come over here, to hold her, comfort her, tell her how he'd do everything in his power to get their child safely home. But he'd broken their bond for reasons that paled in comparison to their missing child. If she got the opportunity, she'd try to work things out with him.

Cash's phone buzzed to indicate a call, and when he looked at it, his face tensed. "It's Orin. If everyone can stay totally silent, I'll put it on speaker."

Holly wanted to shout "No!" Someone would screw it up. How could he trust them so much? But no one seemed to share her fears. People nodded and settled into position, and he clicked into the call.

"Meet me at the diner we talked about. Nobody else better be there, and absolutely no police."

In the background, faintly, she could hear Penny's fretful crying. Her throat tightened painfully.

"And you'll bring the baby." Cash was rigid, every muscle tense, every bit of his considerable intensity focused on the phone.

"Yeah, but you can't have her until we have the money." Orin sounded slimy and Holly felt pretty sure he was going to pull another trick.

Cash's eyes narrowed. He must be thinking the same thing, and she could almost see the wheels turning in his head. She knew the exact moment when he came up with a plan and put it into action. "Hey, if Penny's fussy, it could be because she's cold. She likes to be wrapped up in a lot of blankets."

Holly drew in her breath sharply, but he raised a hand, obviously wanting her to stay quiet.

"Also," he went on, "if she keeps on crying, just give her some Coke in a bottle. She loves it."

Holly's jaw dropped. Some of the other women looked shocked, too. But the men nodded and gave Cash a thumbs-up.

"Yeah, I can have the money in… Hang on." He tapped at his phone. "Two hours. So meet me at five o'clock?"

It would be getting dark then, but he probably needed that much time to get the money together. From the way Tiff had described Orin, he was suspicious by nature. He'd surely count every cent before surrendering the baby.

Orin grunted agreement and then ended the call.

Cash put a finger to his lips and checked his phone, then spoke to the group. "It's okay. He's off the line. And we're on to meet him at five o'clock."

Everybody started talking at once. "Why did you…?" and "That was genius!" and "That baby's going to be a mess."

Holly glared at him. "Why on earth did you tell him she's always cold when the opposite is true? She'll hate the blankets. And giving her cola in a bottle is just going to make her crazy."

"I'm hoping Orin will realize she's too much for him to take care of and give her back, rather than continuing to use her," Cash explained, and the other guys chimed in agreement.

"I can't stand to think of it," Holly said. "She'll be miserable."

"But she'll be with us."

"If all goes well," Rita said. "What if he just gets angry and takes it out on her?"

Holly bit her lip, because Rita had put her own fears into words. She swallowed, but couldn't stop the tears from rolling down her face. She drew in choking breaths, trying to calm herself.

She had to stay calm to help Penny, get her away from that monster.

"Mom." Sean put an arm around Holly. "Did our father ever do anything to hurt us as babies?"

"I don't know," she said, looking helpless. "I don't remember."

"Well, I do. I remember him throwing Cash up in the air and both of them laughing, and I remember him coming home holding Liam, all excited. Cash was jealous, and Orin handed Liam to you and picked Cash up and swung him in the air until he laughed."

Rita's hand flew to her mouth as she gasped audibly. "Was Cash wearing a purple sweatshirt?"

Sean looked at her, his head tilted to one side. "Yeah. He was."

"It's another memory!" She ran over and hugged Cash. "Oh, honey, it's just a moment, and no matter in comparison to what we're doing here, but I just caught another glimpse of you as a little boy!" Her eyes swam with tears. "Oh, my, you were the most adorable thing."

"Hey," Sean said, "me and Liam were adorable, too." There was a round of nervous laughter, then Sean held up his hand. "Point is, I think Penny's safe. I think Orin likes babies." He paused. "It's adult women he has a problem with."

"And don't you worry about Coke in a baby bottle," came a voice from the couch. "That's a time-honored Southern tradition." It was Ma Dixie. Holly had almost forgotten she was here. "It won't hurt the baby none." Ma's eyes narrowed. "Might make her fussy, but that's what you want."

"I just pray you're right." Rita looked over at Holly. "I'm sure you're right. Now, let's figure this out because I want to be there when this exchange happens."

Several of the men chimed in that they wanted in on it, too, but Liam shook his head. "He's likely to be watching the place ahead of time. We can't just have a random bunch of guys go in there. He'll smell a setup."

"No," one of the moms said, "but a few families would just be normal, right? In fact, Mark and I have gone to that diner a couple of times, with the kids. Why don't we go, and if help's needed, Mark can step in?"

"We can go, too," Sean said, but Liam shook his head.

"There's a risk he'll recognize you. The only people who can go and pose as ordinary customers are those he's never seen before."

Quickly, the group got organized. Two families were going to go—not with the kids, that was too risky, but as couples. Liam got on the phone with one of his officers, and Cash was talking to the bank when Holly came over. As soon as he finished his call, she gripped his arm. "I want to come with you."

He shook his head. "No. Orin is dangerous. I don't want you at risk." When she opened her mouth as if to protest, he added, "I need to concentrate on protecting Penny, not you."

"But I can help with her. What if you have to drive away fast or something? Who's going to hold her?" Her spine seemed to sag and she clutched her empty arms in front of her stomach. "I want to hold her."

He reached out and pulled her to him, united in grief and fear as only two parents of a missing child could be.

Finally he lifted his head and looked at Liam, who'd been close enough to hear their exchange. "Can she go?" he asked, and Holly knew what he was asking: Could Liam protect her?

Liam glanced over at Yasmin and then back at Cash, and nodded.

"Okay, honey," he said into Holly's hair. "You can go."

She rested her head against his chest, just for a moment. "Thank you."

"Look, I have to run down to the bank," Cash said to Holly, "but I'll pick you up here, in an hour."

She nodded solemnly, eyes still wet.

"We'll save her, Holly," he said. "I promise, we will."

It was a promise Holly fervently hoped he could keep.

CHAPTER SIXTEEN

CASH DROVE HOLLY toward the diner Orin had chosen. They didn't talk.

There were no words to convey how he was feeling. How they were both feeling. He couldn't stop thinking about Penny, so tiny, so vulnerable, in the hands of a man who had no morals or scruples.

"Look, is that it?" Holly pointed up ahead, and sure enough, there was a big sign: Diner.

This place was generic, and not crowded. Cash had been here once and found that the food wasn't especially good. But today, there were several cars pulling in just ahead of them.

"Those are both people from the parenting class," Holly said. "Is that good or bad? Won't he get suspicious?"

"It's too many people," he said. "He's going to know something's up." But he pulled into the parking lot, anyway, on the side Orin had told him to, then scanned the other side of the lot for a car that might be Orin's, might have Penny in it.

"We shouldn't have let anyone come," Holly said, her voice fretful.

His phone buzzed and they both froze.

"Should I pick up?" she asked.

"Give it to me," he said, and glanced down at it, and then at Holly. "Orin."

"Talk to him."

He clicked into the call. "Cash here."

"I changed my mind about this," Orin said.

In the background he could hear Penny crying, and his heart twisted sharply in his chest. Twisted in a way he knew instinctively that his father's had never done for him. His father had wanted to murder their mother, not sparing a thought for the sons he'd devastate.

He *wasn't* like his father. Not in any real, essential way; the way he loved Penny and wanted to protect her from anything and everything proved it. A huge burden seemed to lift off his shoulders.

But there was no time for that. He had to be smart in order to get Penny back. "What's wrong?" he asked Orin, trying to sound relaxed.

"Let's go on into Safe Haven and do this in the grocery-store parking lot." Orin paused, then added, "Come alone."

"I have Holly with me," Cash said. "She wouldn't stay back. She's Penny's mom, for all intents and purposes."

Orin hung up without answering, which could mean he didn't care or could mean he was furious.

"Text Liam," he told her. "Tell him about the

change. And that we can't have all these people come along."

She agreed and started punching numbers into her phone as Cash did a U-turn.

"I'm texting Rita, too," she said. "And Sean."

"Good." Cash drove rapidly now. Orin hadn't sounded right. He was tense, upset. And Penny had been crying in the background, loudly. That was good, it was what they'd wanted, but he hoped it didn't backfire and truly infuriate Orin.

They pulled into the grocery's parking lot, empty save for a single pickup with two men inside. This little grocery store closed down early, which was probably why Orin had chosen it. In all likelihood, he'd never gone out to the diner. He'd always intended to change the locale. That figured. Orin was no stranger to this sort of activity.

Cash pulled into a spot on the other side of the lot and slammed the car into Park. "Stay in the car. I'll take it from here."

Holly was breathing hard, chewing on her lip. "Can I watch at least?"

"He's already seen you, and I told him you'd ridden along, so I guess it can't hurt."

He got out of the car. Sweat dripped down his back and slicked his hands. He'd never handled anything like this before, and the fact that he'd done so many business deals, the fact that he was a millionaire many times over, didn't mean one thing. He was just a dad now, a dad who wanted his baby back safe, wanted to keep his family together.

He straightened his spine and walked like he knew what he was doing because that was what a father did.

Orin got out of the car and stood, arms crossed, legs apart, waiting.

"I have the money," Cash said as he reached the man, holding out his briefcase. The odd thought came to him that he should have grabbed a cheaper briefcase, not his favorite alligator one.

Orin looked past Cash toward the car. "You *did* bring Holly." He grimaced in obvious distaste.

"She wants the baby back. She can comfort her."

"Shut her up, you mean."

Cash shrugged, trying to stay calm although every muscle screamed with the desire to plow down this scumbag and get to Penny. "Yeah."

"No contact with the baby until I count the money," Orin said.

"Okay." He didn't like how antsy Orin sounded. "Here's the money. Go ahead and count it."

He could hear Penny crying and it tore at his heart. He didn't want her to cry. He didn't want her to ever be unhappy. He wanted to keep her safe, wanted to care for her and play with her and spoil her, to protect her with everything he had.

He wanted to care for her as his own father had never cared for him and his brothers.

Which proved again that he was nothing like the sleazy man in front of him.

Orin seized the money and took it over to the truck. He opened the door, set the briefcase on the seat and started counting.

In the driver's seat of the truck, he could see a younger man, thin, with dark hair, holding Penny and frowning.

Cash didn't like it. Didn't like the look on Orin's face or on the other guy's.

Then everything seemed to happen at once.

Orin glanced back at Cash, shoved the briefcase onto the floor of the truck and started to climb in. "Go, go," he yelled to the other man.

"Take the baby, then!" The other man seemed to be tangled up in Penny's diaper bag, to where he couldn't shift the baby over to Orin.

From the corner of his eye, he saw Holly running across the parking lot. She yanked open the truck's driver-side door and grabbed for Penny.

The two men were shouting, Holly was screaming and Penny wailed.

Instinctively Cash started toward Holly and Penny, but then his brain kicked in. Orin was trying to get a grip on Penny. He had to distract him, disable him if possible. He shifted course, going for the passenger side of the truck. He reached in and tried to pull Orin out, but the man was strong despite his age and he gripped the inside of the truck's door.

There was one thing that would get Orin's attention off Holly and Penny. Cash reached down, grabbed the briefcase of money and ripped it out from under Orin's feet, flinging it behind him. In his peripheral vision he saw bills flying in swirls of wind. Orin made an inhuman sound, somewhere between a curse and a scream. He leaped from the truck, saw that the money was blowing away and went for Cash's throat.

But Cash was faster than the old man, and he dodged away and ran around the truck to where Holly struggled to get past the other man in order to grab Penny. Ridiculous. Holly was much smaller and a woman.

And then... He'd never seen anything like it. Tiny Holly grabbed the man's hair and pulled him screaming out of the truck, then kicked and shoved him to the ground. Now there was nothing between her and Penny, propped on the bench seat, and she dove back toward the truck. But Orin's accomplice was outraged. Just as she grabbed Penny and backed out of the truck, he pulled out a gun.

Cash's life flashed before his eyes and he was running, yelling, diving to protect the woman and child he loved, to cover them with his body, whatever it took, whatever happened to him.

Behind him, a shot rang out.

Guess this is it. But at least he'd die with Holly and Penny in his arms.

Only he didn't. Instead, when he looked back

over his shoulder, he saw the accomplice lying on the ground, dead or at least unconscious, bleeding from the head. Liam was running toward them, weapon in his hand.

"Get them out of here," Liam yelled. He bent toward the accomplice, knocked the gun from his hands and kicked it away, and then took off toward the other side of the truck, where Orin had been.

But Orin had climbed into the truck and was now behind the wheel. He jammed it into Reverse and gunned it backward.

"Look out!" Cash yelled to Liam just as the truck winged him, knocking him to the ground.

"Go help them get Orin," Holly said, panting. She was bleeding from a gash on her face and another on her arm, but she was cradling Penny in her arms, examining her. And from Penny's lusty cries, she didn't seem to be hurt too badly.

Orin U-turned the truck, still going backward. He reached the briefcase where Cash had flung it, jumped out and threw it into the truck. It was probably still half-full of money.

Then he gunned it and the truck raced toward the exit of the parking lot.

RITA WAS RIDING shotgun in Norma's enormous vintage Cadillac, leaning forward, clenching the edge of the leather seats. "I can't believe I'm this close to the man who ruined my kids' childhoods and nearly killed me. And I don't even remember what he looks like."

"Process of elimination." Norma steered onto the street that led to the grocery store. "We should see Cash, Holly, Penny and Liam. Any other shady-looking guy, about our age, has to be Orin."

From the back seat, Taffy yelped agreement. Then she went back to sticking her head out the window.

"Can't believe you made me bring that dog along." Norma rolled her eyes.

"She's protection." Something had told Rita to give in when Taffy had begged to come with them.

As they approached the grocery-store parking lot, sirens sounded in the distance.

"There they are!" Rita could see Cash running after a pickup while Holly hunched over something, probably—hopefully—Penny. Liam was on the ground, as was another man.

"That's got to be Orin in the pickup," Rita said. "He's getting away."

"You want I should stop him?" Norma asked.

Rita sucked in a breath, took in the pickup's size, twice as big and heavy as Norma's Cadillac. "Yeah," she said.

"Hang on." Norma floored it, and the Cadillac leaped forward, neatly blocking the pickup's exit route.

It was coming toward them, not slowing down.

Behind the wheel was a man who looked like every monster that had ever haunted Rita's nightmares.

"We're gonna die!" Rita assumed the crash position.

"This thing's a tank," Norma said, but her voice was shaky.

At the last second, Orin slammed on the brakes, missing them by inches. He backed up like he was going to go to the other exit.

"Oh, no, you don't," Norma said grimly. She spun the wheel and hit the gas pedal hard, and the Cadillac surged forward, crashing into the front of the pickup and spinning it around.

Orin gunned the engine again and again, but the truck didn't move. Something was broken.

Liam was sitting up. Cash ran toward them, but then turned back at a cry from Penny.

Orin climbed out of the truck and took off, carrying a briefcase, trying to hold it closed.

"No way," Rita said with determination. She flung open the door of the Cadillac and went after him on foot.

He was surprisingly fast for a man of his age. He dodged into an alley too narrow for Norma, who was following in the car, to pursue him.

It was dark between the two tall buildings, and Rita tripped over a box of trash and went sprawling, scraping the palms of her hands, pounding her knees hard to the ground.

This was ridiculous. She should leave him to the police to catch. Speaking of, where was her police-officer kid when she needed him?

She looked up just in time to see Orin dodge into a service garage. She was pretty sure Shorty had closed for the day, but that wouldn't stop Orin from stealing a car. He knew how to hot-wire them.

How did she know that?

No time. She was the only one who'd seen where he'd gone. If she waited for help to arrive, it might be too late.

He'd destroyed her family and come close to destroying her son's family as well. She wasn't leaving him free to do it again, to some other victim. She scrambled to her feet and ran after Orin into the dark building.

Inside, in the dimness, she could see three vehicles in the service area. Sure enough, Orin was going from car to car, opening the doors. Of course, he wouldn't need to hot-wire a car if he could find one with keys in the ignition or nearby.

On the last car, he let out a triumphant exclamation, got in and started it up. Then he got back out and looked around the service bay, probably for the switch that would open the big garage door.

If he found that, he'd be out of here.

She ran for the car he'd found, yanked open the door, turned it off and grabbed the keys. He roared his displeasure and came running back. She flung the keys hard, heard them land on the far side of the shop.

Don't let him trap you in a car.

Again, wisdom from deep inside, a fragment of a memory too horrible to let in. She flung herself across the seat and out the passenger door as he grabbed for her from the driver's side.

Her heart pounded and it was hard to catch her breath as she scrabbled across the floor toward the door she'd come in, trying to stay low. She'd succeeded in slowing him down. It would be enough to tell the police where she'd last seen him. What had she been thinking, trying to stop him herself?

She saw the door and made for it, but suddenly he was there, grabbing her by her hair and yanking her head back, smacking her across the face.

Shock and pain and more fragments of memories crashed in.

"You were supposed to die," he growled into her face, and she smelled the same sickening cologne he'd worn so many years ago. Her muscles gave out and she went limp, as limp as if she was that young mom, cowed by an abuser.

"Please, don't hurt me. I won't tell anyone where you are. You can get away."

"Gimme those keys."

"I…I threw them over there." She tried to get her arms free to gesture.

At her words, he drew an arm back and she

cowered, trying to shield her face with her now-free arm.

Behind her, by the door, there was barking and the scratch of claws she heard at home every day. Taffy must have followed their scent. The sound distracted Orin.

If Taffy came in, Orin would hurt her. "Taffy, no! Stay!" she called and hoped the limited amount of training she'd been able to do would be enough to keep Taffy safe.

Orin called Rita a foul name and got up. He reached out as if to help her to her feet.

Out of character. She scrambled to a crouch on her own, her eyes never leaving him.

"Get over there and find those keys." He gave her a shove to get her going, making her fall forward onto her scraped hands, and she couldn't restrain a little cry.

The door opened and she looked up, hoping for rescue, but it was only Taffy. Taffy, running to her, mouth open in her usual delighted grin.

Orin delivered a kick that sent Taffy flying.

Rita's mental screen seemed to fill with the image of a very similar dog, flying through the air, landing hard, its neck oddly twisted.

She looked at Orin and felt some kind of click in her head, enough that she put her hand to it. She blinked, rubbed her eyes. She felt like she was waking up.

Just like that, she remembered everything.

"Not again!" she yelled and ran at Orin, knocking him to the ground in a tackle worthy of an NFL linebacker.

But he rolled her off him easily and then he was on top of her, nearly crushing her.

Outrage filled her, overcoming her fear. That was new. She shifted until she could knee him in the groin, not as hard as she'd have liked but enough to make him grunt and flinch. She drove the heel of her hand into his chin, knocking his head back, and wiggled and squirmed as hard as she could.

She'd sidled out from under him when Taffy staggered back over. She reached out a hand to stop the dog, but Orin grabbed her arm and started to twist.

Her wrist exploded with pain and she screamed.

Taffy snarled and jumped at Orin, going for his face, and he fell back, eyes big and terrified. She kept growling and snarling, fierce in a way Rita had never seen the affable pup.

And then the door opened again and Cash was there, punching Orin in the chin. "You leave my mother alone!"

Orin crashed back to the ground, seemingly dazed, and Cash clicked his phone. "Found him. We're at Shorty's."

Norma was right behind, sinking onto the ground beside Rita, looking at the wrist she was cradling, patting and reassuring her while Taffy licked her face. Then Holly rushed into the garage, holding Penny.

Liam burst in and started toward Rita, but Norma pointed at Orin, still on the ground but starting to stir.

Liam spoke to Cash in a low voice, and a few minutes later, began to read Orin his rights.

But Rita just sat savoring what Cash had said.

He'd called her "my mother."

ON THE MORNING of Christmas Eve, Holly was lying in bed thinking about how everything had changed.

She whispered a prayer of thanks, as she had every morning since the abduction, feeling grateful and blessed that they'd gotten Penny back unscathed. The pediatrician had checked her out, pronounced her fine and praised Holly and Cash for the work they'd been doing with her. She was advancing faster than she'd been expected to, and soon she would be caught up with her peers.

She and Cash had taken Penny to the doctor together, had shared a quick celebratory hug at the good news and then they'd gone their separate ways.

Holly, of course, still wanted more than anything to provide a home for Penny, and she knew now that she wanted a secure home for herself as well. But she'd been humbled. No way could she do any of that in isolation.

Safe Haven was the right community for her and

for Penny, but she couldn't hope to make it work if she stuck to herself. Didn't even want to. The way everyone had pitched in to help find Penny and capture Orin had been support unlike anything she'd ever experienced before.

No one else had seemed to think it was any big deal. That was just how things were here, in this town.

She wanted to stay, to build a life here.

Having seen Cash go on the warpath for Penny, realizing how much he cared, she'd made a decision. She was deeply sorry for her own role in the deception. She should have been honest as soon as she found Tiff's journal. She hadn't been, though, and if she didn't do something, Penny would pay the price. As far as she knew, Cash was still planning to move back to Atlanta and commute to Safe Haven one weekend a month.

It wasn't enough.

She leaned over and looked into the crib, but Penny was still sleeping. She hadn't been able to let the baby sleep in her own room, not after the scare she'd had. The police had gone over her apartment, had seen how Orin's accomplice had gotten in and taken Penny, and they'd made sure that the locks were secure. Rita had offered to stay with them, as had Cash. But she knew she had to get over her fear.

And Cash had sounded so ambivalent that she

turned him down. A forced relationship wasn't what she wanted.

On her nightstand sat a picture of her and Tiff, and she picked it up and looked at it. It was a rare time when they'd both been happy and enjoying themselves, eating ice cream, when they were probably ten and eleven years old, their arms slung around each other, big messy smiles.

"I'm doing the best I can," Holly said to the picture. "But I'm going to have to make some changes. I can't live the way we've been living."

A ray of sun struck the picture, illuminating Tiff's smile, and to Holly, it felt like a benediction.

She sat up in bed. So be it. It was time for a grand gesture.

CASH WAS GETTING into the Tesla after the Christmas-Eve church service when Sean called out to him.

He welcomed the interruption to his thoughts. Ever since Penny's disappearance and recovery, he had been in a very strange place mentally.

He was incredibly grateful that Penny hadn't been hurt and that she was doing well. And he was getting along fine with Holly.

Now, though, he felt at loose ends. Yeah, he'd probably go to Sean and Anna's for a bit of Christmas-Eve cheer, but after that, what? It felt wrong to just go back to his condo; he knew that, really, he should be back in Atlanta. And he would, as soon as the holiday season was over.

But to wake up alone tomorrow, to miss his baby's first Christmas...that just didn't seem right.

"Hey, nice service, huh?" Sean clapped him on the back. "We had a little change of plans. Going to stop by the park instead of gathering back at our place, since it's such a nice night." He looked sideways at Cash. "You'll still come, won't you?"

Cash stretched and faked a yawn. "Think I'm just going to head home."

Sean's eyes narrowed and he studied Cash more closely. "No way, dude, that's ridiculous. Just come. The twins really want you to."

"What are you going to do at the park on Christmas Eve?" Cash knew he was just being resistant, but truthfully, he wasn't in the mood to socialize. Had even been thinking of backing out of the gathering at Sean's house, and to go to the park...

"Have a bonfire and let the kids run around," he said. "Come on. You don't have a choice. Liam!" He yelled the words at their brother, walking by with Yasmin. "Gimme a hand here."

"Oh, no, you don't." Cash started backing away.

"What's going on?" Liam asked.

"Our brother thinks he's too good for a bonfire at the park," Sean said.

"That's not what I—"

But it was too late. They came at him from both

sides and grabbed him, each taking an arm and a leg. The world spun, and then he crashed down into the back of Sean's pickup.

"Hey!" Cash yelled. "It's dirty back here! Watch the suit!"

But his brothers just laughed. "See you at the park," Liam said, and slapped the side of the truck. Seconds later, the truck pulled out of the lot.

The old Cash would have been furious, but now he'd had a major shift in perspective. He stretched out in the back of the pickup and looked up at the stars while Sean drove the short distance to the park, seeming to take the corners extra sharply—more than likely, just for the pleasure of making Cash roll around.

The stars were bright and the live oaks and palms filtered the moonlight, and the sea air blew in.

Cash could admit it to himself now: he loved it here. Loved the people and the land, loved the sense of haven that had given the place its name.

His mother's memory had been restored, and in the past three days she'd spent hours with him, Sean and Liam, talking about their childhood, laughing and crying and remembering together. It hadn't been all bad. They'd rediscovered plenty of good moments along with the scary ones. And Rita had apologized, with heartfelt tears, to all of them. She'd tried to explain what it had been like for her to be so

young, with three little boys and few job skills. She'd
expressed her deep regret about what had happened.

Most of the talk had been with Taffy in the room,
cuddling with one of them. That only made sense,
since the three boys hadn't realized that Orin had
killed the dog they'd had back in Alabama as kids,
that in fact, it was that that had made Rita see just
how dangerous and out of control Orin was. She'd
realized then that he was a risk to them, not just to
her, and had made the decision to take them and run.

A lot of missing pieces of Cash's life had clicked
into place.

It had been a cleansing and fresh start. He'd gotten his mother back.

The truck stopped and he realized he hadn't even
minded the unexpected, jolting ride.

HOLLY LIT THE last candle and checked the foil-
wrapped dinner once more. Her heart was beating
double-time. Was she making a huge mistake?

The big live oak tree was lit up overhead, shed-
ding light on the picnic table where she'd arranged
everything. A breeze stirred the air, but it was still
plenty warm; in fact, Holly was sweating in her
lightweight jacket. A few family groups and couples
strolled nearby, chatting, and somewhere in the distance, church bells chimed.

Now she wished she hadn't had Norma and Rita
take Penny, wished for the comfort of her baby. But

in a way, she was doing this for Penny. She needed to focus. She drew in deep, soothing breaths and rehearsed, yet again, what she was going to say.

There was a triple honk of a truck horn, and then Sean's truck pulled up. A moment later, a very confused-looking Cash walked down the park path toward her, brushing dirt and straw off his classy, nicely fitted suit.

Game time.

She stood and tried on a smile. "Hi, Cash."

He slowed and tilted his head. He didn't smile back. "What's going on?"

Her heart sank, but she had to go through with it now. "I wanted to apologize for not letting you know the truth, earlier, about Penny."

"Not necessary." His words were clipped.

"It is to me. Cash, I'm sorry I did that to you. It was wrong. I should have told you everything I knew about Penny about Tiff, as soon as I found out. Maybe if I had…" Her throat tightened and she had to pause, but he didn't help her out. "Maybe if I had, Orin wouldn't have gotten to Penny."

"Water under the bridge." But his voice was still cool. "What's all this?" he asked, waving a hand to indicate the table.

Her stomach churned. She'd made a ridiculous choice. "Um, well, I thought that just saying I was sorry didn't mean much, so I made you a meal."

He raised his eyebrows and didn't say anything.

"I heard from Ma Dixie and your brothers that you like cornbread and fish chowder, so I made that. There's wine, too," she added hastily, because the fare sounded so humble. "And…I made you a present, too, back when I was doing that, making presents, remember?" She pulled out the hand-painted picture frame, with the photo she'd taken of him, Liam and Cash laughing together as they'd pulled the crab trap from the water.

He took it from her, looked at it for a long time, then met her eyes. "You made me a picture of me and my brothers. And cornbread and fish chowder." His voice had no inflection to it.

"Yeah." She felt like a complete idiot. But no way was she taking this food home with her. "Can I dish you up some? It's best when it's hot."

He looked off to the side as if he was trying to figure out how to frame his rejection of her offering. But she wasn't having that.

Quickly, she uncovered the fish chowder and ladled some up for him, then for herself. Not that she was hungry, but it wouldn't do for him to eat alone. Besides, even with her churning stomach, the rich combination of garlic, tomato and seafood smelled fantastic.

She took the foil off the pan of cornbread and sliced it into pie-shaped pieces, then scooped him out a big one. "Here," she said, "I'll let you put butter on this yourself. I don't know how much you like."

Then she reached into the cooler. "Which would you prefer? Wine, or fresh-squeezed lemonade?" When he didn't answer, she finally hazarded a glance up at him. He was looking at her, his forehead wrinkled.

"I'm just having lemonade, myself. It's really good. Want me to pour you some?" She was babbling nervously and he still hadn't said a word, but she couldn't seem to stop herself. Her hands shook as she poured two wineglasses full of lemonade.

"Have a seat," she said, and sat down herself.

Like a man in a daze, he slowly sank down onto the picnic-table bench. And Holly felt her shoulders relax, just a little. If he was going to completely reject her, he wouldn't have sat down. And now that he had the food in front of him, she was pretty sure he wasn't going to be able to resist eating it.

The way to a man's heart is through his stomach. That's what the cliché said. She sure was hoping it was true.

They ate for a few minutes without speaking. Holly, who'd thought she wouldn't be able to eat a bite, actually found that she had a decent appetite. She could be a pretty good cook, and she'd gone all out getting fresh vegetables and herbs and spices for the chowder, and used her own grandmother's cornbread recipe.

He was already finished with his first bowl before he looked up at her. "This is really good," he said.

"Thank you. I don't think anyone has ever cooked me my favorite meal before, on purpose."

His comment said worlds about the way he'd grown up. Every kid should have their favorite meal cooked for them—pretty often when it came down to it.

He tasted the cornbread, and his eyes crinkled. "Another win," he said. He smiled, obviously enjoying the food, but she felt like his smile wasn't quite reaching his eyes.

"There's something I want to ask you." May as well get this out in the open now, while he was feeling full and happy.

Instantly his smile disappeared. "What is it?" His shoulders slumped a little.

She sucked in a breath and shot up a prayer. "We need you." She stopped. That didn't come out right. "Me and Penny, we need you. Not your money, you. Would you consider staying nearby at least part of the time, for Penny's sake?"

Now that she'd gotten that out she felt like she might faint, but almost instantly it felt good. She didn't know if he would accept her apology, let alone her proposal that he stick around, but at least she was being honest and real.

He put down his spoon. Then the cornbread. Let out a sigh.

"I understand, if you need time to think about it. I just wanted to get the idea on your radar. I think it would be really great for Penny. I mean, it would be great for me, too, but she's what matters the most."

"I do," he said. "Need time to think about it." Abruptly, he stood. "Thank you for doing all this. I appreciate it."

It hadn't worked. He wasn't going to forgive her, and he wasn't going to stay in the area. Her stupid lying and deception had cost Penny a father.

Had cost her the man she loved. "Wait, Cash." She stood and hurried around the table to him, held out her arms.

He looked at her, head tilted to one side. "What?" His tone was gentle but puzzled.

Don't hold back. This isn't the time for that. "I've missed you, Cash. I've missed your companionship and friendship and sense of humor and…everything. I've missed everything about you."

He frowned, and she realized that it was words. Just words, and they weren't enough.

She stepped forward and wrapped her arms around him, lifting her face.

His eyes darkened and he looked at her—first her eyes, then her lips.

She raised herself up on tiptoe, wanting closeness, and then he crushed her into his arms and kissed her. *Really* kissed her.

His lips on hers were hungry, tasting, seeking and finding the comfort they both seemed to need. His hands pressed her to him until she didn't know where her own body stopped and his began. It wasn't disrespectful, though; he wasn't trying to put his hands all over her like some men would. He just seemed to want her close, to move his mouth on hers with gentle promise.

She'd never soared so high. Into the stars, into the possibilities. Hope bubbled up inside her. Could he kiss her like that if he didn't care?

And then it was over. He loosened his grip and created distance, a little and then some more, holding her by her shoulders. He studied her face, her eyes. Then he looked off into the darkness.

They were both breathing hard.

"I still need time to think about it," he said finally. "About living close, I mean. Are you okay?"

She nodded, too quickly. "Sure. Fine." Her voice sounded high and false.

"Okay."

"See you later?" The question sounded pathetic.

"Sure." He turned and walked away, and she sat looking after him until her vision blurred with tears.

CASH GOT BACK to the parking lot and realized he didn't even have his car here. He was going to have to walk back to the church—either that, or call one of his asinine brothers, or hitch a ride with Holly.

And since he'd just walked away from her, that last didn't seem like a smart idea.

He sat down on a park bench that was in the

shadows, away from the illumination of the giant oak tree's Christmas lights. His head was spinning and he needed a little space to settle down, anyway.

He'd had women in his life who were practically celebrities, models, stunning beauties. He'd been proud to have them on his arm. But not a one of them would have taken the time to find out his favorite meal and prepare it.

Holly was a good woman. He knew that now. Despite the lies she told—which were really lies of omission, and all because of her less honorable sister—she was a good woman.

Not only that, but her slim figure also drew him closer, her long blond hair made him want to run his hands through it. Her lips were beautiful, and even as she'd been apologizing, he'd been watching them because he wanted to kiss them. Maybe that was why he had acted so awkward. It wasn't like him.

But Holly wasn't like other women.

A familiar truck pulled over to his side of the parking lot. Sean and Liam. They got out and started to walk down toward where Holly was, and he suddenly realized they must've been in on the whole plan. From his dark vantage point, he watched them go toward her and speak to her. He couldn't see her, he was too far away, but he figured that was what they were doing.

He wanted to know what she was saying, how

she was feeling. He wanted to always know where she was and what she was up to.

If he got her a really nice ring, would she accept it? Would she marry him? Or had she made that apology meal because she wanted to be friendly co-parents?

Who could want a man like him, a man who had his father's rotten genes?

But the moment he had that thought, the thought that had tormented him for years, he knew it was wrong. Knew it, because a vision of Penny came to his mind's eye. Would he blame her for the mistakes her mother had made?

Everything in him recoiled at the thought. Penny carried Tiff's blood, but not her mistakes. Those rested solely at Tiff's feet. Penny was innocent.

Cash didn't think of himself as exactly innocent. He certainly had his share of faults and flaws. But he knew now that he didn't bear responsibility for Orin's sins.

"Where are you?"

"Dude, show yourself!"

Sean and Liam were walking around the parking lot, calling for him and none too quietly. They were going to give up. "Over here," he said, resigning himself to some brotherly wisdom and advice he didn't really want to hear.

"What happened?" Liam asked. "What was that all about?"

"You don't know?" Cash asked. "Thought you two were in on it."

"Holly talked us into getting you here," Sean explained, "but she wouldn't tell us why. Said she didn't want to tell us until she told you."

"Yeah, which made me for one think she was gonna propose," Liam said. "Did she?"

"No. She made me a meal because she was sorry for lying. Not really lying, but misleading me about Penny, and her sister, and Orin…" He had given his brothers the bare outline of Tiff's connection to Orin, and how she'd purposely gotten pregnant. But he hadn't got into a lot of detail, especially about Holly's role.

"And?" Sean glared at him.

"And what?"

"Did you eat her food and then shut her down?"

"No! Well, kind of."

"She's crying," Sean said. "She's down there crying. Are you going to leave her like that?"

"You need to hold on to her," Liam said, "or half the guys in town will get in line to take your place."

"I see how you look at her," Sean said.

"It's obvious that you care," Liam added. "Why don't you go talk to her? Why don't you ask her to marry you?"

"Well…"

Liam fist-bumped him. "You want to! Do it!"

"Can't," Cash said, feeling regretful.

"Why not?" Sean asked the question, but both of them were staring at him like he was out of his mind.

"I don't have a ring. And it's Christmas Eve. I can't go buy one."

"She doesn't care about a ring!" Liam lifted his hands, palms up. "Holly's not like that."

He heard a sound, something rolling up the concrete path. It was Holly. She was pulling one of those old-lady shopping carts with all the supplies from the dinner she prepared. Her head was down.

He'd treated her badly. He'd been awkward, because he hadn't known what to say, how to react. He'd just been so surprised. But the end result was that he'd made her cry.

And he couldn't blame it on Orin's blood in his veins in some fatalistic way, like he always had. He'd just been a garden-variety jerk, all on his own, and he needed to apologize.

Maybe even needed to do more. He started walking toward her, then turned back to his brothers and waved them away. "I got this," he said. He didn't; his knees were literally shaking. But he had to do it, and he had to do it himself, and he had to do it now.

"Need some help with that?" he called to her.

She jerked to look at him. "Oh! You scared me."

"Sorry." He took the supplies from her and pulled them toward her car. "I don't know if I thanked you adequately for preparing that meal for me. That was one of the nicest things anyone's ever done for me."

"I'm glad you liked it." She was looking down.

"Do you have a minute to talk?" He held out his hand for her keys; she handed them over, and he opened the trunk and put the supplies inside.

"Rita has Penny. I imagine she'd like to spend the rest of the evening with Jimmy, so, no, I don't really have a minute to talk."

He whipped out his phone and called Rita. "Hey, Mom, it's Cash. Mind keeping Penny another hour?"

"After hearing you call me 'Mom,' you can pretty much do whatever you want. I'm glad to have her."

"Thanks." He ended the call. "Rita doesn't mind babysitting a little longer." He closed up Holly's car, took her hand and tugged her over toward a bench under the lighted-up tree. "You took me by surprise tonight," he said.

"I'm sorry," she said. "I shouldn't have tried to stage a big apology."

"No, you shouldn't," he said seriously. "And that idea of me staying in town part-time, for Penny? I can't do it."

Her face fell.

"I can't do it," he continued, sinking to one knee, "because it's not enough for me. I want to be with you both, full-time."

Her eyes widened. "What?"

"Holly, you are the best and kindest woman I know."

"I'm not," she said. "I did something awful to you."

"But," he said, "you did it because of your sister, not because of any desire for gain for yourself. I can't blame you for wanting to follow Tiff's wishes. She was a pretty great person."

She bit her lip. "She was," she said, nodding.

"And you—you're an even greater person. You're beautiful," he added, "but that's not why I started having these feelings for you."

She gulped. "You have feelings for me?"

He smiled. "Isn't it obvious?"

"No, Cash O'Dwyer, it's not obvious! You had me thinking that you were still holding a major grudge, down there." She gestured toward the picnic area where she'd served him a meal.

"I'm not always great at expressing my feelings, but let me express this—I love you, Holly." He was still down on one knee, but he took her hands in his and looked up into her face. "I know we haven't known each other very long. I know it may take some time. But the truth is, I really want to marry you."

She sucked in a sharp breath.

"Look, I don't even have a ring. I wasn't really prepared for this. I'm sorry."

She didn't answer. She was probably really disappointed. Women liked big major scenes for proposals, wanted to be able to put a picture of their engagement ring on social media.

He heard a sniffle and looked up at her and realized that she was crying.

"What's wrong? Did I say something wrong?" He took her hand and rubbed it between his own. "I'm sorry. I'll do a better proposal and a great ring. You deserve that."

She shook her head, smiling through her tears. "No, you said something really, really right." She gripped his fingers tightly. "Look, Cash, I don't even care about a ring, okay?"

That was so ridiculous it blew his other thoughts out of his mind. "You're getting a ring. A great big beautiful diamond ring."

"Nope," she said.

Disappointment pressed down on him. "Are you saying no?"

She squeezed his hands. "No, I'm not saying no, I'm saying yes! I want to marry you, too."

"Then…you're getting a ring."

"I'd rather you take what you'd spend on the ring and use it to hire more people to help in your business," she said. "Because I don't want you away from me and Penny all the time, doing deals. I want you at home, being a real dad to her."

He sucked in a breath and let it out and looked into the eyes of this woman who was different from anyone he'd ever known. He opened his mouth to speak.

"And," she said, still wiping tears, "I'm still going to work. I love walking dogs, and taking care of them. And I want to set a good example for Penny. So I'm helping support us. I just want you to know that."

A weight that had been on his shoulders for most of his life seemed to lift off him. Holly *didn't* want him for his money. She didn't even really want his money; she wanted *him*. She loved him, for himself.

At least probably. One doubt remained. "Is it because of Penny, that it'll be good for her?"

She shook her head. "I'd want to marry you even if she wasn't in the picture at all. But I'm so glad she is."

"Me, too." He got onto the bench beside her then and pulled her into his arms. "I'm sorry I don't have a ring. Really sorry."

She put her hands around his face. "Don't you get it? This is all I want. You."

And finally, as he pulled her into his arms, Cash got it. He held her close against him and let the thankfulness settle around him, the happiness, the joy of loving and of being truly loved.

EPILOGUE

One year later

"OH, THAT'S ADORABLE!"

"Let me take a picture!"

Holly turned to see what the fuss was about and then grabbed her phone, too. Taffy, all bathed and groomed and wearing a flower collar, sat up on her back legs beside Rita, who was leaning toward the mirror to adjust her headpiece.

"Hey, I'm the official photographer." Miss Martha from the library pretended she was going to shove them aside, then leaned in and snapped a bunch of photos.

Rita turned, reached down and rubbed the little dog's ears, and everyone took more photos.

The bride's room at the church was crowded, but Holly didn't mind in the least; this was her family. The O'Dwyer wives—Anna, Yasmin and Holly—were serving as bridesmaids for this Christmas wedding of Rita and Jimmy.

They'd all gotten close, calling each other most days, helping out with each other's kids, sharing big family dinners. In some ways, they had the sisterly relationship she wished she and Tiff could have had.

Finally, she had a big supportive family and she loved it. For Penny, of course, but also for herself. No more solitary holidays; no more solving all her problems herself; no more ache of loneliness deep inside.

Rita turned to show them all the full effect of her floral crown. She was stunning in a simple white gown, her hair flowing down her back. "What do you ladies think? Ridiculous?"

"No! You're gorgeous!" Holly reached out to straighten Rita's sleeve.

"I'm not exactly in my twenties. We should probably have gone to a justice of the peace, but I never had a real wedding before."

Anna and Yasmin joined Holly at Rita's side. "This means a lot to your sons," Anna said. "They really like Jimmy, and they want to offer you their support."

Rita's face crinkled into a smile. "They're the reason I can do this at all," she said. "They've helped me work through the past. And all these grandkids have helped me think about the future."

Holly pressed her hand to her still-flat stomach and tried to restrain a smile. She didn't want to steal any of the spotlight from Rita. There'd be plenty of time to tell the family about the baby boy on the way.

"Hey! You about ready?" Norma stuck her head in the door, then came the rest of the way in. "Girl, for an old broad, you look good." She enfolded Rita in her arms, and when they pulled apart, both friends' eyes were shiny.

Rita cleared her throat. "You know, you can still change your mind and be in the wedding. I wish you would."

Norma shook her head. "I have to help Stephen. In fact…" She looked back out the door. "'Bye." She rushed out and helped Stephen into the church, lovingly scolding him.

"His Parkinson's is getting worse, it seems," Yasmin said.

"Yes, but they're hopeful about a new drug he's taking for it." Rita watched Norma ushering him into the sanctuary. "For someone who never wanted a man, she certainly seems to like having one."

Anna peeked over Rita's shoulder at the people now streaming into the church. "Pudge looks good, too. He's lost some weight."

"Ma's making him eat healthy food," Yasmin explained. "He'll always be a big man, but they're walking every day and his doctors are amazed at how well he's doing."

As the others went on talking, Holly tucked herself into a chair in the corner and watched them, smiling. She was so very happy for Rita, who'd become a dear friend and had truly stepped up as Penny's grandmother. She'd gone to counseling after recovering her memory and was doing great, especially now that Orin was expected to spend the rest of his life in prison.

Holly and Cash had married in September, in a beautiful beach ceremony followed by a big bonfire by the cabins Sean and Anna managed. She and Cash had meant to spend their honeymoon there, too, not wanting to leave their family behind, but at the last minute Cash had surprised her with a week-long trip to Tuscany. They'd driven from vineyard to vineyard, explored quaint hill towns and stuffed themselves on fabulous Italian food.

And she'd gotten pregnant.

At first, she'd been terrified. Sure, Cash had accepted and embraced Penny, but she *was* a two-year-old; their hands were full with her. Besides, Cash had only just worked through his issues with his father, realizing that Orin's problems didn't have to be his own problems, that the sins of the fathers weren't necessarily visited on the sons.

She'd worried that he wouldn't want to add to their family so soon, even though he'd been the one to suggest that they let nature take its course.

Which it certainly had and still did. Her cheeks warmed. To her, Cash was completely, devilishly irresistible. They'd made good use of all their doting relatives as babysitters so they could have newlywed time alone, and it was everything Holly hadn't known to hope for.

"Come on, it's time!" Miss Vi, who'd insisted on serving as an usher, beckoned them to the back of the church, and they all hurried out, giggling, fixing each other's hair, wiping makeup smudges.

"The groomsmen just came in," someone said in the church, and all three wives peeked at the front to see Sean, Liam and Cash lined up.

"Those are some gorgeous men," Yasmin said. "Mmm-mmm."

"Yes, they are. Sean's the most handsome, but your husbands are all right, too." Anna looked at Sean with adoration undimmed by their nearly three years of marriage.

Privately, Holly thought that neither Sean nor Liam could hold a candle to Cash. Oh, they were great guys, and she was crazy about them, but Cash had such charisma and spark. She fell more in love with him every day.

"Mama!" It was Penny, running toward Holly, hand in hand with HoHo. "We ready!"

"It'll be your turn in a minute." Holly knelt and hugged Penny, treasuring the fact that she was walking and talking beautifully, all caught up. "Do you want to walk in with Mommy like we practiced last night?"

"Wanna walk with HoHo," she said, pushing out her lower lip and frowning, then checking to see

Holly's reaction. She was just starting to realize that she could disagree with Holly, and she loved practicing the power of "no."

Holly restrained a smile and looked over at Anna, who was straightening HoHo's little bow tie. "Do you think they're up for it?"

"They'll do great," Rita said. "This wedding is for us, not some magazine. It doesn't have to be perfect." She leaned forward to look down the aisle, then gripped Holly's hand. "My boys. All so handsome."

"They're gorgeous. Jimmy, too."

Anna's twins came in then, important in their big-girl flower-girl dresses. Yasmin and Liam's son, now a permanent part of the family but still a little shy, was going to walk down the aisle with them, carrying the rings.

Rita was still squeezing Holly's hand. "When I lost them, when I lost the boys, I never thought I'd get them back, and this… All of this." Rita gestured at the children and then at the wives, her eyes glimmering with tears. "I feel so blessed."

"Stop. You'll ruin your makeup." Yasmin gave the thumbs-up signal to the organist and the wedding march started to play.

Later, at the reception, Holly leaned back against Cash in one of the diner's booths, tired, a little queasy, but so happy. "I'm glad they decided to have the reception here."

"It fits. Are you sure you feel okay to stay?"

She nodded. "To stay, but maybe not to dance." The kids were running around in the aisles, and both Sean and Liam were dancing with their wives on the little dance floor they'd made of the front foyer. Even Pudge and Ma Dixie were slow-dancing, holding each other close.

"I'm happy just to sit here and hold you," Cash said, resting his cheek on her head. "I never thought I'd say this, but I'm learning to love weddings. They remind me of how happy I am to be married to you."

"I love that you share your feelings with me," she whispered back to him. "And I love how caring you are with me, and with Penny."

"And with Cash Junior," he teased, putting a hand on her stomach. "Kidding. I'd never saddle a kid with a name like that."

"I like it."

"You're biased." He ran a finger slowly up her arm and she felt it like a jolt of electricity, bringing her alive. "Guess we can't leave Mom's wedding early, huh?"

She shook her head. "I don't think that would be right," she said. "But, Cash, we have the rest of our lives."

* * * * *

ACKNOWLEDGMENTS

Low Country Christmas could not have come into existence without the help of many, many people.

The team at HQN Books has given fantastic backing to the entire Safe Haven series. I'm especially grateful to Susan Swinwood for taking a chance on these books, and to the sales, publicity and art departments for the beautiful covers and amazing distribution.

Thank you, Karen Solem, for your calm support and ongoing wisdom. At that scary ACFW pitch session back in 2013, I would never have dared to hope we'd do fourteen books together, nor that you would become a dear friend. I'm looking forward to many more years and projects together.

Big thanks are due to my brilliant editor, Shana Asaro, who rolled up her sleeves and helped me improve draft after draft of this book. Her ideas, insight and kindness inform every page.

I adore my Wednesday morning writers' group. Sally, Kathy, Colleen, Jonathan, Jackie and Karen, you give me strong, sharp feedback clothed in kindness and humor. Kathy, I especially appreciate you for reading and providing commentary on multiple drafts. Dana and Rachel, writer friends extraordinaire, thank you for your humor and sympathy throughout the writing of the entire series.

In the "research can be fun" department, a big thank you to my Seton Hill colleague Jeff Bartel for the amazing ride and the insider's view of all things Tesla!

Sue, Ron and Jessica, I love you so much and am beyond grateful for my bookish family. Bill, my travel companion in so many ways, I'm delighted to be on this journey with you. And, Grace, my baby who's now a full-on adult, thank you for being the light of my life.

Finally, I am grateful to my readers, whose kind notes and reviews and enthusiastic support mean more than I could ever express. Thank you for taking time from your busy lives to escape to Safe Haven with me.

SPECIAL EXCERPT FROM

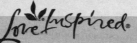

Christmastime brings a single mom and her baby back home, but reconnecting with her high school sweetheart, now a wounded veteran, puts her darkest secret at risk.

Read on for a sneak preview of
The Secret Christmas Child *by Lee Tobin McClain, the first book in her new Rescue Haven miniseries.*

He reached out a hand, meaning to shake hers, but she grasped his and held it. Looked into his eyes. "Reese, I'm sorry about what happened before."

He narrowed his eyes and frowned at her. "You mean...after I went into the service?"

She nodded and swallowed hard. "Something happened, and I couldn't...I couldn't keep the promise I made."

That something being another guy, Izzy's father. He drew in a breath. Was he going to hold on to his grudge, or his hurt feelings, about what had happened?

Looking into her eyes, he breathed out the last of his anger. Like Corbin had said, everyone was a sinner. "It's understood."

"Thank you," she said simply. She held his gaze for another moment and then looked down and away.

She was still holding on to his hand, and slowly, he twisted and opened his hand until their palms were flat together. Pressed between them as close as he'd like to be pressed to Gabby.

The only light in the room came from the kitchen and

LIEXP1019

the dying fire. Outside the windows, snow had started to fall, blanketing the little house in solitude.

This night with her family had been one of the best he'd had in a long time. Made him realize how much he missed having a family.

Gabby's hand against his felt small and delicate, but he knew better. He slipped his own hand to the side and captured hers, tracing his thumb along the calluses.

He heard her breath hitch and looked quickly at her face. Her eyes were wide, her lips parted and moist.

Without looking away, acting on impulse, he slowly lifted her hand to his lips and kissed each fingertip.

Her breath hitched and came faster, and his sense of himself as a man, a man who could have an effect on a woman, swelled, almost making him giddy.

This was Gabby, and the truth burst inside him: he'd never gotten over her, never stopped wishing they could be together, that they could make that family they'd dreamed of as kids. That was why he'd gotten so angry when she'd strayed: because the dream she'd shattered had been so big, so bright and shining.

In the back of his mind, a voice of caution scolded and warned. She'd gone out with his cousin. She'd had a child with another man. What had been so major in his emotional life hadn't been so big in hers.

He shouldn't trust her. And he definitely shouldn't kiss her.

But when had he ever done what he should?

Don't miss
The Secret Christmas Child *by Lee Tobin McClain,*
available December 2019 wherever
Love Inspired® books and ebooks are sold.

www.LoveInspired.com

LIEXP1019

Don't miss the first book in the brand-new
Painted Pony Creek series by
#1 New York Times *bestselling author*

LINDA LAEL MILLER

COUNTRY
STRONG

**A story about three best friends whose strength,
honor and independence exemplify the
Montana land they love.**

"Linda Lael Miller creates vibrant characters and stories
I defy you to forget."
—#1 *New York Times* bestselling author
Debbie Macomber

On sale January 28, 2020!

www.HQNBooks.com

PHLLMCS0919